Einstein's Bones

Charles N. Rice
© 2013

Special Thanks to
John Forse
and
William Rice

Einstein's Bones

Chapter 1

To most, Eastern Wyoming is a vast empty wasteland, best seen from thirty thousand feet at five hundred miles per hour. There are no trees, no lakes, not much for rivers, and nothing is green, especially at this time of year - only barren rolling hills with short brown grass, sage brush and of course, just like Montana, Wyoming's big sky. Why would any *Homo sapiens* set foot on this land except to get somewhere else? More than a few wonder why we took it from the Indians in the first place. Or why not give all of it back to them now? At the very least, why not turn it into one sprawling national park?

But for John Steiner and Charlie Madson it is a small piece of heaven. Once again this year they have made their annual journey west from Minneapolis to the hills and valleys east of Sheridan, Wyoming, to hunt antelope and mule deer. Where some see nothing, no shopping malls, no swimming pools, and no excitement at all, Charlie and John see endless horizons, exquisite solitude, and nature's grandness. Except for the oceans, there is nothing quite so expansive. But most of all, they always see plenty of game, game that's not fenced in, not managed, and game that a hunter has to earn.

They have been coming for twelve years - always to the same ranch owned by family friends - ever since John's twenty second birthday. At first they had come with John's father. He died four years ago, so now they came out mostly by themselves. Once in a while, they would invite another friend, but the friend always seemed a stranger in their special place, usually more interested in drinking, picking up girls in the local bars, or shooting up highway signs than in hunting. John and Charlie were serious hunters. Don't get the wrong idea, they both liked Mr. Jack Daniels, but he had his place - the evenings after the hunting was done - just to warm up the soul a bit. As for fun, Charlie had been married long enough to forget how long, and John, he'd been married once, but it didn't work out. If something came his way, well, that would be just fine, but there wasn't much chance of it out here.

Most of us - those of us in a hurry anyway - like to take the freeways. To go from Minneapolis to Sheridan, chances are you'll drive south on I-35 to Albert Lea and then pick up I-90 going west through the southern part of Minnesota into South Dakota with the highlights along the way being Chamberlain, Wall Drug, and Rapid City. In Wyoming, you pass through Moorcroft, Gillette, and Buffalo. There is not a lot to see from most any freeway, and on this one, there is even less. For most, that's just fine.

But there are other ways to get there, too. Minnesota Highway 7 will take you from Minneapolis to Montevideo where you pick up US 212. It then goes through South Dakota, with the points of interest being Watertown, Redfield, and Faith. The towns are smaller, but you get to see them. The scenery is about the same, but you get to feel it. There aren't many rest stops unless you count that long empty road. If you pull off to the side for a quick nap, nobody seems to mind. Finally, at Spearfish, South Dakota, 212 joins I-90.

Sheridan is fairly large as Wyoming towns go. It has a couple of good motels, several really good restaurants for dinner, and most important, one great greasy spoon for breakfast. If you like your eggs over easy, a thick breakfast steak medium rare, hash browns done just right, and plenty of Tabasco Sauce, then the Silver Spur is the place to go. Every morning before the hunt, John and Charlie made their appearance.

Einstein's Bones

It was now the second day of their Wyoming adventure. The first day the weather had been rough. Cold and rain. Miserable. During the first week of October anything could be expected. One day it might be 90 degrees with a blazing sun frying exposed flesh, and the next day it just as easily could be 35 degrees, with rain and a relentless howling wind. With little grass to hold the soil in place, the ground turns to thick, heavy, greasy muck. Walking can be as tiring as running a Marathon. The goo clings to boots leaving tracks that would make Big Foot pause in terror. And the cold, wind driven rain cuts through anything worn. Minnesota at minus 20 is no match for this kind of Wyoming weather.

By late afternoon of the first day, the storm had ended and a warm front had begun to push in. It was not enough to dry their clothes, but their spirits were raised by Charlie taking a nice buck muley despite the miserable weather. The promise of good hunting weather on the way further buoyed their sagging enthusiasm for the following day.

There was not much need to get out in the field at O' dark thirty. Mule deer and especially antelope are active throughout the day. On the second day of the hunt, they followed their usual routine. They set no alarm clock except for the first light coming in through the motel window.

Sun, or no sun, Charlie always rose early. "Jesus Christ, John, don't you think it's about time to get up, get your ass out of bed, and get the hell out of here? Don't you hear the birdies singing their praises to God - Damn it will you ever get up? "

"Yeah, yeah, screw you. God, I was having this just incredible dream. And you gotta wake me up. I was back in school – Spanish class – and this teacher was really hot. I think I was her special pet. So, she was just about to.."

Charlie cut him off. "Just get up and get dressed. I've been lying here and listening to your damn snoring for the last half hour. You can tell me all about it later."

"What's the hurry, the last time I looked, the Spur served breakfast till noon."

"Get moving."

"All right, all right, I'm up. Where did I put my pants?"

Neither of them was much for early morning conversation.

It took them only about ten minutes to get fully dressed and get their equipment in the truck. They had the drill down well. It was another five minutes before they were at the Silver Spur where they had their usual - two eggs over easy topped with a healthy dash of Tabasco Sauce, breakfast steak on the rare side, greasy hash browns, and strong black coffee. A half hour at the Spur and they were ready for the forty five minute drive to their sacred hunting grounds.

A couple of miles out of town, just beyond what passed for a combination bar, gas station, post office, and part time meat packing plant, the pavement ended. As far as dirt roads go, it was not the worst but it did present its share of challenges. It wound though draws and over hills. There were constant ups and downs with plenty of blind spots. It could be bumpy enough, but if taken at the right speed, about 50 mph, it seemed to smooth out. John always prayed he wouldn't meet another truck, especially on a blind curve or at the top of a rise. The usual trick was to watch for the oncoming dust. On dry days, John counted on seeing contrails of dust a couple of minutes before what ever was on the way got there. John would just put his foot to the pedal and cross his fingers that it was not a semi hauling cattle out of one of the ranches.

Einstein's Bones

But today, with the roads still wet, John took the road at less than his normal speed of 55mph leaving no dust at all in his wake. Regardless, his father would have been on the edge of his seat all the time, crying out at every rut hit and begging for mercy.

"For old times, give me a one of the Old Man's best, Charlie!"

"Umf, slow down, my God, you're going to get us all killed," replied Charlie with a gruff voice and a smile.

With that, John broke into his not so perfect rendition of 'Nearer my God to Thee'. He had sung it many times before when his driving habits had his father on the verge of hysteria. John and Charlie both missed the old man's fretting. A hunt in Wyoming just wasn't the same without a reminder, now and then.

"That was some dream I had, I ..."

Charlie once again cut him off. "So, what's the plan?" he asked.

"Hell, I don't know, one plan's as good as the next. When we get to the ranch, why don't we park the truck just inside the gate and work that draw down to the left? Seems like we almost always see a buck bedded down in that brush. If I walk one side and you walk the other we might just be able to score."

"Some plan, huh. One of these days we're going to have to do something original."

"Yup."

Planning over, they turned to other topics.

"Hear anything from the ex? You're still friends, right?" asked Charlie, knowing that the question would get his friend started.

"Yeah, I thought I told you about that."

"No," was Charlie's reply. "I don't know what you ever saw in her. You two never stopped fighting. And that name of hers - Phyllis. Who the hell names their kid Phyllis anyway?"

"You and most everybody else wondered, too. I don't know. Well, at least she was intelligent and not unattractive, and she could hold up her end of a conversation. I suppose I gave as good as I got. I've kinda forgotten the worst of it, anyway. I kinda miss her in a way."

"I sure as hell don't know why. She must have been good in bed."

"Yeah, she was OK. No complaints. Anyway, just before we left Minneapolis she came over. I thought she might have something else on her mind, but when she came over she told me that she thought I still had some old movies her father had taken back when she was a kid."

"Did you have them? Did you give them to her?"

"No, I didn't have 'em. And I wouldn't have tossed 'em either."

"So you think that's really why she came over? Maybe she did have something else in mind."

"If she did," replied John, "she didn't act like it. I think she just wanted to see how much of a mess I've made of the place since she moved out."

"Mr. Clean you ain't, that's for sure. Sometimes I don't know what she saw in you either."

"Besides the obvious? Well, she's always had a thing for tall slender types with lots of dark hair. Least if I could figure by some of her old photos. Guess that's why she never put a move on you. Square jaws, too. Let me think. A sense of humor and even tempered? Anything else? Well, we both liked classical music,

Einstein's Bones

camping – this is tough. Well, we both graduated from the "U", and . . ."

"And arguing."

"Yeah. Good thing not all women like the same type or what would all you short fat guys do? So, what's yours up to while we're out here?

"Getting things organized so I can redecorate when we get back."

"Now that sure makes me glad I'm back to being single. Too bad your kids aren't old enough to do that for you."

"Or old enough to come hunt with us," replied Charlie.

"Yup, we gotta carry on the tradition. Ya know, I always wonder what I would have been like if I had had any kids," added John thoughtfully. "Would it have changed me?"

"You just never know. You could always get married again, or maybe the next time the ex comes over she won't use some bogus excuse and you'll get her PG. Then you'll have to do the right thing and marry her all over again"

"That's a frightening thought – me getting married to her again," replied John. "You know, you got a pretty good thing going at home."

"I know."

At eight o'clock, they finally reached the ranch gate.

"Get off your fat ass and open it up," said John from the driver's seat.

Not seeming to mind, Charlie got out and slipped the wire off the post and swung the wood and barbed wire gate open. He waited a few seconds for John to drive past and then went back to close it.

Einstein's Bones

"I don't know why, but for some reason, closing it always seems much harder than opening. The ranchers always make it look so easy," remarked Charlie.

"That's because you're a weenie."

Just past the gate, there was a little rise and a good spot to park. John got out and went to the back of his pickup. Reaching for his rifle he asked Charlie, "what ya think you're going to use today?"

"I think I'll use my trusty old 30-06. Don't think I'll need anything else."

"Guess I'll use the same. Loaded up some 165 grainers just for this hunt. You going to use those new bullets you got?"

"Yup! Got to see if they work"

They were ready quickly. They loaded up their day packs with a couple of sandwiches, candy bars, Charlie's Olympus digital camera, and most importantly, a good supply of toilet paper. They slung on their canteens and binoculars. John made sure he had some extra film for his old Cannon F1; they loaded their rifles, and were ready to go.

The head of the draw was about a hundred yards to their left. From there it descended at a gentle rate, but the sides to the right and left were steep. As the ground was still on the wet side from the day before, they would have to be careful not to slip. The last thing they wanted to do was go ass over tea kettle and jam their rifles into the mud. Once that mud dries, it turns into concrete, transforming the rifle into a grenade if you're foolish enough to shoot it without a thorough cleaning.

As planned, John took the left side of the draw and Charlie the right. They walked slowly, all the while looking into the bottom of the draw for movement and, they hoped, a big set of antlers. They looked at each other to make sure that the one did not move ahead of the other. They looked ahead and to the sides of the draw

Einstein's Bones

anticipating that Mr. Big would make a break for it and try to escape up the side of the draw. They said nothing. Hand gestures or a sudden pause were enough.

It took about an hour to work the draw. It was an easy walk, down hill all the way. Off in the distance, they both saw two antelope near the top of one of the ridges. But the range was something over 300 yards and neither of them was that good of a shot, especially without something to rest their rifles on. They both had read and laughed at the magazine articles where the author had bagged his game at 400 yards or more. One such hero even claimed to have taken a deer at 600 plus with a hand gun. But closer was better for John and Charlie. A much greater chance of downing their quarry on the spot and much less possibility of having to track a wounded animal for God knows how far and then the dread of having to haul it out from wherever it ended up. That can be one hell of a lot of work. Neither of them was in favor of a heart attack, especially in the middle of nowhere. If one had the big one, the other would be stuck attempting to rescue him. It might even mean the end of the hunt for the other. Talk about ruining your day!

The end of the draw opened into a small plain at the far end of which, about a mile away, rose a ridge with a high peak in the middle. To either side of the plain, about three quarters of a mile apart, ridges sloped gently up. It was often the case that a good sized herd of antelope would be milling about there. If so, the hunting could be good and fairly easy. Antelope are not the brightest of God's creations and with a little effort, they can even be herded. In the past, when John and Charlie had hunted with a third partner, they had often placed Leonard or one of their friends on the ridge at the far end and had been able to drive the antelope right to him.

But today, no animals were seen.

"So what now?" Charlie asked as they reached the end of the draw.

"First, I'm going to put something in my stomach, and then I think I might have some private business to take care of."

"Well, just make sure you get out of my sight when you do."

John sat down munching on his Snickers bar. Then he reached into his back pack and took out the necessary equipment for his next task. As John went about his business, Charlie took out his binoculars and started glassing. It always surprised him what he could see with a good set of binoculars. Looking at the ridge to his left, he could see four antelope grazing, seemingly unconcerned by the hunter's presence. But one of them was looking right at him.

Not much chance of sneaking up on them, he muttered to himself. To his right he saw two more. Again they were looking right at him. "Damn, but they have good eyes." Ahead of him, about half way up the peak, nearly invisible to the naked eye, he saw three moving to his left and about to go around to the other side. They gave no indication they had spotted the two hunters. "Just maybe!"

"You see any possibilities?" asked John upon his return.

"Yeah, there's some to the right of us and some to the left of us, but I think they've got us pegged. But there's three of them on the peak ahead of us about half way up. I don't think they know we're here. They've moved around to the other side now. I think we just might be able to sneak up on them."

"Ok, so how you want to do it?" asked John.

"If we walk up near the top of the peak and get above them we might just have a shot. Once we get there, you walk around to the left and I'll go to the right. They might still be up there or they might have gone down to the flats below. Either way, I think we should have a pretty good chance. What do you think?"

Einstein's Bones

"Hey, sounds good to me."

The hike across the little plain was easy on their feet, just short grasses and some sage brush. In the middle of the plain were what looked like a couple fallen tree trunks. But there were no trees within thirty miles. However, once they got near to them, they could see them for what they were - petrified trees.

John and Charlie had seen them before. Every time that they came to this spot they would pause. "Can't help but wonder how old those suckers are," said John. "It sure would be interesting to see what this place looked like when they were standing. Kinda puts me back in time. I sure wish my brother could see them, he'd know."

"I can't help wondering why they're left here," was Charlie's reply. "You'd think they'd be fenced in or put in a museum or something."

"Neat stuff."

They walked on. The peak didn't look all that steep from a mile away. But once they got to the base, they knew they had their work cut out for them. A slow ascent was the best. They didn't want to make any unnecessary noise or tire themselves out before they got near the top. A winded hunter is not a good shot.

They arrived with plenty of breath to spare. "Let's take it around the side real slow. Whoever sees a good one, don't wait. Just take it," whispered John.

They separated as planned, John to the left and Charlie to the right. They worked their way slowly. The rocks were loose and the slope steep, so watching where their feet went was imperative. No noise and no broken bones were the orders of the moment.

As he moved to his left ever so cautiously, John could see his prey slowly come into view. They were further down the slope than he had expected. This was a good thing as antelope are less likely to look up than they are to look down. And if he could inch his way forward just a few more feet, he would have a good size rock for cover and a good rest for his rifle. Those last few feet can take an eternity. One misstep and off the antelope would go. But he had done this many times before and had learned the value of patience. Ever so slowly he moved into position. He put his cowboy hat on the rock and carefully put his rifle on top of the hat. The antelope moved very little and showed no sign that they had the slightest clue he was there.

He adjusted his scope to medium power. They were about 100 or so yards below him so the high end of his 2.5 to 8 power scope was not needed. He brought the ocular close to his eye and thought "a perfect shot". Lining up the crosshairs on the closest buck he slowly took up the slack on the trigger and in a millisecond was ready to fire.

But just as the rifle was to do its work, a shot from the other side of the peak rang out. Both John and the antelope jumped. But John's shot was still there and his finger was committed. As he fired, he knew the shot was not the perfect one he had hoped for, but it certainly seemed to be within what he called 'minute of buck' or just plain close enough.

His game ran quickly down the slope and to the left. As John stood, he heard his partner yell.

"What happened?"

Standing, John could see Charlie had also gotten a buck, and that it had dropped where it was shot. "Good shooting, Charlie. Did you see mine?"

"Yeah, I saw him too, but I had a much better view of this one. I saw yours run off and I think you hit him pretty hard. He should be pretty easy to find"

"I hope so. Congratulations. He looks nice."

Einstein's Bones

"Tell you what," said Charlie, "I'll start work on mine and if you need any help finding yours, give me a holler."

John left Charlie to the work of cleaning out his kill. He didn't figure that his antelope would be very far off or that it would be all that difficult to find. But the grasses and sagebrush can easily deceive a hunter. He knew from experience that an animal could be down ten feet in front of him and nearly impossible to see.

But luck was with him. After walking only a few yards, he saw the antelope lying on the far side of the ridge below, next to an outcropping of rock. As he got closer, he could also tell it was quite dead and, like Charlie's, a very nice buck. He thought well of himself. Maybe not perfect shot placement but he had a good excuse. It looked as though there would be plenty of meat between the two of them.

Reaching the buck, his thoughts now turned to the less pleasant task of field dressing the animal. It was important to clean and get it to a meat processor as fast as possible. The day was heating up and an antelope doesn't last long in the sun. It's easy to ruin the meat. Small wonder a lot of hunters' wives don't like the taste of wild game.

The first thing John did was position the animal to make the cleaning more efficient. It was lying with its head facing down the slope. John pulled the legs down so the head would be pointing up slope and then bent down to begin the task. He removed his back pack, then his binoculars, and then his shirt. As he placed the shirt on a rock, something caught his eye.

"What the hell!"

There, imbedded in the rock was something totally out of place, something very unusual. Its color was somewhat lighter than the surrounding stone, but what first caught his attention were the strange patterns on it - high ridges and deep hollows.

Einstein's Bones

"Damn, what the hell is this?"

Forgetting the antelope, he rose to his feet. "Charlie," he yelled, "you better come over here and see this. I found something you've got to see!"

Einstein's Bones

Chapter 2

Charlie had just begun to clean his kill, and now John wanted him to come running. Great! But if John said it was important, it probably was. John was a practical joker in many things, but not when it came to hunting. Reluctantly, Charlie put his knife aside, wiped his hands off on the ground, and began the short trek over to John to find out what was so damn important.

As he approached, Charlie could see his partner on his hands and knees looking at something on the ground, and it was not the antelope.

"All right, what the hell is so damn important?" Charlie asked from a distance.

Without looking up, John said, "You've got to take a look at this."

"At what?"

As he got closer Charlie could see that some rock was the object of all of John's attention. "So what the hell is it?"

John's eyes remained fixed on his discovery. "I'm not really certain, but it sure looks like a fossil, probably a skull. And maybe all in one piece."

Charlie was now at the spot and joined John on his hands and knees. "So what the hell is it?" he asked again, but this time more slowly. "You're right, it does look like some kind of skull, but of what?"

"I'm no expert," was the answer, "but it sure doesn't look like anything I've ever seen before. And it doesn't look like anything recent. I've seen a lot of skulls in my brother's department but never seen a mammal's skull that looked anything like this. It looks more like a dinosaur's." John considered himself a bit of a renaissance man with an interest and some knowledge on most any subject. He could get into a conversation about anything but couldn't always get himself out. "Just a guess, considering that petrified tree back there, but it could be just as old. But then it doesn't look like any dinosaur skull I've ever seen in a museum or on TV, either."

"What the hell is it?" Charlie repeated once again. "Christ, it almost looks human. The top of it looks pretty damn big."

"Damn, you're right, and it almost looks as if it has eyes that face forward."

Charlie's stubby fingers touched the top of the skull. "Man, if there was any kind of brain in there, it looks like it would have been a pretty good sized one. Bigger than the one that your stupid dog has anyway. Course, just about anything has a bigger brain than he has."

John gave his dog, Abe, a lot more credit than Charlie did, but he had to admit, "Yeah, whatever this was, it might have been able to at least figure out how to open a door."

"So, what are you thinking? You want to try to dig it out?" asked Charlie.

"God, that would be fun, but how? I don't know squat about digging fossils and I don't think our knives are up to the job." That it was a fossil of some sort was plain to see, and that it was indeed a skull seemed fairly certain. But as in the case of most finds, less than half of it could be seen. The rest was imbedded in the surrounding rock. "I don't think we should even try. Hell, this could be important and have some value. To do it right takes the right tools, know how, and a lot of time. Shit, do you want to wreck the find of the century?"

"Find of the century? Yeah, right. Well, I don't know about that, but we can't just leave it here," replied Charlie. "Who knows when we'll get back, and maybe someone else will find it and take it out."

"I know, I know," replied John. "Let's think this thing out. Anyway, we've got some animals to clean, and that's what we came here for."

Giving the skull one more look, John returned his attention to the fallen antelope. It was getting hot. The meat on an antelope can turn to glue in the heat, and the processing plant would stop accepting at five o'clock. It was now close to noon. Finishing off the cleaning job would take a half an hour, and getting back to the truck might take two hours or more. And then there was the trip to the plant which would take another hour and a half. They had some time to spare, but not enough to start digging up a fossil now, no matter how interesting it might be.

The cleaning done, Charlie asked John, "Have you figured out what we're going to do with the skull? How about getting some pictures first?"

"Right – we need some photos," agreed John. "Then we've got to mark this spot. We can use the survey marker at the top of the peak and take a compass reading and step off the distance. We should be able to find it again without any problem."

"Jesus, I thought you were smarter than that. Instead of stepping it off, why don't I just take a second bearing? You pile up some rocks over there and I'll take a second reading."

"Now why didn't I think of that?"

Charlie took his Olympus digital camera out of his day pack. It didn't work. "God damn son of a bitch!"

"You sound a little pissed there, good buddy. What's the problem?"

"Damn thing is dead," replied Charlie. "You got your old Canon F1?"

Einstein's Bones

"Hey, I warned you."

With the F1, John began the photography with close-ups of the skull. It was not the first time he had ever photographed a fossil. He had done the photo work for his brother's PhD thesis and several of his other publications. From what was exposed of the fossil skull, it appeared slightly larger than a human's. On its "face" he could see what looked like one eye socket, a short snout, and the teeth, which looked like short pegs. To show scale, John placed a pack of his smokes next to the skull. After taking nearly twenty photos from every angle he could think of, he handed the camera to Charlie.

"Here, take lots, I've got two more rolls. Take some a little way back with me in it and then some from the top looking down, and then..."

"So you think I've never taken a photo before in my life?"

"Sorry," replied John. "While you're off doing your thing, I think I'll have a look around and see if I can find anything else."

After Charlie had taken a few photos of John sitting next to his find, John carefully covered the skull with a few rocks, but not enough to tip off someone else that there might be something underneath them. He then began searching the immediate area for more fossils.

Charlie walked towards the peak, taking photos all the way. The survey marker had been placed at the top in the 1940's. From there, he had a clear view of John as he slowly wandered around, eyeing the ground. Charlie used up the rest of the roll in John's camera and then all of another. Nearly finished with the third, he was satisfied that he had thoroughly documented the site, and then finished the roll with a few photos of the Big Horn Mountains. Beautiful, he thought. Standing on the survey marker, he then took out his compass to mark the direction.

Einstein's Bones

"John, quit screwing around and go stand over the skull," he shouted.

John stood NNW from the marker, or, with more precision, at 325 degrees. Charlie then walked back to the site of the find, noting the number of steps he took. No harm in measuring the distance, too, he thought. He knew it would not be all that accurate as he was going downhill and had to be careful with his footing. But he figured it would be close enough. A GPS unit would have made the job simple, but it requires batteries, and like a digital camera, anything that depends on batteries, as he had recently rediscovered, can fail. Failure in the middle of where Jesus lost his sandals is not an option. A compass does not fail. He then walked off about two hundred yards in another direction, to where John had piled some other rocks, took a second bearing and then returned to the find.

"You find any more?" asked Charlie as he returned the camera to John's pack.

"Nope, Nothing."

"Ok, finish your smoke and let's get going. We've already used up half an hour."

"All done. Just let's not bust our butts on the way back."

The real 'fun' was about to begin. It was at these times that John and Charlie didn't think of themselves as kids any more.

"Too bad about the mud this morning," remarked John. "It would have been a lot easier if we could have driven the truck in."

"Yeah."

They couldn't just drag their animals out in the same way they did when they were hunting in the north woods of Minnesota. They had tried it once before. First of all, there was no snow to provide lubrication. Second, there was not much grass – mostly just dirt and rocks. If they tried to drag an antelope over such terrain,

Einstein's Bones

even for a short distance, they'd peel the hide right off as they had done the first time they hunted Wyoming.

If they had had only one to carry out, they would have tied the legs together and rigged a sling so that they could carry it between them. But with two, the only choice was to carry them over their shoulders, fireman style.

"You see anyone else today?" asked John.

"Why?"

"I don't want some yahoo thinking we're a couple of antelope, and start blasting away, blaze orange or not."

"I had a pretty good look from the top. Didn't see nobody."

Reassured, over the shoulders the animals went. Neither of them ever looked forward to the task ahead, but at least the animals were lighter now than they had been an hour earlier.

"Ya know, we could have just lassoed these bastards and led them out on a rope. Why didn't you think of that, Charlie?"

"Right, smartass," said Charlie smiling. "What are you thinking? Should we let Newcomb know about this?"

"What, the fossil? I guess we should. No, maybe we shouldn't. Who knows what he might do or who he might tell, especially his son, Dale. Maybe they'd dig it up themselves. Hell, I don't know."

"Well, if not him, I guess your brother Willy would be the one. After all, he's in paleontology isn't he," said Charlie.

"You might be right about that, but he's more into tiny fossils of seashells and that kind of shit. But I'm sure he'd get excited about this, and I know he has done some digging of this kind, but not much. Course, I do know some guys in his department who do make this sort of thing their specialty, one in particular. I guess if we let them in on it, they'll do it right. I don't see any other way."

Einstein's Bones

When they got to the base of the peak, they laid their loads down to take a short breather. John took out another smoke. "Damn, carrying that weight down hill might be a lot easier than going up, but my legs are still killing me."

"I just wonder what the hell it is," said Charlie as he took a drink from his canteen.

"Me too. For all we know, some museum's got a hundred of 'em packed up in storage."

"Could be, but I sure don't think so. I've never seen anything close to it before either."

"Shit, Charlie, all the ones you've ever seen were on the Discovery Channel. Who knows what's been found so far."

"And what hasn't been found," added Charlie. "It could be something big." "Yeah, and when you get back home your wife's gonna be waiting at the door to tell you you've won the lottery and Phyllis will be sitting on my front step saying she's so sorry and that she made a big mistake."

"Hey, could be. I sure as shit could use the money and who knows, you might even get lucky."

"Yeah, it's been a while."

John finished his smoke, and the antelope were once again lifted onto the hunter's shoulders. It was as tiring a trek as any, but the thoughts of the skull and what to do with it made it seem easier. Unlike in the past, they did not recount the experience of their recent kill. But they did manage to mention how enjoyable a reunion with Mr. Jack Daniels would be.

They had to stop five times, each time wishing they had some flunky along with them to carry all the extras.

"Damn it, Charlie, I wish I had a lighter gun like yours. This one is really digging into my shoulder. Want to swap for a while? Or at least trade binocs? The strap is rubbing my neck raw."

"Tough shit, John. Why don't you throw out that stupid pack of cards you brought with you?"

"If I had brought any with me I would. But then I'd have to stop, and right now if I stop I'm not sure I could get going again. We're half way back and I'm three quarters dead."

"Ah, thank your lucky Marlboro Menthols."

"Screw you! Get that daughter of yours a boyfriend that looks like Arnold Schwarzenegger."

The sight of the truck only a hundred yards away seemed to make the walking easier. But once again they stopped for a brief rest.

"Makes you wonder how all those guys in the movies carry the girls with the broken ankles half way through the jungle," remarked Charlie.

"I guess they just got bigger balls." John then took a deep drag on his cigarette. "Charlie, I know we've got more than another week of vacation. I hope you don't get pissed or think I'm nuts, but I'm thinking we shouldn't take any more time than we have to to get back home. I don't want anything to happen to our find."

"I understand how you feel, but what the hell difference will another week make? And even if we did end our hunt now, it would take a couple of days to get the meat processed, anyway. Then it's a couple of days back, and anyway, how soon could we get back here with your brother or someone else? Why not just call him and tell him to get his ass out here? They do have phones in Wyoming, you know. Then we can do some more hunting. Besides, that thing has been here forever."

"I know, but no way in hell will Willy ever believe it over the phone. I wouldn't! Sure, he'll believe me that we found a skull of some sort, but I have my doubts that he'd think it all that important. I've got to show him the pictures. As for the meat, I think they will take a rush job. All I can say is that I just want to get back as soon as possible. I won't stop worrying that somebody else might find it or, who knows, it could get washed away."

"Then why not get the photos developed here in town and e-mail them to him? Damn it, I'd hate to cut this short."

"For one thing, I don't know his e-mail address and for another, I don't want anybody in some photo lab here seeing what we've found. I don't like to leave early either, but I just can't stand the thought of leaving it for any longer than we have to."

"Fuck you, it's not like you couldn't look it up. There's got to be some place in town where we can access the internet. They do have a library here you know."

"I just don't want to take the chance. We got one Mulie yesterday. That's enough for me."

"Well, it's not enough for me. I spent a lot of money. I'll be damned if we go back now."

"Calm down, besides, it's my truck. If you want to stay out here hunting, fine, be my guest. I'm going back."

Charlie answered back with a glare.

They carried their loads the rest of the way to the truck in silence. After they lowered the tail gate, loaded the antelope, and threw in their gear, they both once more checked their rifles to make sure they were unloaded. They then performed the ritual of the ranch gate and headed for the locker plant.

It was more than half way to the locker plant before Charlie broke the silence. "Ah, damn," he said softly. "I don't know if you're right, but this sure better be worth it, or you're gonna owe me a really big one."

John did not reply.

Einstein's Bones

"What about Newcomb?" asked Charlie. "He might think it odd of us leaving so soon and he might give us some shit about digging up a fossil on his land. And is it his land or BLM?"

"I think it's all his, or most of it anyway," replied John. "But we'd better take another look at that BLM map just to make sure."

"Yeah, we'd better find out. God, I just wonder what it is."

"Well, a BLM land map is a map that . . ."

"Smartass. The skull."

"I sure hope we can find it again," replied John.

"The map?"

"Guess I deserved that. I hope nothing happens to the skull," said John. "Ya know, your wife might be pleased to see you back so early. Even you might get lucky."

With their thoughts thus occupied, it seemed like no time before they reached the processing plant. Yes, they would accept a rush order for an extra fifty percent. John and Charlie had expected as much. The packaged meat would be ready to be picked up by 1:00 o'clock the next day.

On the way back to their motel, Charlie asked, "Well, what next?"

"Best give old Newcomb a call," Said John. We've always taken him, Margaret, and his son out for dinner at least one night. Best not to break with tradition. We'll have to tell him we're leaving early."

"You think he'll ask why or even give a rat's ass?" asked Charlie.

"Yeah, I think so."

"You think we ought to tell him anything about the skull?" asked Charlie. "I think we ought to come up with some excuse. When we get to the motel, give him a call and see if he's available. In the meantime, think up something."

"No, can't do that if we want to come back again. He's been good to us, and besides, I'm not a very good liar. I just hope he doesn't ask – but he will."

After just two rings, Paul Newcomb answered the phone. Yes, he and his son would look forward to dinner that night, but his daughter, Margaret couldn't make it. Yes, the Sheridan Inn would be fine. Yes, 7:30 would not be a problem. No Margaret was disappointing, especially to John. He had known her for as long as he had been coming to Sheridan and had long had a secret thing for her. Maybe she felt the same way towards him, too, but then they were both married to someone else, and she still was.

"How goes the hunt?" asked Newcomb.

"Great, we got two antelope this morning. Lots better than yesterday!" said John. "Unfortunately something has come up and we have to cut our trip short. We have to leave in the morning."

"I'm glad to hear that you've had some success, especially after yesterday's bad weather, but I'm sorry to hear that you have to go home so soon. We'll see you at 7:30."

Neither John nor Paul Newcomb liked to waste many words over the phone. Not like Charlie who could call his wife and tell her more than fourteen different ways just how much he loved her. But then, maybe that was why Charlie was still married to the wife he started out with.

John, as usual, made sure they got to the Sheridan Inn early; the Newcombs arrived precisely at 7:30. "Good to see you, Mr. Newcomb. How are you, sir?"

The table started out with a couple of rounds of drinks. Manhattans for John and Charlie – dry for John, Scotch for Paul Newcomb. Dale's choice was beer. They all ordered the night's special, prime rib that was nearly two inches thick and wide enough

Einstein's Bones

to nearly cover their over-sized plates, leaving barely enough room for a baked potato.

After ordering, Dale left the table for the salad bar.

"So, you have to leave tomorrow?" asked the elder Newcomb. "Is there anything wrong?"

John answered slowly and in a hushed voice, "No sir. I hate to ask this of you, and I know it is your ranch, but I'm going to tell you something and I'm going to have to ask you to keep it a secret - from everyone." After a pause, he quickly told the elder Newcomb what he and Charlie had found. "We'd like to come back as soon as possible with some professional help."

"I see," replied Newcomb. "You'll have to understand I'll want to call New York."

"New York?"

"My lawyers. I trust you and Charlie, but if others are going to be involved, a few things will have to be cleared up. It was on my land, not BLM, correct."

"I'm fairly certain, sir."

"Alright, that will simplify things. Just do not tell me exactly where you found it."

"Thank you," replied both John and Charlie.

The return of Dale brought the discussion to a quick end.

For the remainder of the dinner, John and Charlie had a difficult time thinking of small talk. When it was over, John took the bill. It came to a hefty chunk of change, but on the other hand, as the Newcomb's were friends and did not charge them for hunting on the ranch, it was a small price to pay.

There was little need for the hunters to rush back to their motel. Tradition called for a stop at the Mint Bar. As taverns go, it is small, but rich in atmosphere. The timber walls are decorated with mounted game and western paraphernalia. Spurs, guns, traps, and

Einstein's Bones

other bits and pieces cover the walls. Into the wooden walls are burned the brands of the local ranches, both past and present. There is a pool table in the back.

They sat at the bar and ordered the usual, Jack Daniels with a short beer chaser.

"Thanks for dinner," said Charlie.

"You could have been just a little quicker on the draw, yourself."

Half of the other patrons there were hunters, too. Many had stories of the fantastic trophies they would be bringing home with them. Others told of the ones that got away and how tomorrow would bring them better luck. As they listened, John and Charlie were tempted. Not to tell of what they had shot that day – it wouldn't be all that much to brag about anyway. No, it would have been so easy to tell of what they had found on the side of the ridge. They knew if they stayed too long and drank too much they just might.

After two rounds, John walked over to the pool table where two of the locals were playing eight ball and put a quarter on the railing.

"Hey, let's go!" barked Charlie.

"Ok," John said as he put the quarter back in his pocket.

The next morning they were in no hurry. After one last breakfast stop at the Silver Spur, they walked down the street to the office of the Bureau of Land Management. They checked the very latest land usage map and could see that the area in question was indeed owned outright by the Newcomb family. That was one less thing to worry about. They finished the morning with Charlie buying a gift for his wife.

By 12:30 they were ready to drive the half hour to the packing plant. They placed the packages in their coolers, paid the

Einstein's Bones

bill, and left. Not much idle chat about how business was this season. Then there was one last trip back to town for dry ice, about ten pounds for each cooler.

At 2:30 in the afternoon, they headed for home. No back roads this time, just freeway. As they began, John was behind the wheel; Charlie put his head back and tried as best he could to sleep. There would be no stopping for a nap by the side of the road this trip. Twelve hours later, with Charlie behind the wheel and John asleep, they arrived back in Minneapolis.

Einstein's Bones

Chapter 3

The office of Professor William Steiner was on the second floor of Pillsbury Hall on the campus of the University of Minnesota. On his walls hung photographs of some of the digs he had been on and several of his heroes in the field of paleontology. There was also a large stratigraphic map of the United States. On the floor everywhere were strewn books, piles of professional magazines, loose papers, a stereo microscope, and rocks, a lot of rocks. Two file cabinets and a large map case took up the remaining space. His large wooden desk was covered with much the same, including several boxes containing small vials of what looked like even smaller rocks. He kept but one small patch open for writing. But, if asked, he could locate anything in an instant. The entire office had the look and smell that it had not been dusted since before Professor Steiner became the occupant. The only things in the office that were cleaned with any regularity were the large portrait of Darwin which hung directly behind Willy's desk and a photograph of his wife somewhere on his desk.

  Professor Steiner, two years older than his brother, had his doctorate in Paleontology, specializing in the study of Ordovician sea shells and other entertaining entities like Brassy Oolites. To John, it all seemed so very dull. He wondered if anyone else in the world gave a shit about any of it. It was nowhere near as interesting as the study of dinosaurs, but to Willy, old seashells like *Diorthelasma* were his world. He had some experience with the bigger fossils, the kind that makes it into TV and the movies. He had helped unearth a few *Titanothere* skulls in the Badlands of South Dakota and had taken out some fossilized turtles. As an undergraduate, he had worked at a few dinosaur sites. He also had a decent collection of small fossilized rodents' teeth. But what he

Einstein's Bones

really liked to do was to go down to the brickyards in St. Paul armed with a screw driver and garden trowel and hunt the Decorah Shale for long dead brachiopods ranging in size from a quarter down to a pinhead.

Hearing footsteps at his open door, Willy turned in his squeaky wooden swivel chair and was not surprised to see his brother standing there. It was not unusual for John to stop by for an unannounced visit. He had been doing so ever since Willy had returned to his home state to become a professor in the geology department. But he was surprised to see Charlie with him.

"So what brings the two of you by?" Willy asked. John had a half smile on his face. He could never conceal his emotions when he had something at least half way important to say. "What, you getting married again?"

"Nope," he replied. "You got any classes coming up, Willy?"

"None. I'm done for the day. In point of fact, I was just about to go over to Annie's Parlor for lunch. I would be honored if you two gentlemen would join me. Then you can tell me whatever is on your mind."

Annie's Parlor, a few blocks from Pillsbury Hall, is a fast food hamburger joint and malt shop with a bit more class and atmosphere than McDonald's. The three of them went to the counter, got their burgers and looked for an empty table. John steered them in the direction of a corner table, one with a little more privacy than the others.

"Aren't you guys supposed to be off hunting in Wyoming?" asked Willy.

"We were. Just got back," replied John.

Einstein's Bones

"So how much venison did you bring me?" Willy was not a hunter and in general did not much like the idea of hunting, but he did love venison.

"Enough."

"I trust you saved the tenderloins for me."

"Yeah, right!" John knew his brother would ask for them. "If you want some, how about a bottle of Louis Roederer Cristal?"

"Sorry, but I just ran out."

"Too bad. But we might just have brought you something much better than tenderloins."

"So elucidate," replied Willy. "I am breathless with anticipation."

"You know where we hunt, don't you?" asked John.

"Sort of."

"We go just east of Sheridan, Wyoming," replied John. "What do you know about the area?"

"So what is this, a guessing game?"

"Just tell me what you know about it, Willy."

Willy turned to Charlie, "What are you two guys up to?"

Charlie did not respond but just looked back to John who repeated, "What do you know about the area?"

"Not much, really. I've been through there a couple of times. Some of the others in the department go hunting fossils not too far from there."

"What kind of fossils?" asked John.

"Old ones," replied his brother with a half smile.

"Really, what kind?"

"Dinosaurs."

"What kind of dinosaurs?"

Willy was getting slightly irritated with the game of twenty questions. "So, have you got something to tell me or not?"

Einstein's Bones

"What kind of dinosaurs?"

"Big ones."

"Be serious."

"I will be, just as soon as you tell me what this is all about."

Finally Charlie joined the exchange between the two brothers if only to end their little game. "We found a fossil and we don't think anything like it has ever been found before."

"What makes you think so?" ask Willy.

Together John and Charlie related the story of their discovery starting with the downed antelope and describing as best they could what looked like a skull. Neither of them had any real expertise, but it was the best that an educated layman could do. John made his best effort to draw the skull from memory, but he was not much of an artist. Neither was Charlie.

When they had finished, Willy responded. "Cockeyed baloney anyway! Hell of a good story, but you really don't expect me to believe any of that BS do you? So why did you really stop by?"

John now played his cards. All along he had known that this was how things would proceed. The brothers knew each other well enough and more than well enough to know how to get under each other's skin if they so desired. He pulled an envelope out of his pocket and placed six photographs on the table. Both John and Charlie were good amateur photographers. The photos were all well composed and sharp.

"Nice photos, so where did you buy these?" asked Willy as he examined them. "Next to that shop that has jackalopes for sale?"

Then Charlie pulled out the rest of the deck and showed him the aces. There were photos of John standing next to the rock and several close-ups of the skull with a pack of Marlboros next to it for scale. If that was not enough, he also pulled out the negatives to show Willy that the photos were for real.

Professor Steiner now took his time for a more careful analysis, handling each photograph separately and deliberately. He looked at them, still wondering if he could discover the joke hidden inside of them. At last, all he could do was to draw a deep breath and slowly exhale.

"What do you think?" asked John with anticipation. "Have you ever seen anything like it before?"

"No, I haven't. This better not be some kind of a joke."

John and Charlie swore to him that it was not.

"Let's go back to my office."

They retraced their steps and once again entered Willy's cluttered office.

Willy went to his map case. It contained both topographic and stratigraphic maps. John had seen the maps many times before and had used some of them to help plan his hunting trips.

"Now tell me exactly where you found it," demanded Willy.

"We were about twenty five miles east of Sheridan."

Willy went through his somewhat unorganized maps. Most of them were of Minnesota, Wisconsin, and Iowa, but he did have a few of Wyoming. "All I've got is a large scale topo of the area. The library should have what we're looking for."

The shelves of the library, in a room about four times the size of Willy's office, were full of more dusty books, more fossils and rocks, and a lot of maps. The first map Willy pulled from the drawer was a small scale topographic. "Now show me exactly where you found it."

John had no problem pointing to the exact spot, as he had the same map at home. "We were within a few yards of right there."

Einstein's Bones

Willy then went to another drawer and this time pulled out a multi-colored stratigraphic map of the same area. "What you found may well have come out of the Lance formation. It's late Cretaceous and near the K-T boundary."

"K-T boundary?" asked Charlie.

"That's the boundary between the late Cretaceous era and the Tertiary, between the end of the dinosaurs and the rise of mammals," John added.

"If you say so," Charlie replied.

"Actually, the Cretaceous is a period, part of the Mesozoic era." The professor did not like interruptions. "As I was saying, if it is from that formation, what you found might be one of the last dinosaurs to have walked upon the earth. That is, if you guys aren't feeding me a bunch of bullshit."

Once again, John and Charlie swore they were not.

"It had better not be! If it's alright with the two of you, I think Dick should take a look at this. He's done some serious digging near where you two were. Again swear to me that this isn't some kind of Piltdown Man bull shit." There was still a hint of disbelief in his voice as he spoke the words.

And again, for what they hoped would be the last time, they swore that what they had brought Willy was no fake.

John knew Dick, Dr. Richard H. Johnson, moderately well. They were by no means close friends, but Dick had been a professor in the department for as long as John's brother and they were the same age. John had gone to some of the same parties and had, on more than one occasion, shared a beer with Dick. Where Willy was lean and very tall, six foot five, Dick was more John's height, about six foot one. But he was much more muscular than either of the brothers. In the summer he always sported a deep tan, the result of his work in the field, and even now, with the field work done for the

Einstein's Bones

year, much of the tan remained, in sharp contrast with his wavy blond hair and well groomed beard. Below the beard and around his neck, he wore a silver chain with a cross. With a patch over one eye and a spear in one hand, he would have looked right at home in a Wagnerian opera. What really impressed people who met him for the first time was the huge size and strength of his hands. They were like hammers. Willy had grown up reading the true-life adventure stories of Roy Chapman Andrews. It was the reason he had gotten into paleontology in the first place. He always thought that if anyone looked the part of an adventuring dinosaur hunter, it was Dick.

Dick's office was the same size as Willy's, but looked smaller. He had even more fossils scattered about the room, and they were larger. Books and papers were everywhere. "Ah, great minds think alike. I was just about to come over to see you. And what brings John? And to whom else do I owe the pleasure?" asked Dick upon seeing his guests.

"Charlie Madson, and the pleasure is all mine." The two had never met before, but Charlie was familiar with Dick's work. John had mentioned him, and Charlie had seen Dick a few times on the Discovery Channel.

"It is we who come to seek you and your sage advice, oh wise one," added Willy with a smile. "I am pleased to see that you are sitting down. It is quite possible that I may be getting my chain pulled, but I don't think so. I hope not. What's the largest cranial cavity you have ever observed on a dinosaur?"

"An interesting question, why?"

Willy turned towards John and Charlie. "Tell him what you told me."

Once again John and Charlie told their story. Once again they were met with a healthy dose of skepticism. And once again they waited until the right moment to produce the photographs. This time, however, they were surprised as Dick took them very seriously without hesitation. "Did you disturb it? You didn't try to dig it out yourselves, did you? I hope not! Can you find it again?"

Dick was assured that they had left it as they had found it and that they had noted its location well. The only fear they had was that someone else might find it. They showed Dick the location on the map. Dick confirmed to them what Willy had said about the age and type of rock in the area. "I spent a summer about twenty miles north of there a few years back. It's a fair area. We've got to get back there as soon as possible, at least to take a look. I trust you can show me the site yourselves?"

"I guess that depends on when you want to go," said John.

"Right now," was Dick's immediate reply.

"Now? Well, we both have some vacation time left."

"I'll just need you to show me where to start digging. Who owns the land? Is it public or private?"

"Private. A rancher named Newcomb owns it. It's a huge ranch."

A look of concern came over Dick's face. "Are you sure he owns it outright and it's not BLM?"

"Yes, why?"

"If it was BLM, I'd get funding, the permits, start digging, and everything would be fine," he replied. "If it really is his land, it's his fossil. No telling what it might be worth. Private collectors might pay a fortune for something like this."

"Can he do that?" asked John.

"Sure, if it's his land, it's his fossil."

"Doesn't sound right. You'd think there'd be a law about that."

"That's the way it is. Anyway, can you go tomorrow?" asked Dick. "We'll take my Beechcraft."

"For how long?" asked John.

"A couple of days, at most," replied Dick.

"I don't see why not, Dick," replied John. "No wife to say no."

"And you, Charlie?" Dick asked.

"Do you really need me?"

"Maybe, maybe not, but I'd feel better just in case John can't find it. Besides, do you think I want to hear his empty chatter the whole way out?"

Charlie had to think about it for a moment. "My wife might get a little pissed, but what the hell, I guess so."

"Can you take off just like that, Dick? What about your classes?" John asked.

"Heck, what do you think my teaching assistants are for?" Dick had a distinguished reputation in his field, so if he dropped everything and said he was off on an important find, it would be unlikely that the University of Minnesota or anything else would stand in his way. He almost always got what he wanted. Suitable weather for digging was nearly past and it would be next summer before any really serious work could begin. But he had to see it for himself now.

"Any idea what it is, Dick?" asked John

"If it really is what we all hope it might be, then it's every bone digger's Holy Grail. If so, it would make the finding of King Tut's tomb shrink to insignificance."

"And it would be Pat Robertson's worst nightmare," added Willy. "I wish I could go, too, but I've got too much on my plate right now."

"John, call that rancher and let him know we're coming," commanded Dick.

"I can do that," replied John.

"What does he know?" asked Willy

"We told him most everything, except exactly where it was. He gave his word he would tell no one, not even his family," said John

"Do you trust him?" asked Dick

"Absolutely."

"I hope so. When in doubt, always tell the truth, but only as much as you need to," was Dick's reply.

Dick then left to make a few arrangements. When he returned, they decided that further discussion demanded a few beers at Caesar's Pub.

"John, first thing you do when you get home, is call that rancher. What's his name again anyway? No, here use my cell phone and call him right now. Do you know the number?" asked Dick.

"I should have it in my wallet." John reached into his back pocket and pulled out a wallet stuffed to overflowing with everything but money. "Let me see, bank deposit slips, ticket stubs from that *Carmen* we saw in Chicago last year – it's got to be here someplace, ah, here it is. When should I say we'll be there?"

"Ask him about tomorrow afternoon."

Dick handed John the phone and he dialed the number

"Hello, Mr. Newcomb, John Steiner."

"Hello John, I didn't expect to hear from you quite so soon. Are you planning to return soon?"

"Well, I've got to admit I have a very excited paleontologist here," said John. "I may have mentioned it before, maybe not, but my brother's a paleontologist at the University of Minnesota."

"It sounds like you want to start digging right away."

"I don't know about doing any digging, but his colleague, Dick Johnson wants to come out right away to take a look for himself."

"Richard Johnson? Yes, I think I've heard of him - seen him on TV. When would you be coming?"

"Tomorrow?" asked John with a slight hesitation.

"I'll be out of town, but I don't see why not. How long do you plan on staying?"

"Just a day or two. We're planning on flying out in the morning in Dick's plane."

"Anything else?" asked Mr. Newcomb

"No sir. I can't thank you enough."

"Have a safe flight."

John hung up the phone with a smile.

"Any problems?" asked Dick

"None, none at all."

"Was he at all concerned about my coming back with you?" asked Dick.

"Didn't seem to be at all. Actually, he sounded excited when I told him you were coming."

"Has he told anyone else?" asked Dick. "Did he ask or say anything about its value?"

"You heard the conversation. I didn't ask, and he didn't mention it either. I didn't have to. The man is a real gentleman."

"I only hope so," added Dick. "Can everybody be at Flying Cloud airport and be ready to take off by 7:00am?"

They agreed.

"Don't be afraid to take enough gear; it's a six seater. I might be able to remove the skull, but it's just as likely I'll have to leave it in place. If that's the case and if it's as important as I think it might be, I'll probably have to leave it until next summer when I

Einstein's Bones

can get things set up. But let's worry about that later. For now, what kind of beer are gentlemen drinking?"

"Who's buying?" asked John.

"I am," replied Professor Johnson.

"In that case, make mine a St. Pauli Girl."

Einstein's Bones

Chapter 4

The thought of flying in a small airplane brought back disquieting memories to John. It was not that he didn't have complete confidence in Dick's abilities or in his plane, but the last time he had flown in a small plane – either a Beaver or an Otter – he couldn't remember which – he had been forced down due to icing on the wings and after a somewhat iffy landing had been obliged to spend the night in the woods in the middle of nowhere. That had happened several years back on a moose hunting trip in Ontario.

John was up early that morning. He packed lightly – except for his photo gear – and was quickly on his way to pick up Charlie. He arrived at Charlie's in about half an hour. As usual, Charlie was ready and waiting. All of his gear, which like John's was not much, was all packed and stacked neatly by the garage door. As John drove up, Charlie was walking out the front door with a cup of coffee in his hand.

"Good morning, John," he said.

"You got an extra cup of that stuff for me?" asked John.

"Help yourself, there's plenty. You know where it is."

"You all ready to go?" asked John.

"Yup, just one last thing."

"Ah, Jesus Christ." John knew what that would be. "Did the wife give you any grief?"

"Some, not much, but she let me know she wanted me to go shopping with her for new curtains today."

"And you gave all that up for this?" asked John with a smile. "What sacrifices you make! Well, I guess you better get it over with."

Charlie went back into the house for the long mushy goodbye. He always did and John always teased him about it, but

Einstein's Bones

at the same time could never help thinking that if he had done a bit more of that with his wife, they might not have parted ways.

Flying Cloud airport was forty-five minutes away. Even though he knew that he had more than enough time, John kept worrying about being late. They arrived at the airport early and could see that Dick already had the plane out of the hanger and was busy getting it ready for take off.

"So what took you guys so long?" asked Dick.

The plane was a twin engine Baron Beechcraft model 58 that could seat six. With a cruising speed of about 200 knots and a range close to fifteen hundred miles, they would be able to reach Sheridan, about 700 miles by air, sometime later that morning.

After a few minutes they were on board and at the head of the runway. As Dick manipulated the throttle, John felt a slight twinge, but once in the air, his calm seemed to return. It felt good to be on their way.

When they reached their cruising altitude, Dick asked, "Anyone up for some Wagner?"

"What you got?" asked John.

"The *Ring*."

"Solti's?" asked John.

"Is there any other?"

"The *Ring*?" asked Charlie. "How long is it?" He liked classical music as much as the next guy, that is to say in small doses, but wasn't all that crazy about opera, which he seemed to recall that the *Ring* was.

"Not sure you want to know, but it's more than long enough to get us out there and back," said John.

"OooK," was the reply. "I guess I can always spend the time reading this magazine or just looking out the window, but what the hell, I'll put the head phones on for at least a while." Charlie

Einstein's Bones

recalled that on their trips to Wyoming, John always played *Siegfried's Rhine Journey* as they crossed the Missouri River.

"The *Ring* always gets me in the spirit of adventure," added Dick.

The weather was nearly perfect for flying. The temperature was in the sixties, cloud cover was minimal, and the winds were calm. The forecast was that it was to remain that way all the way to Sheridan and that it would remain so for at least several more days.

With an unscheduled stop in Rapid City for a minor repair and fuel, they landed in Sheridan in the early afternoon. The airport there is very small. There are no covered gantries, and no cocktail lounges in the bus-stop size terminal. The commercial jets unload their passengers on the tarmac. Only a couple of passenger jets come in every day, part of a circle route from Denver to Gillette to Sheridan and then back to Denver.

Once on the ground, while Dick secured the plane, Charlie and John loaded up the waiting rental pick-up truck.

Before they left for the ranch, Dick stopped to pick up a carton of Pall Malls. It always struck John as odd that someone as educated as Dick not only smoked, but that he smoked Pall Mall straights. But then, John knew he might have to bum one or two of them if he ran out of his own brand. At the edge of town, Dick asked John to tell him the odometer reading. Fifteen minutes out of town and the truck was on the dusty road.

As John drove, Charlie would point out a mule deer or an antelope. Dick paid little attention to that. His eyes were fixed on the hills and gullies. As he made notes, every now and then he'd ask John the mileage. Once past the ranch gate, with the ground now well dried out, they were able to park within 250 yards of the site.

"Are you sure you can find it?" asked Dick.

Einstein's Bones

"Should be no problem," said John as they began walking towards the spot. "If we do have any problem, Charlie took several bearings to zero us in. You do have those with you, and a compass, too, don't you?"

"Yes, I do."

It did not take them long to reach the spot. It turned out that there had been no need to have taken the elaborate bearings; no need for Charlie to have come along. John was almost as familiar with the area as he was with his own back yard. But it was best to have played it safe.

Besides the photo gear, John and Charlie assisted in carrying out some of Dick's equipment. Dick's bags resembled those that doctors used back in the days when they still made house calls.

At the site, Dick put his bag down and opened it. Inside the bag was a variety of hand picks, trowels, brushes, a whisk broom, chisels, several hammers, a couple of bottles of some liquid, a wide assortment of dental picks, a few spoons, several different sizes of plastic bags and wrappers, and a couple of gadgets that looked like compasses. The collection of dental picks was extensive - Dick's grandfather had been a dentist.

"Holly shit!" exclaimed Dick as John uncovered the skull. John and Charlie just smiled.

After a long silence, Dick spoke again. "Well, I guess you weren't bull shitting me after all." He dropped to his knees to examine the skull more closely. "A new species? I do think so. I've never seen or heard of anything like this."

"Do you think it might have been intelligent?" asked John.

"It's possible," replied Dick thoughtfully.

Dick sat beside the fossil, drew a deep breath, and lit up another Pall Mall. In his excitement, he lit two. Once he realized his error, he offered the second one to Charlie, who, of all things,

Einstein's Bones

accepted. John had seen Charlie enjoy a cigar now and then, but a cigarette, never.

Dick sat examining the fossil from every angle. At first he almost dared not touch it.

Finally, Dick asked, "I know it's highly unusual to do it in the field, but have you ever thought about a name?"

In a subdued tone John replied, "Me? Well, I have to admit that I have given it some thought. The best that I have come up with - ."

"You know, of course that you can add your name to it."

"No, I keep on thinking Sapienasaur, "Thinking Lizard". I haven't been able to come up with anything better. What do you think, Charlie?"

"I'll pass," said Charlie. "I don't know a damn thing about naming dinosaurs."

"Ok with me, but Sapienasaur actually means wise lizard," was Dick's comment.

"Whatever," John replied to Dick's correction.

"So Sapienasaur it is but perhaps with a slight change for scientific reasons," was Dick's definitive rejoinder. "It just so happens that I have a bottle of Wild Turkey in one of those black bags. The sun is certainly well past the yardarm, so I think now is a good time to pause and enjoy a libation or two."

With that, the bourbon emerged from the black bag and three paper cups were at once filled.

"To Sapienasaur!" said Dick in toast.

"To Sapienasaur!" they answered.

"To Mr. John Steiner, the discoverer of Sapienasaur!" added Dick in a second toast.

And once again they all replied, "To Mr. John Steiner!"

Einstein's Bones

"Ah hell, why not one to my good buddy Charlie?" added John.

Charlie had a quizzical look on his face. "So why do you suppose something like this has never been found before?"

"I can't tell you that," answered Dick, "but then maybe it has. For one thing, there are a lot of fossils that have been dug up and removed and never really examined. Museum back rooms are full of them. Or maybe someone didn't know what he was looking at. Maybe just fragments were found. Happens all the time. Then again, maybe we are the first to ever see one of these. Who knows?"

The toasts completed and the whiskey drunk, Dick began working on the skull, while John and Charlie busied themselves taking photographs.

Removing a skull from the ground is slow, laborious, and exacting work. It is done as much by feel as it is done by sight. The trick is to determine what is surrounding rock and what is bone which had now become rock. The differences can be subtle and the process frustrating. But color and texture will tell the expert what is to be saved and what is to be discarded. And the discard pile would be examined again and again. In this instance, the fossilized bone was somewhat lighter in color than the surrounding rock matrix and was smoother in texture.

Dick began with an old Boy Scout jack knife, then a trowel, dental pick, and brush. After he had cleaned off a small area, he made use of the contents of the several small bottles John had noticed in the black bag, applying the liquid to the fossilized bone.

"What's that stuff?" asked John.

"Liquid cement – keeps the bone from breaking up," informed Dick. "When we take it out we'll wrap it up in burlap and plaster of Paris."

"Are you going to remove it now?" asked Charlie.

"No, I just want to see a little more and we need to protect it," he answered. He then began to laugh. "This sure is going to mess up my plans for next summer."

As Dick finished his preliminary work, John kept taking photos. In an hour, Dick was finished, carefully protecting the skull and then covering it with a few rocks.

As he raised himself up, he said, "I'm gonna have a look around and take some measurements. John, you and Charlie, why don't you walk around too, and keep your eyes to the ground. If you find anything, just let me know."

"What the hell do we know about fossil hunting?" asked John.

"I know," replied Dick, "but you found this one. Besides, you have gone out fossil hunting with your brother, right?"

"Yeah, but that was for sea shells, and I didn't find much of anything anyway."

"That's alright, don't worry about it. There'll be plenty more eyes here later. And if you do find something, be sure to look up-slope as the skull might have been washed down hill."

Dick then took out two maps and two of the compass-like gadgets that John had seen in his bag. "What are those?" asked John.

"A pocket transit and a Brunton compass."

"I'll take your word for it."

While John and Charlie spent the rest of the afternoon walking slowly with their eyes on the ground, Dick was more concerned with the surrounding rock formations, the uprisings, the dips, and other similar outcroppings, all the while taking notes, looking at his maps, using his two gadgets, walking and measuring. And constantly smoking Pall Malls. Every so often, he could be heard to say, "Yes, yes," or "that looks interesting," or, "John, can you come over and take a picture of this or a picture of that."

Einstein's Bones

By the end of the day, John and Charlie had found several rocks they thought might be fossils. None were.

"Time to head back," said Dick. "I've done about all I can for now. Hope there's a decent motel room or two to spare in town."

Early the next morning they boarded Dick's Beachcraft for the flight back to Minneapolis. The next summer couldn't come soon enough.

Einstein's Bones

Chapter 5

For Dick, the rest of the academic year was busier than usual. First, he had to cancel a scheduled dig in Montana, a dig he had planned two years before. He had to let his three graduate students know about the change in plans for the summer without telling them too much. And then there was funding, always the funding. And to get funding there were grant proposals to write. He always hated doing it - hated begging for money, but the university budget was very limited. Of the several he wrote, only one, the one to the National Geographic came through. Telling them only that he had made an interesting find, they were more than generous. Dick had never let them down in the past. Finally, there was Newcomb. Would he keep the secret, or would he take the discovery for himself? After several phone conversations, he received papers from Newcomb's New York lawyers and breathed somewhat easier. By spring, everything seemed to be in order.

While still excited about his discovery, John gave little thought that he would be returning to Wyoming anytime soon. Maybe if they were still working on it, he'd see it next hunting season, or perhaps he'd see something about it on the news. He was surprised when Dick called and asked if John could spend the summer at the site as the official photographer. Dick liked the photos John had taken so far, and Dick thought that the camera work John had done for his brother was first class. Still, there was a minor problem. John had a job in the city. He hated it, but it paid the bills.

"What will it take to make up your mind?" Dick had asked.

"Other than money, nothing," John had replied.

Dick then told him about the funding arrangements and that they included John. The pay was good – more than he was making now. Saying "yes" was easy. Sure, he'd have to get another job when the summer dig came to an end, but he reasoned he couldn't find a worse job than he had now. He'd be a fool to pass on what might be the adventure of his lifetime.

As soon as the academic year was over, John was on his way back to Wyoming, this time riding shotgun in the fully packed geology department van with Dick behind the wheel. Dick had considered flying, but decided the extra set of wheels was more important.

John had little idea what equipment Dick had packed. John brought along, besides his clothing, all of his photo gear which included a new Canon digital camera with various lenses and accessories, compliments of the National Geographic.

They started out at 5:00pm, planning to drive non-stop, with a cooler full of thick ham sandwiches, chips, and several cans of beer. Behind them by an hour or so, hauling a fifth wheel trailer, were two of Dick's graduate students, Hezekiah Thompson and Colin Yeager, better known in the geology department as Stan and Ollie. Hezekiah, who liked to be called Zeke, was the tall skinny one - his tall, underweight frame made more striking by his thin angular face which was covered by a short sparse red beard. Colin was clean-shaven, but his florid face matched the color of Zeke's beard. Dick's third graduate student, Karen Peterson, would follow in a few days.

When they reached the South Dakota border, they ate the first of their ham sandwiches. At the Missouri River, they had another and changed drivers. A few miles past, Dick popped open two beers and handed one to John.

"Just don't speed," he said as he handed it over. He then dialed his cell phone and talked with Colin. They had fallen a little further behind.

Einstein's Bones

"Nice guys," said John as Dick put away his phone. "I guess I've seen them once or twice around the department before all this, but I don't know if I've ever met Karen. What's she like?"

"If you'd ever met her, you wouldn't need to ask the question. She's very good at what she does and I need her here, but I'll just leave it at that."

John leaned a little further back in his seat, took a swallow of beer, put the can in the cup holder and then fumbled for a cigarette. As he slowly exhaled, his mind drifted back in time and a slight smile appeared on his face. But John did know her. He knew her in that special sense of the word. Right after he broke up with Phyllis, there was Karen. A chance encounter in the Geology department when she asked him right out if he'd like to go to bed with her. He didn't refuse. It wasn't anything with any special meaning, no thought of anything permanent, just some of the best quick sex he'd ever had, and then, with no explanation, she moved on to someone else. If nothing else it helped him through a difficult time. That was fine with John That Dick didn't know anything about it was a surprise, but John had done his best to keep it secret, fearing it might make matters worse with his divorce. Perhaps his brother knew, but if he did, he never said anything. "Karen Peterson," he thought to himself. "I wonder who she's screwing now. He's gotta be one happy bastard - at least for a while." As he exhaled again, he wondered what was going to happen next. He looked over at Dick and thought, "I wonder if he ever slept with her."

A few miles past the Wyoming border, they pulled into a rest stop to try to get an hour or two of sleep. Only partially successful, they were on the road again in two hours. Numb from the drive, they pulled into the Sheridan Holiday Inn at 8:30 that morning, quickly unpacked, left a message for Zeke and Colin, and went to bed.

Four hours later, the hotel phone rang. It was Zeke. He and Colin had stopped just west of the South Dakota/Wyoming border to catch some sleep in the fifth wheel. They were fully rested and ready to get going.

All that Dick said was, "we'll be ready in ten minutes." He put down the phone, picked it up again, and called Newcomb. After the short conversation was over, he told John that Newcomb and his son, Dale would meet them at the ranch.

Leaving the fifth wheel in the hotel's parking lot, all four piled into Dick's van. The only stop in town was for a fresh carton of Pall Malls.

Just out of town, Dick turned to John and asked, "A little disappointed?"

"What do you mean?" he replied.

"I mean that Margaret isn't coming. Hell, you never stopped talking about her the whole way out."

"The hell I did. Did I really?"

"Just about."

"Bull."

"Bull? You want me to start at the beginning? Let me see. She's about five foot ten inches tall, slender, has the darkest brown eyes you've ever seen, very intelligent, looks great on a horse, she's the best female friend you've ever had, her favorite movie is *Casablanca*, she likes classical music and is a history buff, you've been secretly in love with her ever since you first saw her, you love her voice, she likes all things outdoors, she - - - shall I go on?"

"I guess not."

Einstein's Bones

"Now is there really anything going on between the two of you?" said Dick.

"How could there be," replied John. "First of all, she was married, and then I only saw her a couple of times each year on hunting trips. Hell, I didn't even get to see her last year."

"You didn't answer my first question. Are you disappointed especially now that she's divorced?"

"Yeah, I suppose a little, but I guess I'll see her soon enough."

Dick took out another Pall Mall and turned the conversation to the work ahead. Now, for the first time, he revealed all he knew to Zeke and Colin. John passed them a stack of photographs.

"Jesus," was Zeke's only comment as he passed them to Colin.

"Interesting *foramina*," said Colin nonchalantly.

"Whatever you say," said John.

"Now here's the plan," said Dick. "John, of course you'll be ready with your cameras at all times while Zeke and I work on the fossil. Colin, I want you measuring out the site and looking for more specimens."

He made further elaborations. They also made several brief stops along the way to examine rock formations and for John to take photographs. By 1:30, they were at the ranch gate waiting for the Newcombs to arrive.

They waited only long enough for Dick to finish one cigarette. From the driver's side of a green Ford F250 stepped Dale Newcomb. With his mustache and cowboy hat, he looked like he could double for the Marlboro Man. He belonged on a horse. It took Paul Newcomb a little longer to emerge from the passenger side. He didn't quite fit the western image. Maybe he looked too buttoned-down, too eastern, too much like an accountant. Or maybe it was his thinning grey hair. But, all that didn't matter. He might not have looked the part, but John always thought he acted with the ideals inspired by any good John Ford movie.

John and his three companions walked over to the pick-up. "Hello Dale. Glad, as always, to see you Mr. Newcomb." John never called him "Paul".

John started the introductions with Paul and Dick Johnson. Newcomb could not conceal a broad smile. "I've been reading a couple of your books since last fall. Very interesting and very well written. It's too bad you and that Shunk fellow can't agree on much of anything."

Shunk. Carl Shunk. "Shunk the Skunk" to Dick. Sure, there were many things on which they could agree, but there were also major differences. Were birds really dinosaurs? Was it really a comet or meteor that wiped them out? For Shunk the answers were an unqualified "yes". For Johnson, a cautious "maybe". And there were differences in style. Shunk lived for the publicity and the fame, or so thought Dick Johnson, while Johnson thought all of that was just nonsense that got in the way of doing the real work. There was more. He never had trusted the Skunk, the Skunk who was too quick to take the work and ideas of others as his own. The Skunk who was always quick to see where a profit could be made.

For now, Dick kept these thoughts to himself. "Well, maybe one day we will, Mr. Newcomb," said Dick in reply.

"Please, just call me Paul."

John made a final introduction. "And this is Hezekiah Thompson. He goes by Zeke."

"Jesus, what drugs were your parents on when they named you?" asked Dale as he looked at Zeke.

A short silence followed as Zeke ignored the question.

"Well, let's go," said Newcomb.

Einstein's Bones

On the short drive to the site, Zeke asked John, "Is he always like that – always rude?"

"I suppose he can be. I know his sister has never had anything good to say about him – thinks he's a real asshole. But I don't really know. I've never had all that much to do with him."

Once again, they were able to park within 250 yards of the site. As they walked, carrying their equipment, John hoped that the site had not been disturbed. He was not disappointed. Once again, Dick slowly uncovered the skull.

Almost immediately, Colin and Zeke dropped to their knees to get a closer look. "Son-of-a-bitch, I can't believe it," said Colin.

Zeke joined in with, "No shit, I never imagined I'd ever see anything like this."

Paul Newcomb stood silent, but Dale added, "I wonder what it's worth." No one replied.

"Just look at the size of the cranial cavity," noted Zeke.

"Maybe?" questioned Colin. "Not all that much is out yet. But, yes, the possibilities, the possibilities."

After they had all had their turns looking, Dick and his graduate students took out their tools. As Colin began his search for more specimens, Dick and Zeke got to work on the skull, Dick with a jack knife and Zeke with a pick and brush and a small trowel. The more they cleared away, the more of the skull that they revealed, the more they were amazed by the apparent size of the brain cavity.

"My God," said Zeke, "it's not all that dissimilar from the size and shape of a human skull. Do you think it could have been intelligent?"

"How can we ever know?" replied Johnson. "John, take some shots of this. How close can you get? How much film you got?"

Einstein's Bones

"I got lots, and ya know I've got this digital camera too, so don't worry. Just tell me what you want and I'll shoot it. With this macro lens I can get just about as close as you want."

"Here, get a close up of this. And this, too. Be sure you get the ruler in for scale."

As the work went on, the day became hot. Dick and Zeke digging, picking, brushing, and cementing. Colin measuring, taking notes, and every so often getting on his hands and knees for a better look as he worked the ground for more specimens. John taking both digital and conventional photographs. All the while, the Newcombs watched, fascinated, and every so often brought a beer to the thirsty workers. For several hours they continued. Richard Johnson and Zeke knew their work well. Except for the rear most portion, the head was almost completely exposed by now and Dick soon ascertained that the neck of the creature, who he was now calling "Einstein" was also *in situ*. What was further amazing was that the neck seemed to join the skull at its base in the same manner as in humans, as opposed to at the rear as it does with most mammals and all other known dinosaurs.

"Just look where the f*oramen magnum* is," noted Dick. "This bad boy not only had to have walked on two legs like a lot of other dinosaurs, but he must have walked upright and erect almost like a human."

"Certainly it is a new species," said Zeke. "A new genus, too."

"Might even be a new family," replied Dick.

It was getting late. Zeke got up to join Colin and John who were looking at an interesting outcropping of rocks and enjoying a beer, leaving Dick alone - the Newcombs having left two hours before. For what remained of the daylight, he would continue to excavate as much of the skull as he could, while at the same time continue to expose more of the neck vertebra. If the neck was in such good condition it stood to reason that the rest of the skeletal structure might be well preserved also.

As Dick chipped away at the neck with one of his grandfather's old dental picks, a bright yellow color caught his eye. He applied a mild concentration of HCl then chipped a little more. He repeated the process several times. A few more chips and dustings with a brush, and there was no doubt as to what it was. Gold!! What was gold doing here? He began to sweat. He chipped away more urgently, his mind buzzing now. A few more probes with the pick and a few more strokes with the brush and more came into view. So far he had uncovered an area of gold about an inch long and an eighth of an inch wide. Once again he dusted it and then took out an eight power loupe. He dared not believe what his eyes now told him. He looked hard once again, and then again to be sure, leaving the magnifying piece on the streak of gold until he at last believed.

"Holy living fuck!" he blurted out.

Dick was never thought to be a prude, but his use of that word was unusual.

"What?" they all asked.

Now the sweat was pouring from his face. Dick took several deep breaths, for he could hardly believe what he was about to say. "A gold necklace! This son of a bitch is wearing a gold necklace. Holy living Fuck!"

Einstein's Bones

Chapter 6

Zeke, Colin, and John walked quickly over to Dick who was intensifying his efforts on the necklace.

"Holy shit," exclaimed Zeke as he dropped his beer bottle.

"Don't just stand there gawking, start taking photos," said Dick to John who was standing frozen.

John bent down with the macro lens on his camera. "Could it be that Einstein here really is wearing a necklace? Damn, I was pretty sure I had found something that was important, but never anything like this."

Dick chipped away and exposed more of the gold, this time washing it off with a squirt of water. "I don't know what else it could be. If anyone has a better explanation, please tell me."

"Well, whatever it is, it shows pretty damn good craftsmanship," said Colin. "And if it really is a necklace, what else are we going to find?"

"You sure you got enough film, John?" asked Dick.

"Like I told ya."

"I'm thinking," said Dick.

"About what?" asked Colin.

Dick ignored him as he continued to pick and dust. He then took out his cell phone and punched in a number. Nothing. He tried again. Still nothing. "Guess we're out of range. Have to wait till we get back to town. OK, let's get this wrapped up."

When they reached the van, Dick turned to John. "Thank you, thank you, thank you. If I ever doubt you again, just shoot me."

"Well, this ought to make you famous," said John.

"I already am," deadpanned Dick.

"Anyway, it sure is gonna make the National Geographic happy. If this doesn't rate a special, I don't know what will," said John.

"If you don't mind, I'd like to keep them out of this for now," replied Dick. "The last thing I want right now is a bunch of unwanted strangers running around, getting in the way and telling me what to do and how to pose for their silly pictures. I've been through all that shit enough times before. Can't get a damn thing done. We'll worry about all that PR crap later."

"You're old buddy the Skunk's gonna be pea green."

"Yeah, I suppose he will. But I don't want to even think about him now. Where's a good place to eat?"

"Who's buying?"

"I am – as usual."

"In that case let's go to the Sheridan Inn. Did you ask the Newcombs about tonight?"

"Yes I did, but they had something else going on," replied Dick.

Three miles back towards town, Dick tried his cell phone once more. For the third time there was nothing. Ten miles nearer, he finally made contact but there was no one at the other end, so he just said, "Dear, call me as soon as you can, I love you."

"Just can't wait to tell the wife, can you?" asked John.

"Something like that."

Back at the hotel, Dick called his wife again, but still she was not home. He left the same message. They all cleaned up, changed, and headed for dinner.

All through the meal, Dick kept his cell phone on the table. As the waitress handed him the bill, his phone rang at last. At first he sounded angry, "Where have you been?" There follow a short silence, then, "I'm sorry. I need you to look up the number for

Einstein's Bones

Barbara Allen. It's in that green book on my desk in the study." He waited with his pen poised on a napkin. John watched as he wrote out the number, a number which did not have a normal area code. When Dick was finished, he said, "Thanks. I've got a lot to tell you, but can't do it right now. I love you."

"Barbara Allen?" asked John. "Is she from Scarlet Town? I don't suppose she has a boy friend named Sweet William, does she?"

"I don't know anything about that. She's an English cultural anthropologist."

"How do you know her? Have you ever worked with her? I can't imagine you would have."

"No, we've never worked together, but we've met a number of times – attending lectures, some meetings of the Geographic. I like the work she does, and she likes mine. And with what we found today, well, that might be right up her ally. I'm going to give her a call and see if she can come over and help us out."

"Right now? If it's 10:00pm here, what time in the morning is it there?"

"It can't be that early there. She seems like a pretty good sport. I don't think she'll mind. I'll call her from the room."

By the time they reached Dick's room, they had come to the conclusion that it must be about five or six in the morning in London. "If she's not up by now, she should be," said Dick as he passed out beers and pulled his cell phone from his pocket.

The other end of the line answered almost immediately. It was Barbara Allen. "If I woke you, I apologize," said Dick after he identified himself. He had not. In fact she had already been up for an hour. For ten minutes he told her what had been found. Even without hearing her end of the conversation, John could sense her excitement. When Dick put the phone down, he said, "She'll be here next week."

"So, you gonna call your buddy Shunk and invite him here too?" asked John with a laugh.

"Sooner or later that bastard's going to find out. And when he does, I think I can keep him out of here, but he's sure as hell going to try to horn in one way or another," said Dick as he took a swallow of beer.

"So, how in hell is he gonna be able to bother us, anyway?" asked John.

"He has his ways," replied Dick. "He might start digging nearby in some of those formations we saw that looked promising. If he finds something, he might try to steal the show. But I'm not worried about that."

"So?" ask John.

"What worries me is that he might try something with the Newcombs."

"I don't think you have anything to worry about there."

"Maybe not with the old man," replied Dick, "but what about that son of his? I do remember him asking about how much all this might be worth."

"You don't think he'd let the Skunk in, do you?"

"I sure as hell hope not. Tell me everything you know about him."

"Well," said John, "I know the old man pretty well. Always liked him. As far as him doing something, I really doubt it. I've talked with him enough times, seen his library, and know he has a good sense of history and science. And what with his ranches, his oil, and his gas, he's got more money than he knows what to do with. Dale? Like I said before I don't know him that well - hardly at all really. All I know is mainly through what Margaret has told me.

She's not overly fond of him - thinks he's a shit. But anything specific? No, no she's never been specific. That comment about how much it was worth? A little scary, but hell, I don't know."

Colin broke in. "Yeah, it worried me too, but I suppose it's a natural enough question."

"Yeah, just how much would it be worth?" asked John.

Dick sounded resigned. "For now, let's just hope they all keep their mouths shut. And with nobody guarding the site, we don't want any lookers-on or looters."

John reassured Dick, "As long as the old man is in charge, we'll be OK. He won't stand in the way of science."

"Yes, we'll just have to trust them - for now," Dick concluded.

They continued the discussion for one more beer and then called it a night.

The next morning, all four were up early and ready to go a half hour before dawn. As he passed through the lobby, Dick left a message for Karen, just in case she showed up. "Karen – sit tight, we will be back from the field some time before dark and will come back here first. If it's not too late we'll all go out for dinner."

Once again they piled into the van, John driving. Before they got out of town he stopped to let Dick grab a couple of packs of Pall Malls.

There are few things as beautiful as a sunrise on the high plains. The rich red glow of the sun blanketing the warm brown of the hills sparkling with dew. Breathtaking – as long as you were not driving right into it. Ahead of them and off to the sides they saw cattle, a few mule deer, a flock of turkeys, and every now and then an antelope off in the distance.

"I can see why you and your buddy keep coming out here," mentioned Zeke to John.

"Yeah, it's great. You a hunter?"

"No, never have."

"How about you, Colin?" asked John.

"Just a couple of times with my father."

"So," asked Dick as he turned to John, "how'd you like to do a little field work today?"

"What the hell do I know about digging up bones? I didn't touch old Einstein when I found him and I sure don't want to screw things up now," said John.

"Don't worry, you won't. I'll guide you. It won't hurt you to learn. Besides, you've helped your brother, haven't you?"

"That wasn't like this."

Dick just smiled.

John was both excited and nervous at the prospect. In another twenty minutes they were at the ranch. About a mile past the gate and after innumerable twists and turns and ups and downs, they once again reached the point where they had parked the day before.

"You might not believe it, but they actually bring semi's in here during the round-up to haul out the cattle," observed John.

"I'll believe anything you tell me," replied Dick.

"Well, it's still here," said Zeke as they reached the site.

Dick seemed to take forever examining what they so far had done before he determined how to proceed. Though Dick was the expert, he earnestly solicited his student's advice and listened to their recommendations. To John they might as well have been speaking Armenian. "*Distal* this, *maxillary* that, or *quadrate* this." "Just look at the *sclerotic* plate. I bet this fellow had good vision."

Einstein's Bones

"I don't have a clue what you guys are talking about. Latin right? All I seem to remember from my high school Latin is *futue te ipsum et caballum tuum*. I guess that's just enough to get me punched out."

"Stick around long enough and you'll pick it up," replied Dick. "Maybe even enough to impress Margaret. If you really want to learn those terms, I've got a book back at the hotel. Shall we begin?"

"John, Zeke and I are going to start you on your lessons. But keep that camera ready. Colin, go get some of those marker flags out of my kit over there and start looking for more fragments. Flag anything that looks like it might be one of Einstein's friends. And if you find something, don't forget to take a look up-slope for a possible source. Just go slow, take your time, and keep your head down. If you miss something, don't worry, a lot more looking is going to be done."

"What, ya think I've never done this before?" asked Colin.

"I know, I know," replied Dick. "Sorry."

Dick reached into his black bag and pulled out his familiar picks, bottles, knives and brushes. He handed John a squeeze bulb. "Your first lesson will be how to blow off the dust,"

"I guess I can handle that. So why look up-slope?" asked John.

"If you find something, there's a good chance it washed down from above."

"That makes sense."

No one could ever accuse Dick of working without a sense of style. Along with the usual professional equipment, he brought along a bottle of wine, some cheese, and a portable CD player with a good supply of Mozart. John couldn't help wondering what some stranger might think if he heard the *Jupiter Symphony* drifting through the hills.

Once again the weather was perfect for digging. A bit on the cool side at the start, but soon it became hot.

As Colin began to search the hills, Dick and Zeke resumed their excavation in earnest. By now the skull and neck were completely exposed. They now concentrated on exposing the rest of the necklace. They soon discovered that it was lying on top of the ribcage and, unlike any other find, besides so far appearing to be complete, the remains appeared to be in line. Unlike other finds, they were not twisted or contorted nor were they in any way scattered about.

"Not only is this young man wearing some pretty heavy metal, but so far it seems that he was laid out with a purpose," observed Dick.

"Almost as if he were buried by his friends and relatives. After what we've seen so far, I guess I'm not really surprised," added Zeke. "I have the feeling that we're not through with surprises."

"Nor do I. You want to try your hand at a little chipping, John?" asked Dick. "Follow the line, and just don't force anything. I will be watching."

John took up one of the dental picks tentatively. "You sure about this?"

"More or less. You'll be fine. You've been paying attention to what I've been doing? Just do the same. Pretty easy to tell the bone from the matrix. Wait, hold the pick right there. I'll take a picture of you for a change."

Before John could do any damage, Dick handed the camera back to John. "Get some good close-ups of that, and that, too."

Einstein's Bones

By now, they had exposed about six inches of the necklace on either side of the neck. "Amazing how new it looks," observed John.

"It's gold you know. It doesn't exactly rust," said Zeke.

"Yeah, I knew that."

"Time for a break," said Dick. "Now where the hell is Colin? I don't see him anywhere. Call him in."

With that, John bellowed out a long and loud "COLIN," which was soon answered with a much softer, "What?" He was not all that far distant, just hidden by a nearby ravine.

"Hungry?" asked Dick. "Find anything yet?"

"Yeah, hungry and thirsty, but haven't found anything I like yet."

"I gotta a strong feeling you will."

The break lasted only fifteen minutes. It was now getting quite warm and the flannel shirts began to come off.

"You want to try a little more, John?"

"Sure."

John took up a pick. Dick sat beside him with a wisk-broom and advice. "You're doing fine. Careful there. Clear off a little more of the *uncinate* process."

"Huh?"

"That there. That rib strut."

"Got ya. I'll have to remember that one – for Margaret. Ah, I don't seem to remember that we have these, do we?"

"No, birds and some dinosaurs. Zeke, work that trowel and see if you can figure out how wide this is. I don't want this out in the field any longer than it has to be. Well, OK John, the lesson for today is over. Time you got back to what you know best."

"Thanks, Dick. Wish my brother could see this."

Einstein's Bones

"Maybe he will, if I can pry him away from his Decorah Shale. Zeke's found some interesting shells."

Colin had not gone more than forty steps over the same ground he had looked at earlier, when the sound of a distant rifle caused him to look away and then back at the ground. Something caught his eye. It was no skull just lying there ready to be picked up, but a small nearly concealed fragment of bone.
"I think I found something here."
"Mark it and keep looking. John, go over there and take some photos before someone steps on it"
"Ok, boss," was Colin's reply. He was a little surprised that Dick didn't rush over at once, but he knew that was the way he worked. Ten more steps and, "I think I've got another."
"So mark it already!"
"Will do," and so he resumed his search after having planted two flags. Colin was getting excited. It was like fishing. Nothing raises spirits faster on a slow day than to catch that first fish or two. Too bad for him, but that was his last find for the day. Another hour of carefully examining the ground produced nothing.

By early afternoon the work had proceeded down the rib cage to where the chain ended with what looked to be a gold medallion about the size of a half dollar. The chain itself totaled about thirty inches in length.

"From the way this chain is laid out, I'd swear this boy went to a funeral," said Zeke. "Maybe we should bring out some flowers next time."

"Take a closer look at this medallion. Seems to be some design on it," said Dick as he washed it off with a squirt of water.

"Yeah," remarked Zeke as he brushed away some of the matrix.

It took ten minutes of careful work to reveal the design. "This is really getting way too unbelievable," said John. "It looks like some kind of sunburst design."

"Yeah, and a circle and a triangle. What the hell is it?"

"Holy shit, I know," said John. "It's fucking Masonic."
"Oh bullshit. It can't be. Are you sure?" asked Dick.
"As sure as anything."
"Holy shit is right. It seems as though we just might not be the first to find one of these bad boys, after all. Either that, or this son-of-a-bitch was a Mason."

Behind them in the distance they heard the sound of a pickup coming towards them. It was Newcomb. This time he had his son and both of his daughters with him.

"Good to see you, what a beautiful day," said John.
"Howdy, John, Dick, Zeke. Where's Colin?" replied Mr. Newcomb.
"Off looking for buried treasure," replied John. "Good to see all of you." He smiled. "I don't think you will be disappointed." He called Colin in, but Colin had heard the trucks too, and was back with the group quickly.

Einstein's Bones

"From what I can see now, I'm sure we won't. Hello, Colin."

"Good afternoon all."

One of the Newcomb daughters approached John. She was about his age, only a few inches shorter than John, with medium length brunette hair, deep brown eyes, slender, but not skinny, very attractive in her blue jeans and a red and black checkered flannel shirt, and from her tan, it was obvious that she was an out-of-doors type of woman. She was also recently divorced, though John had always thought that she and her husband got along just fine. She and John had been friends, good friends – nothing more – ever since John and his father first started hunting on the ranch. As for Newcomb's other daughter, Carol, John had never laid eyes on her before. She too, was quite striking, but as far as John was concerned, from what he had heard about her from Margaret, she was not really his type. Not into the same kind of music, the same movies, or watching PBS specials. And besides all of that, from all accounts, she was very happily married.

Colin looked at Margaret then nudged John and whispered, "Hot."

"Great to see you, Margaret. Sorry to hear about you and Bob."

"Thanks, but no need to be sorry about it, he wasn't all that much anyway. Thank God we never had any children."

"Still, I don't like to hear about such things." Now that was about as big a lie as John had told in at least a month. There was nothing he would like better than to be able to give Margaret his best shot. As long as she had been married, there had been no point in spoiling the great hunting setup he and Charlie had. Margaret had never given any indications of interest in him before – at least as far

Einstein's Bones

as John ever noticed, but now, maybe the door was open. He could only hope. "You're looking great."

"Thanks," she said as she looked straight into John's eyes. "It looks as though you boys have been hard at it."

Dick now took over the conversation. "Take a close look. Interesting, is it not?"

"It looks like a necklace. Did you put it there?" asked Mr. Newcomb half seriously. It was obvious to him that Dick had not, but what other easy explanation could there be? He might be a rancher, but being a rancher did not keep him from knowing what was going on in the world. Without really getting close he thought it was just possible it might be a prank for his benefit.

"Take a really close look. Use the magnifier."

"I'll be dipped in shit." His son and daughters also took their turns, saying nothing - for a while, but what they must have been thinking could easily be imagined by the looks on their faces, as if they were staring at some great religious icon for the first time.

It was Dale who broke the silence. "I wonder what *Antiques Road Show* would say?"

As Margaret gave him a knowing glance of disgust, John thought to himself, "That bastard."

Without acknowledging Dale, Dick spoke. "I'm going to call in some more of my students, some of my best undergraduates to help out. I think that this might get to be a very big dig. It could go on for quite some time."

"I believe I know where you're headed," interrupted Newcomb. "It's a big ranch. I've talked with my lawyer - if you will guarantee to repair the land after you have finished and cover any liabilities, go ahead, and do what you have to. I'm not about to stand in the way of something like this. Just let me know what you're going to be doing so we can keep out of the way."

Einstein's Bones

"I think there's going to be a lot of digging and even more people. I've invited a colleague in England."

"Jane Goodall?" asked Newcomb hopefully.

"No, Barbara Allen," replied Dick.

"Her I've never heard of. Just keep me informed and I would appreciate a ringside seat for me and my family."

"Done. Thank you. Again, I'd like to keep this quiet at least until we get the site secured."

"I agree. There's no point in being flooded with tourists! I certainly don't want the ranch overrun," Newcomb added.

With this informal understanding, Dick opened some of the refreshments brought out in the morning and some which the Newcombs had brought with them.

"How old do you think that is?" asked Carol.

Margaret turned to John and said in a low voice, "Here we go again."

Dick answered Carol's question. "I can't tell for certain, but judging from the local formations, I'd guess about sixty five million years old."

"How can that be?" she asked.

"What do you mean, Carol?" asked Dick.

"How can something be that old? How can it be older than the Earth?"

Dick had been through this routine before. "You and I have different points of view, and there's not much point in arguing either. But, as you can see," he said as he lifted out his cross, "one can believe in God and science both."

Carol began to reply, "I think God would be - - -".

"That's enough for now," interrupted Paul Newcomb. "Maybe you can take this up later."

Dick resumed his digging.

Einstein's Bones

"Colin, would you mind taking photos for a while," asked John. "I want to show Margaret what else we've found."

"You've got fifteen minutes," said Dick.

The remaining Newcombs sat around the ever-widening dig, soon re-joined by Margaret and John. Before they had given it much thought, it was two hours later. The excavators were near the base of the rib cage. The Newcombs, except for Carol, kept up a conversation with many questions both about what was going on in front of them and about the experiences of paleontologists in the past.

"Was that character in the movie really based on you?" Margaret asked looking Dick's way.

"No, but I've met him many times, and we've been on a few programs together. I bet he'd sure like to be here now. He's a real hog for publicity."

"And you're not?" asked Zeke.

"Well, maybe a little."

"Have you ever found anything at all like this before?" asked Dale. "What do you do with them after you get 'em out of the ground?"

"All I have found in the past is nothing next to this. Or what anyone else has ever found. At best, all I have ever done before has been just good training for this," answered Dick. "It's something I could never have even dreamed about. Never in my wildest fantasies. No telling what else might be here. And as for what will eventually happen to this, after much study, I'm sure it will end up in some museum."

"This is just fantastic," replied Newcomb. "I could stay here all day, but I've got to head back to town for a meeting with my bank. If we leave right now, I just might not be too late."

Einstein's Bones

After they had gone, Dick asked John, "Did you really show her anything?"

"Not really."

"She's certainly quite the eye-full. So give me the low down, what gives?"

"Are you two exclusive?" asked Zeke.

"Does she need a boy friend?" ask Colin.

"Ok, everybody back off. If either of you two want to ask her out, be my guest." John knew that wasn't true. "All we did is walk and talk a little. I've got no claim on her. Just remember, she is the rancher's daughter so don't be stupid. Anyway, she's probably got seventeen other boy friends in town and half of the rest of Sheridan lusting after her – and her money, too. So, think what you want."

"You going to see her tonight?" asked Dick.

"No. Enough already."

"Well, I know you are going to see her."

"And just what makes you so sure of that?"

"We're all having dinner together," replied Zeke as he worked the brush for Dick.

"Really?" John could not help but be pleased. "What time are we going to close shop and go back to town?"

"In a hurry now?"

John laughed and took a swallow of beer.

"We're going to meet them at seven," said Dick, "so we ought to leave here around six so we have time to clean up. Especially you. In the meantime, get back to work."

"As you command."

As six o'clock approached, Dick and his grad students once more began the work of protecting the by now nearly half exposed creature. Once finished, they returned to the van for the drive back

Einstein's Bones

to the motel. The conversation on the way back was a mixture of the fossil, Margaret, and a little about Carol. "That type, you can't avoid them. Nothing you can do except pass them off with a smile."

At the motel, Dick checked to see if Karen had arrived. She hadn't. He left her a note, then it was off to dine with the Newcombs.

Einstein's Bones

Chapter 7

Dinner was almost finished when a very attractive young woman sauntered over to the table. She was of moderate height, about 5' 7", with light brown hair, striking green eyes wearing a tank top that did a poor job at modesty, and cut-offs above a pair of long silky legs. No one was able to take his eyes off of her.

"Have a seat, Karen," said Dick.

"Hi guys," she replied. "Looks like the party's just about over. Am I in time for dessert?"

John thought he heard Dale whisper, "Girl, you are the dessert."

Dick quickly introduced Karen Peterson. "You're not exactly dressed for dinner. I thought I'd made it clear that it was casual, but not that casual. But, if you're hungry, order what you want."

"I'm starving. I'll have a Tequila Sunrise to start," she said as the waitress came over. "And a T-bone medium rare."

"So, what do you do?" asked Dale, his eyes fixed on her firm unfettered breasts.

"Whatever Dick wants me to do. And what about you? What do you do for fun?"

"What ever you want me to do. And punch cattle, too."

"Punch cattle? That sounds like way too much fun. Are you married?"

"No."

Dick then turned to Karen and in a low voice told her briefly what had been found.

"You're shittin' me," she said when Dick had finished. "So what have you really got?"

"John, show her the pictures from today."

John handed Karen his digital camera. As he did, he felt her index finger lightly stroke the side of his hand. It wasn't accidental. "Oh my, this is really hot. Now I'm sorry I got here late." She glanced at John and Margaret. "Really hot."

John looked at Margaret to see if she might have caught any hidden meaning in Karen's words. If Margaret had, she didn't show it. Maybe John was just imagining that there was some concealed message in what Karen had said and that Karen had given both John and Margaret some special look. How would she know about them anyway? He felt very uncomfortable. Was Karen going to tell everyone – especially Margaret – everything? "Just stay cool," he thought to himself.

The dinner now seemed to drag on for John with each glance from Karen. He thought every little nuance in her smile was directed at him – or maybe at Margaret. Did she really wink at him, or was he going crazy? Was she having a silent conversation with him and did she want to take up where they had left off? He wished he had never shared a bed with her in the first place, but she was oh so impossible to resist.

Finally, Karen finished her steak and dinner was over. As they rose from the table, the Newcombs promised to stop at the dig sometime the following afternoon.

"You doing anything tonight?" Dale asked Karen as they were leaving.

"If the bar's still open, why not?" was Karen's reply.

John felt an immediate relief.

"Don't stay out all night, you'll have plenty to do tomorrow."

"Yes Dick."

John had cleaned up as best he could for the dinner and was pleased that Margaret had arrived wearing an attractive, yet modest light blue dress. It was the first time that he could remember her wearing stockings. He liked what he saw. They had said little to each other during dinner. But now, as they left, Margaret and John hung back a little from the rest.

As Karen and Dale walked into the bar and the others walked out the front door, she moved close to him. "Do you need a ride back to the motel, John?" she asked softly.

"No, but I'll gladly take one. Did you drive here by yourself?"

"You don't mind if we stop off at the Mint first, do you?"

"Not at all. Boy, am I going to get some looks from the others!"

"You, too?" she asked.

"We ought to make up something really juicy."

"Yes, I suppose we will," she replied as she lightly touched his shirt, her voice getting even softer.

There was nothing for John to say. He could remember the old salesman's adage that he who speaks last, loses. He just smiled, waved to the others, and got into the car with Margaret.

The new day promised to be warm and sunny. For John it began with a wake-up call from Dick. "Time to get up, there Romeo. We're just about ready to leave"

"Right, I'll be right there."

John quickly dressed, and then headed down the hall to Dick's room.

"Did you and Margaret have a good time last night? You came back late enough."

"How'd you know that?"

"Hell, the whole motel heard you come in."

"Yes, we had a very nice time."

"Just please, please be careful. There's way too much riding on this. You screw things up with her, and you're going to screw all of this up."

"I know. I know better than that. I don't think anything too drastic is gonna' happen anyway."

The conversation ended with a knock on the door and the entrance of the three graduate students.

"I got a hold of some of those undergrads we talked about last night," said Dick. "I've got four of them on hold ready to come out if I want them. I talked to your brother, too, John. He's tied up right now with his own projects, but he would like to come out and see what we've got here before we get it into the lab. If he can find the time, he might come out for a couple of days."

"Any idea when?"

"He's going to have to make it soon if he wants to see Einstein before we get him out of the ground."

"How soon will that be?"

"As soon as we know the extent of his remains. Well, time to get on the road. Zeke, you go with Karen in her truck," said Dick as he handed the van's keys to John.

John handed the keys back to Dick. "No, you drive. I'm still a little fuzzy from last night." As he spoke, he could see Karen's eyes light up but she said nothing. He wanted to ask her what she and Dale had done last night, but didn't.

As Dick drove he tried to ask John a few questions about the night before, but gave up when it became apparent that all John wanted to do was to try to get some more sleep. John was gone to the world five minutes out of town. Not even the gravel road was able to wake him. The next thing John knew was Dick poking him in the ribs and asking if he would be so kind as to get out and open the ranch gate.

Einstein's Bones

Once at the site, John turned to Dick. "What ever you do, don't be having me do any more field work. I'm just fine with the camera, but I don't think I could manage anything else."

"Don't worry about that. I think I've given you enough lessons already, and I don't think my nerves could take it any more."

Instead of going to Einstein, Dick proceeded to where Colin had planted his first flag. He and his three graduate students began working on it with pick and brush.

"Damn, this almost looks like the "hand" of another Einstein," said Colin.

"I don't know about that," intoned Dick. "Heck, we haven't uncovered Einstein's hand yet, so how would we know. But it does look in a way almost human. And I've never seen anything like this before. John, are you getting photos of this?"

"Yes," replied John as he alternated between taking pictures and writing down notes on what he was photographing.

"If this is another Einstein, do you suppose –"

"That we've found some sort of grave yard?" interrupted John. "Sorry Zeke, go on."

"As I was saying, do you suppose we might have found a grave yard? Hell, if we have, who knows what?"

"Possible," said Dick, "but then there are a lot of other sites where mass burials have been found which imply nothing of the sort. All you have to think of is Dinosaur National Monument just west of here. But, you are certainly right, there is that distinct possibility. If Einstein over there was buried with a purpose, as he appears to have been, why not? Zeke, you and Karen work on this. Colin, let's go over and check out that second flag."

John joined Dick and Colin as they proceeded to the second flag. Here they found a bit more exposed than at the first flagged site.

"Amazing," said John.

"Absolutely amazing," echoed Dick. "Incredible! Hard to believe nobody found this all before."

"I guess somebody has to be the first one to find it. Maybe it was the rains last fall, or maybe just nobody ever gets up here," mused John.

They didn't have to do much work to know that they had found another one of Einstein's friends. Glancing off to his side, Colin spotted another possible just a few feet away.

After a quick examination, Dick called them all together. "You guys stay here. I'm going into town to call those undergrads. We're definitely going to need more help." Dick put down his tools and started towards the van. As an afterthought, he returned and spoke to Karen. "I'd like you and Colin to work together on the original and have Zeke work at flag number one. Be careful. I know you won't, but if you guys get into any trouble, just stop. I should be back in a couple of hours. As long as you're working, keep John busy with his cameras, or you might have him help out by doing a little trenching, but nothing more."

"Got ya. Too bad our cell phones don't work out here. You know the way now?"

"I've been out here several times now, so I sure should."

"I hope so," said John as Dick turned once more towards the van. "I've been coming out here for years and I still get a little confused sometimes."

It was apparent from the cloud of dust left in his wake that Dick was not about to waste any time. Even after the van itself disappeared, the trail of dust could be seen making exceptional time.

"I hope he's right." said Colin.

"About this being a cemetery?" asked Zeke.

"No, about knowing how to find his way back."

"If he's not back in four hours John's going to have to go find him."

"God knows where he might end up," replied John.

"How about something to eat?" asked Colin. "I'm starving. What did we bring out?"

"Do you ever think about anything but food?" asked Zeke.

As they all sat and ate the sandwiches and drank their coffee, Karen looked over to John and asked, "Well, did the two of you have fun last night?"

"Margaret and me? What about you and Dale?"

Karen smiled. "I know he did. You want to know more?"

"No."

"Let's get back to work," said Colin.

With Dick gone, the work proceeded at a more leisurely and cautious pace. They didn't want to make any mistakes while the master was away. At the first site, Karen and Colin concentrated on widening the area away from the fossilized bone. As Karen worked, John thought to himself that yes, she was good at what she was there for, and yes, she was not any less pleasant to look at than when he first saw her – maybe even more so. As she bent over facing away from John, he had some difficulty thinking only of his camera. His mind snapped back to photography with a command from Karen.

"John, get down here and get a close up of this."

"What is it?"

"Fossilized wood," she replied.

After it was photographed and cataloged, Karen carefully placed it in a plastic bag and continued digging. "Here's more."

Einstein's Bones

Ten minutes later she came to a more substantial piece of the fossilized wood and now realized where the small pieces had come from.

"This is bitchin'. Colin, what do you think?" She raised her voice. "Hey Zeke, get your cute little buns over here!"

"What you got?" asked Zeke.

"It all fits. They put this stud muffin in a coffin!"

"You sure?"

"Take a look for yourself and tell me what you think. And take a look at what's in these bags."

"No shit. So it does."

"Let's all of us work on seeing if we can find the limits of this thing. Forget the other site for now," said Karen. "How was that one going?"

"Good. I got a bit more of the 'hand' exposed, and found the skull. It looks pretty much like this one."

"The two of you work that side while I keep at this. You know, I'm not really all that surprised and I don't think Dick will be, either. I hope he gets a hold of every body he wants to. We're sure going to need them now. Shit, when the Skunk finds out about this he's gonna' pee his pants. He doesn't know, does he?"

"I don't think so. Not yet anyway," said John. "I think, I hope we've kept a pretty tight lid on it. How could he?"

"He has his ways. That bastard would sell his own grandmother's bones for a buck," said Zeke.

"You really think he'd sell fossils?" asked John.

"Think it, shit, we know it. He's done it before," stated Karen. "Big money for this stuff, and, of course, big money for all the 'comic' books he sells."

"You think Dick might call his friends at the Geographic?" asked Colin.

Einstein's Bones

"He might," Karen replied, "but it's a little early for that. If he does, we are going to have to start looking pretty, TV and newspapers and all that," she said as she pushed out her breasts. "And John, you're going to have to clean up more if you want to get into Margaret's pants – if you haven't already."

John did not reply. He just kept taking photographs.

After two hours, they had revealed a fairly large portion of the coffin. It was now clearly exposed on both sides of the fossilized remains, extending from near the top of the skull to nearly the point where the necklace ended. Measurements showed that it was a uniform inside width of approximately ninety centimeters. What the width would be further down would have to wait. The lower portion of the remains (if they existed) was under an ever heavier layer of overburden which was going to require more work and possibly some heavier equipment. But that did not concern them now. They had plenty to work on right in front of them.

"Anybody mind if I put on some music?" asked John.

"No, go ahead."

John found a CD with his favorite aria from Mozart's *Ziede*, forgetting that he had played it just before he and Karen had been intimate for the first time.

Karen's eyes widened and she smiled. "That's oh so sexy," she said. "It brings back some memories of a very enjoyable evening."

"Jesus Christ," added Colin. "You like this stuff too? There's gotta be something else in there."

"Indulge me. How about a break?"

"I think we need a group photo," said Karen.

"Without Dick?" asked John half seriously.

"Sorry, but he's been gone too long."

Einstein's Bones

John set his Cannon F1 on the Tilt-all tripod and the four of them made a semi-circle around their horizontal friend. Just before the shutter clicked, Karen gave John a light stroke with her hand on his ass.

"Maybe a good idea to take that one over," said John.

He repeated the procedure and so did Karen.

The photos over, they broke open the food again along with a few bottles of beer to wash it down. Then back to work.

They exposed more and more of the coffin, working deeper down and also towards the top end. It was not long before they discovered that it extended about ten centimeters beyond the top of the skull and that the sides and the top portion of the coffin met at right angles. So far, the width remained consistent. The thickness of the fossilized wood was about 2.5 centimeters and so far no variations in this and the other dimensions were noted. As yet they could not determine how the various sections were joined, but more digging would soon reveal some clues.

"Well, it certainly doesn't look like they jammed the old boy in too tight," observed Zeke. "They seem to have left him plenty of room."

"Maybe he was just fat," thought Zeke. "Maybe they needed a weight watchers group back then, too."

A little more digging done and it was close to noon.

"Dick certainly is taking his time!" remarked Colin.

"Or lost," added Zeke. "If he's not back here by one, maybe you should go looking for him, John."

"Now I just wonder where the best place is to start looking," said Karen with a smirk directed at John. "I'll bet he's having a cool one at the Mint with little miss Margaret while you slave for him here, John. Anybody up for another sandwich or a beer? This work is good for my appetite."

Einstein's Bones

No one else was hungry except for John. Feeling much better, he took a beer, too. As he took his last bite, he saw a pickup on the way in. It was not Dick, but the Newcombs.

Once again all four came. After the usual greetings were exchanged, Karen acted as host. She showed the Newcombs what they had found so far that day at both the original site and at the others. The Newcombs were impressed

"My God," said Mr. Newcomb, "I've ridden and walked over this ground all my life and never had the slightest idea that all this was here. It's all so strange."

Karen couldn't wait to see how long it would take John to get Margaret alone. John was well aware of what would be going through her nosey mind, so he took his time, keeping with the group for fifteen minutes. But when Karen took Dale for a short walk, he decided to do the same with Margaret.

They did not need to go very far. Just out of sight so they could have a private conversation.

"Did you get any teasing, Margaret?" asked John.

"Sure, a little. A few questions, that's all. Don't worry, they all like you, and after Bob, they owe me some slack. You?"

"Dick asked a little, mainly trying to impress on me not to piss you off. And Karen – well."

"What's with them?"

"Dick's OK with it, he just wants to make sure you guys don't boot us out of here. I don't blame him. I sure ain't gonna do anything that makes you guys do that. But Karen, I don't know about her."

"I think Dick should be more worried about your friend, Karen."

"You think so?"

Einstein's Bones

"Knowing my brother, who knows? With women he's had his problems. He and dad don't always see eye to eye with his choices. How well do you know her?"

John hesitated for a moment. "Karen? Oh, I've seen her around the geology department a few times and I think we were at a party together once. But what do I know about any woman?"

"I guess we'll see. Anything else?"

"Yeah, do I smell OK? I didn't take a shower this morning and I've been out here and sweating like a pig."

She moved as close to him as she could with out touching, put her nose to his neck, and inhaled deeply. As she did, John instinctively put his right arm on her shoulder and she did the same.

"Well, not great – could be better, but remember, all my family is used to being on horses and working the ranch all day."

"Thanks, I think. Did you enjoy last night?" he asked. "I did."

"Yes, what I remember of it."

"It's a relief that you got back home OK. I should have called you when I got back. I felt a little guilty about that."

"That, and anything else?" she asked with a smile.

"Nothing else. Are you up for anything tonight?"

"As long as it's not too late. Tomorrow being Sunday, we're all having brunch at my sister's. Why don't you come?"

"Thanks for the invite, but I think they might have other plans for me. I think we best head back and join the others."

"If my brother has brought back your friend," she added.

"I'll give you a call tonight when we get back into town."

"Don't forget!"

"I wouldn't worry about that."

Margaret gave him a little laugh and smile.

Einstein's Bones

Back at the dig site they waited a few minutes for Karen and Dale. As they returned to the group, Margaret looked at her brother and then at John with up-turned eyes. John looked back questioningly.

"So what trips your trigger, Margaret?" asked Karen. "Horses? Music? What?"

"Both"

"John?"

Margaret didn't answer.

"You'll have to teach me how to ride sometime, unless Dale wants to."

"Any time," said Dale.

Margaret came closer to John and stage whispered, "I sure don't want to see those lessons."

"Well, then maybe you should teach John," said Karen. "I'm sure he'd like that."

"Maybe sometime I will."

Karen gave her a wink. "Don't wait too long."

The conversation was ended with Dick's return. They met him about twenty feet from the first site. "We were getting a little worried you got lost or something," said Karen.

"I did get a little turned around. I've got Mike Curtin, Lani and Jeff Basarus coming. They'll be here day after tomorrow. Josh Nandrew should be coming in a week. I also called Keith Mersky at the Geographic. Zeke, I want you and Colin to get that fifth wheel out here. We'll set up a schedule for sleeping here. And that means you, too Karen, if that's alright with you, Mr. Newcomb." Paul Newcomb gave a nodding approval. "Two in the trailer at a time should be enough. I don't want anyone to get too lonely or too filthy. So, anything new while I was gone?"

Einstein's Bones

"Oh, nothing much. Not much at all really, but just maybe you ought to take a look at this," replied Karen as she walked Dick towards Einstein.

"O holy shit again," said Dick when he saw the coffin. He then looked at Paul somewhat sheepishly.

"Don't apologize," said Paul. "I said the same thing when I saw it."

"Sure looks like a coffin."

"That's what we all figured, boss," said Colin.

"This just keeps getting better and better," said Dick.

"It's discovering a whole new world!" said John.

As Dick's team began to confer, the Newcombs made their departure. John again assured Margaret he would call.

Dick turned to Karen. "You did bring the GPR with you, right?"

"Well shit, I wouldn't forget that," she replied.

"GPR?" asked John.

"Ground penetrating radar," said Dick.

"Oh yeah, I guess I've seen them on TV. How do they work?"

"A radar pulse goes into the subsurface, and we get an image. It's the same principle as any radar."

"How far down can you see with that thing?" asked John.

"It all depends on the type of soil," replied Dick. "If we really get lucky it could see down maybe fifteen meters, but I don't think we'll get that deep here."

"Can you really see what you're looking at? Do you get like a picture? I saw some movie and the image on the monitor looked plain as day."

"No, that's bull," replied Dick. "What we get is a tomographic image. It takes a little time to figure out what it all means. It's not perfect, but it gives a good idea where to start looking. We'll start using it tomorrow and you can see for yourself."

Dick looked down at the coffin and then at the other finds. "How much plaster of Paris and burlap did we bring up here anyway?"

"I think we might just need a little more," answered Zeke.

"Well, the tarps and canopy we've got should be OK for now, but we better check out a local source when we get back to town. And for burlap and plaster of Paris, too. Colin, you can do that and Zeke, find out where we can get some fencing to keep the cattle out of here. Check with Newcomb first. Maybe he's got some. Anyway, he should. Right now we've gotta start getting this site laid out and organized. Stakes and string are in those big cardboard boxes in the van. You three start laying it out. I'm going to show John how to do some trenching at number 1. Now, let's get to work."

"You want me digging again? You sure?" asked John.

"Any idiot can do that. We're just going to dig a trench away from the coffin to keep the water out. You interested in staying here a little longer?"

"You mean tonight?"

"No, I mean maybe past summer."

"How far past?"

"Not sure. Maybe a lot longer – through the winter? If we keep finding more I'll want some of you to stay here. Just think about it. I don't need an answer right now."

"Can you get work done in the winter? That could be a mess."

"If we have to. We can set up some tents and heaters."

With Karen doing the sighting, Colin and Zeke began pounding in stakes and connecting them with string. As they laid out the next to last grid, they found what looked to be another piece of fossilized wood, maybe a part of another coffin. They noted the location, called it out to Dick, and moved on. Colin took no more than three steps further and saw another. Then so did Zeke. Dick entered all of the grid coordinates in his journal and then turned back to their first discovery and resumed trenching around the coffin with John. When the graduate students finished with the grid, they returned to the site where they had found the "hand".

"Ya know, Dick," said John, "If we work here in the winter that ranch road is really gonna be a bitch."

"You don't have to remind me. We'll think of something."

"This one's in a coffin, too," said Karen from the second site. "So Dick, what are we gonna do with 'em?"

"I think we should rent some space in town to set up a lab. After that, I'll talk with Newcomb."

"Hey, this one's got more jewelry. Just a guess, but since they're alongside the skull, they could be earrings. Ears on a dinosaur?"

Zeke shook his head in disbelief. "Why not?" he added.

Colin's examination of the hand revealed that it had what appeared to be an opposable thumb and three main digits. There was a fifth digit which was much smaller, probably vestigial, perhaps not even visible on the living creature - similar to a dog's dew claw. Or maybe it was just a deformity.

Quitting time was a little after 6:00. "Let's have a beer and get this covered up and get back to town. Colin, you and Zeke can start staying out here tomorrow night," said Dick.

Einstein's Bones

Chapter 8

Back in his motel room, John called Margaret. She feigned surprise that he had not forgotten. Yes, dinner would be nice. He told her that everyone was going to a Korean restaurant, Aye Suck, and that she was welcome to join them.

"I'm not really into Korean food, and besides, that place is kind of a dump. Why don't you come over here and we'll decide what to do. How soon could you be here?"

"In less than an hour. By the way, just in case I can't use one of the trucks, can you pick me up?"

She could. After he said his good-bye, John walked down the hall and borrowed the keys for the pick-up that had brought out the fifth wheel. Back in his room, he took a long hot shower, watching all the dirt from the day's work swirl down the drain. He then shaved, added a touch of after shave – something he almost never did, put on his one good pair of dress slacks and one of his three good dress shirts and then headed out.

In less than ten minutes he was at her door. Margaret lived on the edge of town where she kept three horses and a few goats. John could never figure out why she kept goats. She didn't drink goat's milk. Though he had been there many times before, this time he felt very different, like a school boy picking up his date for the Prom. As she opened the door, wearing a mid-length red dress, he realized too late that he had brought nothing with him for her.

"Well John, are you just going to stand there?" she said. After a pause she added, "I hope you're planning to come inside." She took him by the hand. Almost pulling him inside, she moved close to smell his neck. "Much better," she said with a soft laugh.

"I got cleaned up as best I could just for you. The cleanest clothes I've got and I even polished my shoes. I wanted to look at least half way presentable for dinner." He then backed away from her slightly and slowly looked her over from top to bottom. "Wow, nice, very nice. You look absolutely beautiful."

"Polished your shoes and put on clean clothes? How thoughtful."

She led him the rest of the way in and to the sofa where she offered him a Manhattan. After she poured one for each of them, she brought the pitcher back to the kitchen. She returned and sat beside him and asked, "So what was the rest of your day like?"

John relaxed. "Well, I found out I'm gonna be sleeping out on the range. And a couple more interesting finds. Maybe even some earrings."

"Earrings? What do you think they'd look like on me?"

"A little strange looking, but ya know, there's an idea. I don't think you'd like 'em but there might be some money in making copies. It might keep your brother happy."

"I don't know," she replied. "I have a feeling, and I hope it's wrong, that he's seeing some really big dollar signs. Would you like me to put on some music?"

"Sure, what ya got?"

"Country, some Stones, classical? Whatever you'd like."

"How about DeBurgh?" he asked.

"DeBurgh?" she asked with a quizzical smile.

"Chris DeBurgh, *Lady in Red*."

She smiled. "Sorry, no have got. Do you like Nora Jones?"

"Sure."

She put in the disk then went into the kitchen and came back with the pitcher of Manhattans she had made before he had arrived. It wasn't the first time that they had had Manhattans at her home, but in the past his father, or Charlie, or Margaret's husband, or all of them had been present.

Einstein's Bones

As she refilled their glasses, she said, "Here's to your discovery and making you guys famous."

"I'll drink to that. And here's to whatever might be."

She slightly cocked her head to one side as if to ask what he meant, then gave him a light kiss on the cheek. They both sat for a moment speaking only through their eyes. After another sip he returned the kiss.

"I suppose after working all day you must be hungry," she said.

"You know this town a whole lot better than I do. Where would you like to go for dinner? Sure you don't want to join everybody at Aye Suck? Where on earth did they ever come up with that name?" he asked with a laugh. "It's not too late you know."

"I hope you haven't lost your sense of smell. Can't you smell what's coming from the kitchen?"

"I got a pretty good whiff from the outside, but it's never a good idea to assume," he replied.

"I hope you like Italian."

"Absolutely. Gina Lollobrigida has always been one of my favorite."

"Funny. Help yourself to the Manhattans while I put the spaghetti in."

As she walked back into the kitchen, he couldn't help but admire the view. After she turned the corner, he leaned back to enjoy the music, the smells, and to burn her visage into his brain.

With dinner came a bottle of good Chianti and some light dinner music. "This is very good," he told her. "Next time, I'll to have to have you try mine – an old family recipe. I might not be the world's greatest chef, but I grill a mean steak, too."

"I know, you grilled some here a couple of years ago, did you forget?"

Einstein's Bones

As they ate and talked, he told her that the pick-up he drove was needed to bring the fifth wheel out in the morning.

"Do you have to bring it back tonight?"

"I'm afraid so."

"That's too bad."

They smiled, touched their glasses, and then held hands across the table. The only thing missing was candle light. When they had finished, they cleared the table together.

"Would you like some help with the dishes?" he asked.

"They can wait."

Back in the living room, John called the motel, and assured Dick he'd have the pick-up back that evening. Once off the phone, he told Margaret, "Well dang, he does want it back."

"That's a shame. A penny for your thoughts?" she asked.

He gave her a kiss

"That's not what I asked for!"

He took a deep breath and exhaled slowly. "I had hoped he'd have said he didn't need it."

"Well, there goes my plan for the rest of the evening," she said.

He hesitated and just smiled. Had she really asked him to stay the night? He thought so, but was not absolutely certain. He tried to put the thought out of his mind. "Am I still invited for breakfast tomorrow? Dick said I could have the day off if I wanted, or at least part of it, though in the afternoon I might have to meet a bunch of students in town and take 'em out to the ranch."

"So? What? You get a whole half day off? My, that's generous. I hope you like what you're doing. And no, you're not invited for breakfast, it's brunch. Be here by 9:30."

"Yes boss."

Einstein's Bones

They stayed on the sofa listening to music until nearly midnight, when John reluctantly returned to the motel, humming to himself *Lady in Red*.

Einstein's Bones

Chapter 9

John awoke at sunrise – earlier than he had expected. He casually turned his head to the left and then to his right, regretting that he was in his motel room bed and that he was the sole occupant. At least he was not hung-over and that he had gotten up in time to ask Dick if he really could have the day - or at least half of it - off. He raised himself out of bed and after putting on his bathrobe, called Dick to find out for sure. He could have the morning off, but would have to be back at the motel by 1:30 or 2:00 to meet the undergrads. As for transportation, he could borrow Karen's pick-up.

"Well, relax," he thought to himself. He had a few hours to kill before he went back to Margaret's. Maybe he'd go for a walk. Where? Not much to see or do early on a Sunday morning in Sheridan. Maybe he'd open his lap-top and update his photo log, or maybe he'd write some e-mails and send a couple of his recent photos to Charlie. He'd like that. Or just read a book. Yes, that was it. He had a biography of Charles Lindbergh by Leonard Mosely that he had just started. He liked reading histories and biographies.

He went to the dresser and dug under some dirty clothing and a few papers until he found the book and then returned to bed and began reading where he had left off the morning before, at chapter twelve – just after the point where Anne Morrow and Lindbergh got married. Five pages into the chapter there was a knock on the door. He got up from the bed with his index finger between pages 146 and 147 and opened the door. It was Karen dangling her keys from her fingers at shoulder height.

"You're going to need these if you want to score with Margaret," she said as she shook them. "Or have you already?"

Einstein's Bones

He did not answer the question. "Thanks for the use of your pick-up. I'll fill it up for you."

She smiled and turned back, turned to John again and then walked suggestively towards her own room. There was something about her smile, something teasing, he didn't like. Or did he? But he had the keys and a book to read. He closed the door and returned to his bed and his book. He'd be able to read for a few hours before he had to clean up for brunch. He thought to himself that he would rather be doing something other than reading a book in bed – alone.

It made no difference what the occasion was, John hated to be late for anything – work, parties, going to see an old friend, or especially a date. Even though it was only a ten minute drive to Margaret's and he knew that he could do all he had to do to get ready in less than half an hour, when 8:30 came he put down his book and showered, shaved and dressed. When he was ready, he looked at the clock and it was only ten minutes to nine. He opened up the book again and read for another twenty minutes. At 9:15 he was in the motel parking lot and realized that he didn't remember what Karen's pick-up looked like or even what color it was. It seemed like everyone in Wyoming was driving a pick-up. He looked down at the keys. At least he knew it was a Ford. And, oh yes, it had a remote beeper. It worked.

"You're early," said Margaret as he walked through the door.

"Only a couple of minutes. Guess I always am. I didn't interrupt anything, did I?"

"No, no. I just have a few more things to do before I'm ready. Make yourself comfortable while I finish. There's some juice or milk in the fridge if you want some."

As Margaret headed into her bedroom, John went into the kitchen and poured himself a glass of milk. He sat down to drink and looked towards the sink and thought to himself that he hoped she didn't stay up too late cleaning things up. He no more than finished his glass when she entered.

"Let's go," she said.

He looked at her with an approving eye. "You look pretty good in blue jeans, too. I don't know why, but I feel a little nervous about seeing your family today."

"Now why on earth would you feel that way?"

"Stupid, but what with our seeing each other, I guess I'm a little worried they might look at me in a different light."

"I don't know why you should be worried about it. It's not exactly like we're living in sin. And even if we were, so what. They all like you. You'll have a good time. Did Dick change his mind and give you the whole day off?"

"No, still just half of it," he replied. "Ya know I gotta meet those students coming in, so maybe we should drive separately."

"Don't worry about that. If you have to leave early I can get a ride back. Carol's only a quarter of a mile from here."

He need not have worried about his reception. Mr. Newcomb met him at the door and asked him if he'd like to start off with an eye-opener.

"I'll give it a try," replied John. What's in it?"

"First try one, and then you tell us."

Whatever it was, it certainly did open his eyes. Maybe he took just a little too much that first sip.

"Wow! Gin and lemon juice for sure. Triple Sec? Just remember I've got some work to do this afternoon."

"What kind of boss makes you work on a Sunday?" asked Mr. Newcomb.

"The same kind that makes this family work that ranch of yours. A real slave driver."

Einstein's Bones

After he finished his drink, John joined the others at the table. There was ham, eggs with béarnaise sauce, sausages and waffles. To drink, there was champagne.

"I hope you didn't go to all this trouble just for me," said John.

"No, we do this about once a month," replied Carol's husband, Jason.

John found himself the center of conversation. How did he get to know Dick? How long had he known him? How long did John plan to stay? Did he have any background in paleontology? Was he, or had he ever been a professional photographer? What did he do for a living before he started working at the site? He told them that he had met Dick through his brother about seven years ago when his brother had become a professor in the geology department at Minnesota. Dick was originally from Wisconsin and had gotten his PhD from Pennsylvania. No, John didn't have any background in paleontology other than what he had picked up from his brother, from Dick, from watching TV and reading about it occasionally. His interest in photography began early. He had been a photographer for his high school newspaper, had worked at a portrait studio part time while in college, and until he started working at the site, he had done weddings on the weekends. The job he had left? It was in sales and was glad to be gone.

"About the only thing like this I ever did before was taking the photos for my brother's thesis and some of the articles he wrote, but I never knew much, if anything, about what I was taking pictures of."

"And how long are you going to be with us?" asked the senior Newcomb.

"Through the summer at least, Mr. Newcomb. Maybe longer depending on how much more we find."

Einstein's Bones

"Please, just call me Paul."

Carol then turning towards John with a serious look. "Do you people believe in God? Do you read the Bible?"

John was surprised by the question and hesitated. Looking around the table he felt that the other members of the family, except for Carol's husband, wished she had not brought up the subject. He didn't want to answer and he didn't want to start an argument. "I'm not a biblical scholar if that's what you mean. But, yes I have read it. I think everyone should."

"But do you believe in God? Don't you believe that God created man in his own image? Do you believe in what the Bible tells us? You say the rocks you are digging up are sixty million years old. Do you really believe that?"

Again he hesitated. "I'm just not much up on all that. I'm just the photographer. If you really want somebody to talk with about it, maybe you should ask the boss, Dick. He's pretty religious and at the same times goes along with evolution." After John said that, he regretted it. Would she now start pestering Dick?

"Does he believe that we just came out of slime? Aren't those rocks you call fossils proof of the flood? Did we descend from chimps? And if we really did, then why can't they talk? Where are the missing links?"

"I really don't know the answers to any of that," replied John cautiously. "I don't know of any paleontologists who believe we descended from chimps. What they do believe – rightly or wrongly – is that we both descended from a common ancestor millions of years ago. Talking chimps? I don't know anything about that. Maybe in a couple of million years, if they're still around, they will. As for missing links, a lot of important finds have been made and I'm sure a lot more are yet to be found. Not many bones survive over all that time. It's a matter of luck."

Einstein's Bones

Jason now joined with his wife. "You sound like you're not sure about the answers yourself. We'd like to help you out. We're going to a Bible study group this afternoon and you're welcome to join us."

"You forget," said Margaret, "he's got to go pick some people up. How about another waffle, John"

"One more and that'll fill me up," he replied as he said 'thank you' to himself.

"Before you leave then, would you like something to read?" asked Carol.

"Sure," he replied, knowing that if she gave him any handouts they'd more than likely serve as nothing more than book markers. He looked down at his watch. It was 11:30 and brunch was finished. The undergrads were at least a couple of hours away. There was no need to rush, but he was feeling uncomfortable. "I hate to eat and run, but I have to head back to the motel. Boss's orders. Thanks so much. It was great. I can't tell you how much I've enjoyed this." As he got up to leave, Carol went into the living room and brought back a short pamphlet titled *Evolution or Creation?* He thanked her and said he would read it that night. If he had nothing better to do, maybe he really would.

At the door, Margaret said, "Wait a minute by the truck. I'll be right out."

In less than a minute, Margaret joined him at the pick-up. "I'm sorry about that," she said.

"For what? Your sister? Forget it."

"She and her husband are always doing that. Ruining a good time and scaring everybody away. Nothing we've ever said has ever made them quit."

"Don't worry about it. Yeah, I guess it made me a little nervous - scared we'd really get into it. Always does when the subject comes up. I sure don't like to get into arguments over religion. Nobody wins, nobody ever changes his mind. I don't care what anybody believes in just so long as they don't get in my face about it and just so long as what they believe doesn't hurt anybody else. And, believe it or not, in a way I envy your sister with her strong beliefs. Sometimes I wish I believed in something that strongly."

"I hope you had a good time otherwise. Are you going to be busy tonight?"

"Oh, I had a great time. Not sure about tonight. I'll call you. I'd give you a kiss, but I'm afraid everybody's looking."

"Oh, go ahead."

John returned to his motel room and to his book, sorry that he had left Margaret before he had to, but glad to be away from a potential argument over religion. He read a few pages. They left him disturbed, learning that one of his heroes was far from perfect. He marked the page, put down the book, and dialed Margaret's number, getting only her answering machine. He left only a short apology for leaving early, and then returned to his book. Interesting, but depressing. At 1:00pm he called the front desk. No, the students hadn't checked in, but yes, they'd let John know as soon as they did. Instead of returning to his book, he glossed over the tract Carol had given him. "Whatever," he muttered to himself as he put it inside the book cover, intending to use it as a book mark. He called the front desk again at 2:00pm. No, not yet. He called Margaret again. She had not returned.

Ten minutes later there was a knock on his door. John opened it to find four scruffy looking students standing before him. "Are you John Steiner?" one of them asked.

"That's me. Are you guys ready to go?" They nodded in agreement. "Well," he said without asking for any names, "give me a minute. One of you ride with me."

John entered the cab with his unknown and somewhat corpulent companion. "And you are?" he asked.

"Mike."

"Last Name?"

"Curton."

"And the others back in that little car?"

"Lori, Josh, and Jeff."

"And do they have last names?"

Lani Katiama, Jeff Basarus, and Josh Vandreu."

"So, which is it, Lori or Lani?"

"Lani."

"You sure about that?"

"Yup, Lani."

"If I have to ask you their names again, sorry, I don't remember names very well, but you don't seem to be much better. I hope they don't have any trouble driving that little car into the ranch."

Those were the last words John was able to say for most of the drive to the ranch. Mike was a senior in geology. Besides being overweight, he had an over-active mouth. It didn't matter what he talked about. He just talked and talked and talked, telling John way more than he wanted to know about every subject that Mike had time to expound upon. He was an expert on everything. John was enlightened with the knowledge that Gandhi was a racist and a pedophile, and the Tucker was the greatest automobile ever built. We were wrong to have entered World War Two and especially World War One. And that there was nothing more fun and

Einstein's Bones

informative than attending a Star Trek convention. John's usual replies were just a 'yes' or a nod of the head.

So far, Mike asked John nothing about what was going on at the dig. A mile before they got to the ranch, Mike asked, "Karen's here, right?"

"If you're asking about Karen Peterson, yes she is."

"God, she is so beautiful – so hot."

"Yes, she certainly is that."

"Is she here with anybody?" asked Mike. "You aren't dating her, are you?"

"No."

"Anybody else dating her?"

"I don't know anything about her personal life."

"I think she really likes me. Has she said anything about me?"

"No," replied John as he thought to himself, 'unless it was just to say how much of a total nerd you are'.

"Every time I've been with her she likes to get so close to me."

"If you say so," replied John as he thought that she probably did that with everybody. "Well, here we are. Now why don't you get out and open up the gate."

Mike got out and fumbled with the gate. "What an idiot," said John under his breath. He raised his voice. "Ok, you drive it in and I'll take care of the gate." After he opened the gate both vehicles drove in and kept going, not stopping until they were 100 yards past John. "Idiots," he muttered. He shook his head and walked the 100 yards and asked Mike, "Where did you think you were going? Were you just going to leave me there?"

"I thought we were here."

"Move over and let me drive the rest of the way." Until they reached the site, John learned all the benefits of being a vegetarian. He couldn't have cared less.

John parked Karen's pick-up next to the others and looked back as the small Honda drove up, amused it had made it in. "We gotta walk just over the top of that peak a couple hundred yards. Get your stuff."

Dick and Colin were working on the original find which by now was almost ready for removal. Zeke was walking back and forth with the GPR unit as Karen watched a monitor. When the new arrivals saw what Dick was working on, they said nothing, their jaws dropping to their chins. Dick just laughed. "So, was it worth the drive out?" asked John.

Dick stood and gave the newcomers a quick tour of the site. As he did, Mike kept looking over to Karen with a smile and a wave. She returned his smile once.

"So what's new, Dick?" asked John when Dick returned.

"We'll be taking this one out soon, and the GPR, I think, has found a lot more of his companions. And we found that number two has a ring on his pinky." He looked at the four new workers. "You guys are going to be very busy."

John took some photos of Dick's recent work and then some of the ring. Like the medallion, it was gold, but with some green stone inlaid. Finished, he went over to see what Karen was doing. He looked at the monitor. "So what do all those squiggly lines mean?" he asked her.

She pointed to a few blips on the screen and showed him some of the print-outs. "See this," she said pointing at what made no sense whatever to John, "It tells us where to start looking for another stiff. We've found a lot of 'em"

Einstein's Bones

"I'll have to trust you. It doesn't look like a damn thing to me. So tell me, what's with that Mike guy?"

"Ya mean Tubby?" she said with a laugh.

"Yeah, he has quite the thing for you."

"He's harmless," she said with a smile.

"Karen, Zeke, why don't you quit for now," called out Dick. "Everybody over here." He passed out cold beers. "Karen, I think you two have found enough to keep us busy for quite some time." He paired off the grads with the undergrads and assigned finds to work on. Dick paired himself with Lani. Mike's face made little effort to hide his disappointment in not being paired with Karen. John moved from fossil to fossil taking photos and when he was not, helped dust them off with a four inch paint brush.

"Do you have an idea yet how big this is going to be?" John asked Dick.

"No, not yet. It's all very regular - orderly. All the remains are laid out in same northeast/southwest orientation. And so far as I can tell from what we have uncovered and from the GPR, very regularly spaced." As he spoke, Colin and Jeff, who were working a meter away from Dick and where the GPR had indicated a possible find, discovered another burial. Soon, Karen and Josh announced another – one meter beyond Colin's find.

"Good thing Keith's coming out for a look see tomorrow," said Dick.

"Who's he?" asked John.

"A big shot from the Geographic. He's coming to look after his investment. I'm going to ask him to up it."

"They aren't going to want you to go public, are they?"

"I hope not – not for a while at least, but 'he who pays the piper, calls the tune'," said Dick as he removed a piece of matrix with his knife.

Einstein's Bones

It was near quitting time when Zeke called out that he had found another medallion. John went over to take photos. The design on its face looked to be the same as on the first. But there was a difference. This one had what looked like writing around its edges. "Damn," said John. "Writing? Do you think we might ever understand it?"

"Just about impossible," replied Zeke, "unless we dig up a dino to English dictionary, too."

"But just imagine what we might learn if we could," said Dick who had come to see it for himself. "You can't help wonder what they looked like and sounded like. Well, time to get this thing wrapped up and head out." He raised his voice. "Ok, listen up everybody. As I said earlier, Zeke and Colin are staying here tonight and are going to wrap Einstein up. When we get another trailer out here, we'll all stay here. Now let's get this buttoned down." Ten minutes later he spoke again. "Tomorrow we have a back hoe and truck coming to take this specimen out. When they are here, it's going to be important to keep everything covered up. We don't want everyone knowing just yet what we've got here. So we've got to remember to keep those tarps close by. And when we all get back to town," he said looking hard at the undergrads, "I don't want anyone talking to anybody about anything. Now if anybody should ask what you are doing here, you are on a department field trip as part of your course work, nothing more. And keep this in mind, because they will ask, we're just going to tell the help coming here tomorrow that we have found a few fragments of some as yet unidentified dinosaur. Nothing special. The last thing we want here is some big circus. Are we all on the same page?" They all nodded in agreement. "Ok." He looked at Colin and Zeke. "See you in the morning."

Einstein's Bones

With that, they turned towards their vehicles leaving Colin and Zeke behind to encase Einstein in burlap and plaster.

"Mind if I ride back with you?" John asked Dick. "Five more minutes with that Mike guy and I'm gonna go ballistic."

"Believe me, I do understand."

A mile down the road, John asked, "I don't want to sound like some kind of mercenary and that all I care about is money, but I've been wondering if sometime maybe I could publish my photos. Maybe in a book."

Dick laughed. "Well, just remember we have to consider the Geographic first, but after that you don't think I'm not going to make a buck or two on this myself do you? I already have my publisher lined up, and your photos are going to be in it whether you like it or not and with a generous cut coming your way. After that, publish all you want. I can't say you're going to get rich, but you won't be hurting, either.

"Another question. How do you deal with people who get after you about religion and evolution - paleontology? You must get that a lot."

"Why do you ask that?"

"Carol."

"Margaret's sister?"

"Yeah, she started getting on my case about it this morning."

"I don't get it that much. People are going to believe what they want to believe. I keep my views on the subject to myself for the most part. Just remember, even Darwin never denied God."

Einstein's Bones

Chapter 10

Back in his motel room, John laid himself on the bed, lit up a smoke and called Margaret.
"Are you smoking?" she asked.
"Ah, yes," he answered sheepishly.
"You are going to quit aren't you?"
"Yes."
"When?" she asked.
"Soon."
"I hope so. There's nothing worse than kissing an ashtray."
"If you put it that way, I'm gonna have to. So are you up for anything tonight? I don't want to push my luck about borrowing a car again, so if you don't mind, why not come and have dinner over here. It looks like they have a nice dining room right next to the pool. Have you ever eaten there? Is it any good?"
"I've been there two or three times. Good, but a little pricy, if that's OK with you. Can you give me about an hour?"
"Sure. Why don't you meet me at the pool?"
John hung up the phone and finished his smoke. "If I'm gonna be making a habit of kissing Margaret, maybe I better quit," he admitted to himself. He showered, shaved, even used the hotel's complimentary mouthwash, put on fresh clothing and headed for the pool.
He stopped first at the bar and brought his drink – in a plastic cup – to the pool. Lying down in a recliner was Karen and next to her, sitting straight up and talking non-stop was Mike. She waved John over. "Mike, why don't you be a good boy and get me another Tequila Sunrise," she said as she handed him a twenty.
Mike obeyed instantly. When he was far enough away not to hear, she said, "You got to help me get rid of that fat blabber

Einstein's Bones

mouth. Dale's going to be here soon and I'm worried he just might invite himself to join us."

"Why don't you just tell him to get lost?"

"I would, but I have to work with him."

Mike returned with Karen's drink. After he handed her the change, John pulled him off to the side. "You haven't met Dale Newcomb yet, have you?" Mike shook his head in the negative. "Well, he's coming over to see Karen in a couple of minutes and if he sees you anywhere near her he's gonna beat the crap out of you. I've seen him in a bar fight and I wouldn't fuck with him. If I were you, I'd go back to my room and read that book."

Mike returned to where Karen was relaxing, picked up his book, said good-bye, and left quickly. "What did you say to him?" she asked.

"I lied. Ya know, if you weren't lying around here in that skimpy bathing suit and were a little more modest, maybe he wouldn't hang around you so much."

"I dress for myself, nobody else." She took a long sip of her drink. "So what are you doing tonight? Are you going to get into the farmer's daughter's panties? She's hot and she's got lots of money."

"Karen, Karen, Karen. It's not like that."

"Sure it is. Have you forgotten I know you? You still have a penis don't you? You men are all such pigs. If you have a penis, you're a pig. All you want to do is get laid." John did not reply. "I bet she wants it too. How long has it been for her? For you?"

"I think we're better than that."

"Right. She might be, but I do know you." She looked past John and saw Dale walking towards her. "Here comes my pig. And Dick – the boss Dick - too."

Einstein's Bones

"Do you have any big plans for tonight, John?" asked Dick. "I want you to do some work for me. Like I said this afternoon, we've got Keith from the Geographic coming here tomorrow and I need you to make up a slide presentation for him that he can take back to Washington with him. You can do it, can't you?"

"Easy enough. I can burn a CD for him on my lap-top. About how many photos you think I should put on it. You want titles or anything special?"

"Fifty ought to be plenty. Just a short description of what they are should be enough. Nothing fancy. Can you bring it out with you in the morning?"

"Good as done."

"Great. I'll see you guys in the morning," said Dick who then left.

Karen and Dale left together a few minutes later, leaving John with his drink and debating if he should light up another smoke. He finished the drink, returned to the bar for another, sitting down in Karen's vacated recliner on his return, contenting himself to watch a couple of kids in the pool. To his right he saw an ash tray and lit up another smoke. He closed his eyes for a moment then felt a tap on his shoulder. "Kinda early aren't ya Margaret?"

"What, afraid I'd catch you with that cigarette? Let's go eat."

John carried his drink to the dinner table. Margaret ordered red wine. "We're gonna have to make the evening short. Got work to do." He explained what Dick wanted.

"You're in luck. I have everything you need at home. We can do it all there and I can get to see if your photos are any good," said Margaret.

Einstein's Bones

He conveniently forgot to tell her that he could easily do it all on his own lap-top. "Perfect. I didn't know what I was going to do otherwise."

After dinner they walked to John's room to pick up his lap-top and camera. She didn't know he had a lap-top. "Burner doesn't work very well and the software ain't so hot," he explained. "You did say you had wireless, didn't you?" She did.

She scanned his room and shook her head. "Thank God you have a maid come in here every day."

"If I'd a known you were gonna see it, I'd a cleaned it up a little."

She looked down at the ash tray beside his bed and shook her head again. They left as soon as John retrieved what he needed and ten minutes later were at Margaret's.

"Want a beer?" she asked.

"Just one if I'm gonna do a decent job on this."

With beers in hand, they walked into her den and set up the computers. An hour later they had put together what they both thought was a pretty good presentation.

As usual, John awoke at sunrise. Before he lifted himself out of bed, he turned his head to the right and then to the left. Alone in bed again.

"You have time for breakfast?" he heard Margaret ask from the foot of the bed.

"A quick bowl of cereal, maybe," he replied as he looked at his watch. "Can you give me a ride back to the motel?"

"I guess I'm going to have to, unless you want to walk." She left and went into the kitchen. John quickly dressed and joined her there.

"You look so beautiful in the morning," he said with his arms around her.

"That's more than I can say for you. You sure you don't want anything more substantial than just a bowl of cereal? I can make you some bacon and eggs. It won't take long."

"No, if I'm gonna catch up with the others I better hurry. And I can't work in these clothes, either."

He wolfed down his breakfast – such as it was, then headed outside to Margaret's Suburban. He hesitated. "What?" she asked.

"Silly me, I almost forgot all my stuff and the CD. I'll be right back."

They were too late getting to the motel. All the vehicles had left. "Shit," John muttered, "Sorry to ask, but can you give me a lift out to the ranch?"

"Sure. Being I'm a teacher, what the heck, I've got the whole summer off anyway. Are they going to give you a hard time?"

"No – well maybe Karen will," he said with a laugh as he jumped out of the Suburban. "I'll be back in a flash." In fewer than five minutes he was back from his motel room with more photo gear and wearing his work clothes.

"Don't you ever wash them?" she asked. "I hope I didn't get you into any trouble," she said as they headed out of town.

"No, we couldn't have missed them by much, and they don't get right to work anyway. They like to sit around and hob-nob for a while and figure out what they're gonna do all day. They can't get pissed at you anyway, being the owner's daughter and all."

They drove for a few minutes without speaking. "So, are you going to stay in that motel all summer?" she asked.

"You got something better in mind?"

"Maybe," she said with a slight smile.

"Well damn. If what you're asking means what I think you're asking, well don't it just go to figure. We got another trailer comin' out and Dick is gonna have us fix up and clean up that bunk house down by where we park. Looks OK. So, it seems I'm gonna be sleeping out there for the most part along with everybody else. But, we'll all be comin' into town to clean up every now and then. But thanks for the offer, if that's what it was. I hate to turn it down."

"So what did you think I had in mind?" she asked with a laugh.

"Well, I just figured – So what did you have in mind?"

"That you should clean up the old bunk house."

As they neared the ranch they saw several vehicles ahead of them. The last one in line was Karen's "Either you drive too fast or they drive too slow," said John. "At least I'm not gonna be late and have Dick kick my behind." By the time they reached the ranch gate, Margaret had caught up with the others. "You can just drop me off here if you want."

"No, I think I better make sure you guys are getting some real work done. Besides, I've got nothing better to do."

As the last vehicle entering the ranch, it was John's duty to close the gate. As she drove through the gate and past John, Karen called out, "So, seems like you took my advice there, Tiger."

When they arrived, Colin and Zeke were already at work at the site. Einstein's coffin, about two meters long, sixty centimeters wide, and about the same deep was almost fully encased in burlap and plaster leaving only the underside, which was still attached to the deeply undercut rock, unprotected. It looked like a very long toadstool. "It doesn't look all that stable," observed Margaret. "Aren't you afraid it's going to break? How are you going to get it out?"

"It won't break - if we're careful," replied Dick. "I've never broken one – at least not yet. We'll put some cables under it and when the back-hoe puts a little strain on it, we'll cut the rest of the rock away. My only real fear is that somebody might get a finger or hand smashed." He held up his left hand and showed her that the tip of his little finger was missing. "This is what happens when you get careless."

"They gonna be on time with the equipment?" asked John.

"They should be and they're bringing that other trailer for us, too. As soon as we get that bunk house cleaned up, we can all stay here."

John looked at Margaret and then back to Dick. "I got that CD done. Ya want it now?"

"No, hang on to it. He won't be here until this evening. How'd it come out? Any problems?"

"No problems," replied John, "took me all night – with a little help." He paused as he saw a few raised eye brows and a smirk on Karen's face. "Anyway, I think – who is it? Keith? I think he'll like it."

As Dick and his team got back to work, Margaret stopped to see in detail what was being done at each find. She pulled a small camera out of her purse. "You don't mind, do you?" she asked looking at Dick. "I teach fifth grade and I know my students would love to see what's going on."

"As long as you keep them to yourself until we go public, no problem at all. You can use some of John's too if you think his are any good."

"What really fascinates me," she said, "is that you use such ordinary equipment, knives, paint brushes, trowels, nothing you couldn't get at the hardware store to do what you do – except for those dental picks."

"What did you expect to see?"

"I don't know. Something more scientific I suppose."

"You haven't seen 'em use the radar yet. That's pretty scientific," said John. "You gonna use it today, Dick?"

"After the truck leaves."

"So where you sticking this thing anyway."

"For now Karen and Dale got us some space in town we can use as a lab and for storage. After that, it isn't decided."

"What are all those flags sticking in the ground for?" Margaret asked John.

"That's where the GPS thinks there might be more bodies buried. Did I say GPS? I meant GPR – Ground Penetrating Radar," replied John.

"That many?"

"Looks that way."

Margaret stayed at the site for another hour, taking pictures, asking questions, and making notes as Dick and his teams chipped and dusted, brushed and sifted. When she was ready to leave, John walked her to her Suburban. "I really enjoy this. I'm learning a lot. Tonight?" she asked.

"Maybe not dinner anyway what with this Geographic guy comin' in. I'll give you a call if it's not too late, but don't stay up all night on my account." He kissed her good-bye and watched her drive off. "Don't screw this up," he said to himself.

The heavy equipment arrived at noon. Two trucks, one hauling a back-hoe and the other, a flat bed which the cargo was to be loaded on, pulling a trailer. The trailer had "Lyman & Sons Constructions" painted on its sides. Dick got it cheap. It would be a combination office, mini lab, and Dick's sleeping quarters. When it pulled in, all the active sites were covered with tarps. All that

Einstein's Bones

remained visible was the 'toad stool' encased in plaster, several steel cables, and some heavy timber.

Once unloaded, the back-hoe moved the several hundred yards up the slope and then down again to the object it was to remove. The flat bed had to stay behind. "You worried, Dick?" John asked. "There're gonna have to carry that thing a long way back to the truck."

"No, not too. Done it before. We'll take it slow and keep it from swinging around too much with those ropes."

The 'toad stool's' stem had two holes drilled through, which were for two of the steel cables. Two more would be used to support the ends. The wooden timbers were placed between the cables and the coffin to even out the strain and keep the cables from digging into the fossil. At Dick's word, the cables were hooked onto the back-hoe. He stood to one side, ready to shout orders and give hand signals. "Ok, up a little, a little more, a little more, that's it." When the slack was taken up and the cables began to bite into the wood, he shouted and signaled, "Ok, stop! That's good."

"Alright, you three start breaking it free. Everybody else on the ropes." When Dick thought they had removed enough rock, he shouted out, "Ok, that's enough. Let's give it a try. Everybody clear out." He looked back at the operator. "Now give it a little more." The back-hoe pulled up again. Nothing. The back-hoe's struts began to push into the ground. "Stop," he said as he raised his hand. "Let's cut it some more." He waited patiently. "I think that's enough. Everybody back." Again he signaled to the back-hoe. This time, with a sharp crack, it broke free, twisting counter-clockwise, but quickly stabilized by the students on the ropes.

"So far, so good," said Dick nervously. "Now for the fun part."

Einstein's Bones

There were over two hundred yards of uneven and rocky ground between the back-hoe and the waiting flat bed. The coffin made a slow journey, escorted by the students manhandling the ropes and Dick walking along side, supervising its transportation. Not until it was lowered on the flat bed and securely strapped down did Dick show any signs of relaxing. But he was still worried. "Take it slow and easy going back. We're in no hurry." Colin and Karen would accompany it, Colin with the flat bed driver, and Karen in her pick-up.

As the caravan slowly and cautiously drove away, Dick smiled and motioned towards the department van. "Time for a little celebration. There's a red cooler in there. Bring it out."

One of the undergrads obeyed. Inside were four bottles of champagne. "Open 'em up. And save one for Karen and Colin when they get back."

As Dick poured out the champagne, everyone shook hands. "Bring out those sandwiches, too."

They sat in front of the construction trailer. "Man, that had me worried," said John.

"You rookie," replied Zeke.

"You never really lost one, Dick?" asked John.

"Nope, never." He looked at the undergrads. "Time you started getting that bunk house in shape. Remember, you're going to be the ones living in there. And when you get done with that, you can start on this, too," he said as he motioned towards his new office and sleeping quarters.

It was another hour before they resumed work and another hour before Colin and Karen returned. They assured Dick that Einstein had arrived safe and sound and that the space where he now resided had been locked down tight. Dick then motioned for the remaining bottle of champagne.

Einstein's Bones

"Where's everybody else?" asked Colin.

"The coolies are hard at work cleaning up the bunk house, or maybe if they're done, they might be working on Dick's new palace," replied Zeke. "I hope at least one of them is a decent cook. I tried my hand at it in the trailer last night. I don't think anybody was too pleased."

"Anything new of interest since we left?" asked Karen.

Zeke showed her a pair of earrings they had unearthed just before she had returned. She picked them up. They were still encrusted with rock. "They're actually quite pretty." She put them up to her ears. "What do you think, John? Do they go with my t-shirt?" She handed them back to Zeke.

"That's about it, and a few more fragments of wood. But now that you're back," said Dick who saw the undergrads approaching, "and now that they're back, maybe we can get some work done before we shut down for the night." He looked at the undergrads. "Is it livable?"

"All we need is some bedding, and we're set," said Mike.

"Well, then go into town and get some. You guys can all stay there and the girls can stay in the fifth wheel."

"Does that mean they do the cooking?" asked Mike.

"No," was Dick's only reply.

It was near quitting time before another significant discovery was made. Chipping into the area of a pelvic bone, Zeke noticed a ball of reddish brown color. It was located where the femur joined the pelvis. Not only did the color look out of place, but the pelvis seemed wider and presented a very distinct socket for a corresponding ball from the femur. A ball and socket joint was to be expected. It is found on most dinosaurs. But this particular ball and socket joint appeared to be very human like. Zeke called Dick

Einstein's Bones

over. As Dick examined Zeke's new find, it struck him that the ball was likely made of an iron compound.

"Anybody got a magnet or a compass on them?" Dick asked. He remembered that he had a compass in one of his pockets. He pulled it out and moved it over the reddish ball, watching as the needle turned. "It's iron, alright. I think it's quite possible that this old boy had an artificial hip joint. This just keeps getting curiouser and curiouser."

John moved in to take photographs of the new discovery. "Christ, what next? And my old buddy Charlie wondered if we really had found something all that special. Your buddy Keith's gonna shit his pants."

Dick looked at the sky over the Big Horn Mountains. It looked like rain. "Let's get this wrapped up really tight tonight."

A few minutes later they were on their way back to town and a last sleep in a soft bed for a while.

Einstein's Bones

Chapter 11

"There's a Mr. Merskey waiting for you in the bar," the desk clerk informed Dick.

He thanked her and walked into the bar. Sitting on a bar stool was a prematurely gray haired man of about thirty five years putting a double vodka up to his lips. Sitting on a bar stool to his right, drinking what looked to be a large glass of straight bourbon, was the last person Dick wanted to see in Sheridan, Wyoming. He was short, fat, and balding with a salt and pepper beard. He looked like a prospector who had lost his mule. He was Carl Shunk.

Dick greeted Keith and then turned towards Carl. "What are you doing here?"

"Word travels fast," he slightly slurred. "Join us for a drink."

Dick sat down to Keith's left and ordered a Rob Roy. "How long have you been waiting here? You didn't bring him with you, did you?"

"He was here when I came in about an hour ago. I think he's been sitting here since early afternoon, drinking." Carl lifted his glass in salute. "I think he's pretty tight."

"I can see that," said Dick as Carl lifted his glass again. "How about you come back to my room to look at some things?"

"Give me fifteen minutes. Room number?"

They got up to leave. Carl attempted to follow, but couldn't. He awkwardly resumed his seat at the bar. "Now if he'd only stay that way," said Dick.

John was just getting off the phone with Margaret when Dick knocked at his door. "Come down to my room."

"I got time for a shower?"

"No."

Einstein's Bones

John entered Dick's room to find the whole team assembled. "I'll make this short and to the point," Dick began. "Carl Shunk is here and . . " There was an audible gasp. "And I don't know how he found out and I don't know what he's up to, but I can guess. Regardless of how much he knows or how much he thinks he knows, I don't want any of you even thinking of speaking with him. He'll try to buy you dinner and drinks and who knows what else just so he can find out what's going on here. For sure he's not going to buy it that we are here just on a summer field trip. Say nothing. Avoid him. That's all. Now go have dinner some place other than here. He's in the bar dead drunk and probably staying here, too. At least this is our last night here." John began to leave with the others. "John, go get your photos and come back. Keith will be here in a minute or two."

"How do you think he found out?" asked John. "You think he knows what we've got?"

"Who the hell knows? Somebody opened their mouth. Oh, and don't repeat any of this to Keith. The Geographic helps him out now and then, too."

"Do ya think Keith might have told him?"

"I doubt it."

John left and returned to Dick's room in less than a minute. Keith Merskey arrived a minute later. "I hope you don't think I brought him," Keith said as Dick opened the door. "I wouldn't do that."

"I know," replied Dick. "So are you ready to see some very interesting pictures?"

Every photograph that John showed was punctuated with a "wow", or a "fantastic", or an "unbelievable" from Keith. "I can't wait to see all of this for myself. I'll be flying back in the afternoon, so it will have to be in the morning."

Einstein's Bones

"That'll be fine," replied Dick.

"Let's get something to eat," suggested Keith. "You too, John. How's the food here?"

"Not here," insisted Dick.

They went to the Sheridan Inn. Keith began the discussion. "Those photos you took were great, John. Good composition, good lighting. You have a very good eye. "I'd like to use them in the magazine." John thanked him and smiled. Keith turned to Dick. "The people back at the Council and our big donors are going to be very pleased. I doubt upping your grant will be any problem at all. Are you going to need any more help?"

"I don't think I'll need any more just yet - maybe some later. I did ask Barbara Allen to come over and I suppose she'll bring an assistant."

"Good. I like her. How long do you think you'll be working on the site?"

"From what we've found so far, into next year anyway. Maybe even longer."

"How soon before you have a preliminary summary. When do you want us to break this? I'd like to get a little something in not too far down the path."

"I'll send you a report in a week or so." Dick thought for a moment. "As for making it public, you guys are footing the bill, so it's your call."

"How about something at the end of the summer?" Dick nodded assent. "In the meantime I'd like to get a film crew out here as soon as I can. And a writer – no offense Dick. As for the stills, John's work looks good enough for me. Or is he part of the grant? I don't recall."

"Yes, he is," replied Dick.

Einstein's Bones

"An unusual move for the Expeditions Council, but then so is the rest of your grant."

"How big a film crew? I don't like a lot of people getting in the way, you know."

"I'd say four at the most."

"I don't want to sound greedy," said John, "but OK, maybe I am, so do I get anything extra out of this?"

"I don't know if Dick explained any of this to you, John, but we, the National Geographic, have the right of first refusal on all your photographs. What we don't use is yours to do with as you please."

"Sort of what I figured. Sounds fair enough to me," replied John.

Dick asked the question that was uppermost on his mind. "Did Shunk tell you why he was here? Did he bring anyone with him? Did he say how he found out?"

"Hard to tell, really. He was pretty drunk when I got there. He just kept rambling on and on about getting in on something really big. Big find, big fame, big money, and how he was going to shock the world. That's about it. I don't remember ever seeing him quite so juiced. I don't like him that much either, but do you mind if I ask you what is it between the two of you?"

"I don't mind if you ask as long as you don't mind if I don't answer."

It was after ten before John got back to his motel room. He called Margaret immediately. "I didn't wake you did I?" He hadn't. "Sorry it took so long. I don't think we can do anything tonight. I gotta get all my stuff ready to leave in the morning."

"You really think you can get that mess cleaned up all by yourself? You need some help. Besides, it might be your last night in civilization for a while."

Einstein's Bones

Before checking out the next morning, but still reserving one room, the team met as usual in Dick's room. "You all go ahead," said Dick, "I'm going to take Keith out for a nice greasy breakfast." The Silver Spur was quieter than normal, only about half full. It was too early to be filled. Keith was not overly impressed with either the decor or the smells emanating from the kitchen. It was a long way from Washington, D.C. He ordered toast and coffee.

"I can see those letters to the editor pouring in now," said Keith, "and a few cancellations, too."

"But you're sure as hell going to sell a lot of magazines and I'm guessing you might make a dollar or two from your other revenue streams – books, TV specials and big fat cat donors."

"No doubt. So how much of a storm do you think this is going to cause?"

"Big, I imagine. Right up there with *The Origin of Species* is my guess." Dick took a few bites of a sausage. "I just wish that some people wouldn't insist that you have to either believe in God or in science. I believe in God, not in the same way they do. I believe he took his time with all this – not just six days. The Bible? There's a lot of good history in it, good thoughts to live by, and some very interesting symbolism. Take the story of Adam and Eve. They're running around innocent and naked in the Garden of Eden until they take the bite out of that apple. All of a sudden they discover they are naked and go shopping for fig leaves. And they discover good and evil. For me, it represents man's transformation from an innocent beast to what I hope is a more intelligent creature that knows the difference between good and evil, between right and wrong. At some point in time we bit the apple and became human. You?"

Einstein's Bones

"Something like that. It's been a long time since I went to temple."

"No matter what we find, I doubt any of this is going to change anyone's mind."

As they got up to leave, Keith left a buck on the table. "Hey, I'll have to eat here again," said Dick as he threw down another couple of bucks.

The drive to the site was unremarkable until they were a mile from the ranch. A quarter of a mile off the road where Dick had spotted some promising out-croppings the autumn before, a half dozen pick-ups and a full size trailer were parked. Dick slowed the van and stopped.

"What's going on over there?" asked Keith.

"I don't know. It's all new to me," replied Dick as he strained his eyes. "Grab those binocs out of the glove compartment, will you." Dick rolled down his window and steadied his elbows on the door frame. He took a long look. "Jesus Christ, the Skunk. Damn it!" He watched for another minute. "He certainly came prepared."

"You think he's going to find anything?"

"I took a quick look at it last year and it does look promising, but that's no guarantee. If he does, he does, but I don't want to think about it. With any luck, he'll just tell me where not to dig." He put the van back in gear and drove to the ranch.

At the site, Dick approached John. "Did you see what was going on back there when you drove in?" He had. "Do you by any chance know who owns that land?" John didn't. "I suppose there's nothing we can do about it, but go into town and find out."

"Right now?"

Dick handed the van keys to John. "Yes, right now." Dick then turned to Keith. "Let me show you around."

126

Einstein's Bones

Two hours later John was back at the site. He didn't see either Dick or Keith. They were in Dick's trailer. He knocked and entered, finding them looking through some books and drinking coffee.

"Did you find out?" asked Dick.

"Yes, and of all people, it belongs to Dale Newcomb."

"What? Are you sure about that?"

"Yeah," replied John. "I even called Margaret about it. She just found out about it herself this morning."

"Did she tell you anything more?"

"She said Dale was getting paid but she didn't know how much."

"So did she say if it was her brother who told Shunk?"

"She wasn't sure about that, but that was her guess. Odd, all the years I've been comin' out here hunting and I never knew Dale owned any land of his own. So, you think this is gonna be a big problem?"

"Not much. Maybe a little competition is a good thing. Oh, by the way, you don't mind taking Keith back to town, do you?"

"How soon?"

"About noon."

John returned to his work followed shortly by Keith and Dick. "Did you get some photos of this yet?" asked Dick as he knelt beside a find that Lani was working on.

John went over and took several photographs. "What the heck is that?"

"It isn't part of any Sapienasaur, that's for sure," she replied as she brushed dirt from fossilized bones, bones that were beside those of another Sapienasaur, but much smaller and more delicate than all those of a Sapienasaur. "It looks to be about the size of a chicken."

"Do you know what it is?" asked John.

"Nope," replied Lani, "and neither does the boss. He's been looking through all his books and can't find it."

"I thought you knew em all, Dick" said John with a smile.

"Not hardly."

"Looks to me like it was put inside the coffin. What do you make of that?"

"We'll never know why. Some kind of offering? A ritual sacrifice? It could be a favorite pet for all I know. You can make of it what you want. Everyone is going to have their own theory."

At noon, John drove Keith back to town, stopping briefly to observe what the Skunk was doing. Eight or nine bodies were scouring the ground and at least two were working with a GPR. If they had done any digging, John couldn't see it. When he passed again two hours later things looked much the same except that several flags were planted. But still no digging.

There were several remarkable finds when John returned to Dick's site. Two more coffins were now ready for removal, and three more pieces of jewelry had been found, one of which had more writing on it. And Karen was very excited about what she might have found with the GPR. She asked John over so she could pose over some of her recent print-outs.

"For God's sake, don't bend over so much," said John, "some of these are gonna end up in the National Geographic, ya know."

She shook her torso ever so slightly and then halfway straightened herself. "That better?"

"A little." He moved in to take some close-ups of the radargrams. "So what's so exciting? More bodies?"

"See this hyperbolic reflection?" she asked. "That's another body. I've found a lot more. Now take a look at this." Even to

John's untrained eye there was a big difference. "It's something really big," she continued. "Something very much out of place compared to what we've seen so far."

"So where is it?" he asked. She pointed up-slope. "Why aren't you digging there yet?"

"It's too far down, see," she said pointing to lines on the radargram.

"Yeah, even I can see that. How soon we gonna start working on it?"

"As soon as we get in a back hoe that we can keep here for a while," she replied. "So, I hear Dale's gone over to the other side?"

"Yup."

"Well, he was fun while it lasted."

That evening was John's first in the bunk house, to be followed by many more. He and Charlie had pitched a tent nearby on several hunting trips in the past, but they had never slept in the bunk house itself. There was little that was modern about it. It had six bunk beds, a small table, a counter with a dry sink, and two cupboards. Kerosene lamps provided the lighting, and the toilet facilities were an old outhouse. Water was furnished by a hand pump twenty yards away. Two of the bunks would be empty that night. Colin and Zeke had the night in town.

After dinner – canned beef stew – John walked up towards the peak and looked down upon their camp. "How incredibly peaceful," he said to himself. There were no city lights, just a dim orange glow coming from the bunk house. But that was overwhelmed by the brilliance of the night sky. There was no moon that night, just countless stars. He studied them and knew why men believed in Gods. He wondered if they had had the same effect on the creatures whose long forgotten bones they were now unearthing.

Einstein's Bones

They must have. How different did the sky look then? And it was so quiet. He could hear some laughter and some talk coming from the bunk house where a card game was in progress, but it did not disturb him. Even the occasional howl of a coyote only added to the sense of quiet – or maybe of loneliness.

    Was he there for half an hour? Longer? His little escape seemed forever. His dreamlike state was broken when the bunk house door opened and someone shouted, "Are you going to stay up there all night or are you coming in?"

    He walked back down the hill, passing Lani and Karen who were on their way to the fifth wheel and Dick who was going to his private quarters. In the bunk house, while the others were getting ready for sleep, Mike was explaining something about English history. John put up with it, but soon had enough. "Lights out and quiet," he said. The lamps were put out but Mike kept on with his history lesson until someone shouted, "Will you shut the fuck up." For a while, John enjoyed the silence until he heard the rustling of a plastic bag and the crunching of corn chips. Again someone shouted out, "For Christ sake, Mike, put down that bag and go to fucking sleep." Quiet at last. John strained his ears for the sound of a distant coyote only to be traumatized by ear splitting snores. "It's gonna be a long summer," he thought.

Einstein's Bones

Chapter 12

John had to endure Mike's know-it-all lectures and chip munching for another week before it would be his turn, along with another member of the team, to spend two nights in town, cleaning himself and his clothing and escaping the nightly beef stew. He was only slightly bothered to find out that his partner for those two nights would be Mike as John knew he had an alternative to sharing a motel room with Mike.

Between that first night spent in the field and his two nights in town, several new faces appeared. The first addition was Barbara Allen, the cultural anthropologist from England. Along with her came her assistant, Kathy Stokes. Barbara was older than John expected – in her mid-fifties, very slender bordering on skinny, a sharp featured face with her gray hair pulled back in a bun. Perhaps John thought she looked older because his only notion of what she looked like came from the jacket cover of one of Dick's books, a book more than ten years old.

Kathy Stokes was much younger, not much over twenty. She was shy and unobtrusive, very ordinary in appearance, nothing at all to distract any of her male co-workers, especially with her horribly aligned front teeth.

The day following the arrival of Barbara and Kathy came the film crew from the National Geographic along with a writer, Diane Snyder, who spent her two days at the site doing interviews and taking notes. John spent an hour with her telling her how the original discovery had been made and showing her copies of his first photographs. He made it a point to let her know that they were his and were taken before he became part of the team. What interested John more was the film crew. He did his best to avoid being in front of the camera. What fascinated him was their equipment. All the latest video gear and a couple of film cameras, too.

The film crew did not have the satisfaction of filming any startling new discoveries. They recorded the removal of three more coffins, the unearthing of two more fossils, more jewelry, interviews with Dick and some of his crew, and the day in and day out work with shovels, trowels and brushes. Some of their footage was devoted to the everyday life at the camp – meals, card games, and bull sessions. They left the same evening that John and Mike left to spend their two nights in town.

John's drive back to town that night was a non-stop lecture in history, political science and the movies from Mike, interrupted only when Mike grabbed another handful of chips and stuffed them into his mouth. John didn't complain or try to interrupt. He had only the drive back and forth from the ranch to worry about. He had a better place to spend his nights.

As soon as they reached the motel, John called Margaret while he held up his hand, trying to get Mike to stop talking long enough so he could at least hear the phone ringing. He got Margaret's answering machine. He left his room number and then motioned to Mike. "Go take your shower." He called Margaret again. Still just the answering machine. He got it yet a third time after he himself stepped out of the shower. He called Margaret's sister. Carol told him that Margaret was gone and would not be back the two nights that John was in town. It was disappointing, but not nearly as much as the thought of spending two nights in the same motel room as Mike. He put down the phone. "Grab you dirty clothes and let's go eat."

Dinner with Mike was tolerable, sitting with him at the laundromat was borderline, sleeping in the same room was torture - listening to his endless talk and the crunching of chips. For some reason the drive back to the ranch was enjoyable. The reason being that Mike said almost nothing.

The thought of another night in a hotel room with Mike all to himself was too much for John. That evening, when they got to the motel room, John picked up the phone and pretended to call Margaret. "Yes, of course I'd love to spend the evening with you. I'll be right there." He hung up the phone and smiled. "I'll be back in the morning for ya," he told Mike. He walked out the door and down the hall to the front desk. He got a room for himself. Too late, he remembered he'd left a book behind. He wasn't about to go back and get it.

Mike was not as quiet the next morning as he had been the day before. And the subject of his jabbering had changed. This morning it was all about Kathy Stokes. At least someone thought she was attractive.

"What about Karen?" John managed to ask.

"She's too old for me, so I told her I wasn't interested."

Nearing the ranch, John slowed for a look at the Skunk's site. There was digging now, but John couldn't see any details. He asked Karen when he got to the site if she had heard anything, but she didn't know any more than John. "So, are you all broken up, Karen?" he asked her.

"About what?"

"Mike says he dumped you."

"He did? Well shit, then I'm just crushed. Thank God Stokes is here to get him out of my hair. So how was your sweetie?

"Keep it to yourself, but she wasn't home. I had to tell Mike I spent a night with her so I could get a room by myself. What a relief"

Dick approached. "All your equipment working?" he asked John.

Karen laughed. "I don't think he found out."

"Sure," he replied. "Something special going on today?"

Dick pointed to an area that had been marked off with yellow plastic ribbon, the same area where the GPR had indicated a large anomaly. "We're going to start excavating there today."

"Are we going to get it out?" he asked.

"No chance of that. It looks way too big and about three meters down. By the end of the day we might have some idea of what we've got."

A back hoe arrived an hour later and was positioned at the edge of the cordoned off area. Everyone but John grabbed a shovel or a hand pick or some other tool. After conferring with the operator, Gene, for ten minutes, the back hoe's engine revved up, its arm went down, and a scoopful of overburden was lifted out of the ground and dumped in a designated area where two of the undergrads examined it. The new hole was examined by Dick himself. He took a few swings with his hand pick and turned the debris with a garden trowel. Finding nothing, he signaled for another scoop. Gene again paused his machine while Dick took another look. Nothing but Wyoming dirt. He looked at Karen. "Are you sure the area around this is clear?"

"Like you and I have gone over it before, there's nothing off to the side for at least twenty meters and nothing above it."

Satisfied, Dick ordered another scoop-full taken. Nothing was done quickly. Each time Gene removed another scoop, Dick and most of his team were on their hands and knees picking and brushing. Four feet down and nothing but rocks and dirt. It was deep enough now that the sides had to be cut back and crude steps dug for access. And then another foot down, and wider still. Two hours later they were down eight feet and getting thirsty enough for Dick to order Colin to bring up some water.

Dick worked more slowly now. Instead of full scoops, only a few inches at a time were being removed. And the picks and brushes were more careful, too. Again the shovel went down followed by Dick and his team. Still nothing. Still another shallow layer of over burden was removed. Karen took three or four swings with her hand pick. Work stopped at the sound of a distinctly metallic ring. "I do believe I have something here," she said.

As the others watched, Dick knelt beside her and brushed away debris. There was something flat and gray in color. He rubbed it with his finger. It felt perfectly smooth. "Here, give me that," he said to Karen as he took her pick and used it to expose more of whatever she had found. "You hit it here?" he asked. She nodded yes. He examined it closely with his naked eye and then with his loupe. "There's not a mark on it." He tapped it lightly with the blunt end of the pick and got the same metallic ring. "Damn interesting," was all he said.

He climbed out of the pit, directing Gene to widen it and dig it down to a depth of just a few inches above where the metallic object was found.

They worked past noon without stopping, and would have kept at it without a break, but at 2:30 it was time for Gene to return to Sheridan. The roughly square hole was now about twenty feet on each side and more than eight feet deep. At several points they had uncovered more of the mysterious object. It was all the same. Gray, flat, smooth and metallic. It showed no signs of rust, pitting, or corrosion of any kind. It looked as though it could have been made yesterday.

"I'm starving," said Zeke. He was seconded by Mike.

While the others had been busy digging, John had been busy with his camera, taking wide shots, close-ups and photos of the dusty diggers. He had many shots of the strange object but had not

Einstein's Bones

yet felt it. As the others walked back to the camp he decided to touch it for himself. What was it he would be touching? He reached out his hand but hesitated, then moved his fingers forward and very slowly, as if not to break it, pressed his fingers down. It was cold, exceptionally smooth, and very hard. What was it? What was it made of? He drew his hand back and then touched it again. It seemed flawless - and mystic. He lingered a moment longer then got up to join the others for a late lunch.

John grabbed a beer and sandwich from the cooler, sat on the edge of one of the bunks and joined the discussion. "Any guess what that is?" he asked.

"None whatsoever," answered Dick.

"Any idea what it's made of?"

"Not that either," answered Dick. He turned to Barbara. "You have one of those satellite phones, right?" She nodded. "I'm going to call a metallurgist friend of mine and have him come and see if he can help us out. And get that film crew back here, too."

"It's Krell steel," volunteered Mike.

"Krell steel?" asked Colin.

"You know, that's the metal the Krell used on Altair IV."

"I'm still not following you."

"You know, the movie *Forbidden Planet* from the 50s"

"If you say so," replied Colin.

Dick handed the phone back to Barbara. "The film crew and Snyder will be back tomorrow, the metallurgist in a couple three days. Let's get back to work."

By early evening most of the twenty foot square had been cleared, made easier by the happy fact that nothing stuck to the metal with any tenacity. There were no variations in the metal. No markings, no seams, just solid, smooth, flat gray metal. Curious, Dick hit it several times with the sharp end of his pick, each time using a little more force. Finally, he hit it with all of his strength, resulting in a blunted pick, but still not even the slightest mark on the gray metal.

"Yup, Krell steel," said Mike.

Jeff, working on the west side of the excavated area, shouted out, "I've got an edge here."

Dick moved over a few feet to investigate, feeling the edge with his index finger. It was at a right angle to the top of the metal slab and gently rounded. He dug deeper and called for assistance, stopping a half of a meter down without finding a bottom. "We'll wait for the back-hoe. Let's get the rest of this cleaned off."

At the next morning's first light, most of the team, including Barbara and her assistant, were back at work examining the remains of the Sapienasaurs. Colin busied himself by circling the area just outside of the yellow ribbon with the GPR while Karen watched the monitor with Dick vulching and smoking his Pall Malls. Every few minutes he would point to the screen and ask Karen, "What do you think? Is it anything?" To each query she replied in the negative - that there was nothing within twenty meters of the gray metal slab, just as she had reassured Dick the day before. But he was never fully satisfied; he still had his concerns about destroying something significant when Gene arrived at 7:30am. To be on the safe side, he'd proceed slowly and carefully. Exposing the west side of the slab would be more than enough for the day's work.

As before, each scoop of the shovel was followed by a careful examination. The first five seemed to take forever. Maybe it was carelessness on Gene's part, or it could have been a problem with the machinery. The sixth time the shovel went down it landed with full force on the smooth gray metallic surface.

"God damn it," yelled Dick. "Get that bucket up."

Einstein's Bones

Gene lifted the arm and set it to one side as Dick raced over to inspect the damage. "I'll be damned – still nothing. Not even a scratch." He walked over to Gene. "You came close to seeing me lose it. You - we were lucky. Watch what you're doing, will you, but I think we can speed things up some."

Gene now took five or six scoops before Dick and his team re-entered the ever deeper, longer and wider trench. Some poked and prodded the soil while the others cleared debris off of what now looked like a wall. By the time the back-hoe quit for the day they had a trench twenty five feet long and ten feet deep, with still no bottom found, just the same seamless gray metal.

It would take most of the rest of the next day to excavate the entire west side, witnessed by Margaret and her father. It measured forty feet wide and twelve feet high. Margaret and her father could not stay very long. She did manage to tell John that she would not be leaving town anytime soon and that any time he came into town, he could stay with her.

And they continued to dig, but now with the returned writer and film crew. Two days on the north side. It was the same as the west. For two days it was the turn of the east side. Again, forty feet long and twelve feet high. The first day on the south side was more of the same. The same smooth and seamless gray metal. At 10:00am the next day there was something different. At the midpoint of the wall, Josh worked his hammer and wide chisel, patiently exposing more gray metal with each stroke. Another stroke and his chisel came to a sudden stop. He lifted his chisel again and moved it a few inches to the right, exposing more of the wall. Then he turned it sideways towards what had stopped it two strokes before. Again it came to an abrupt halt, but this time exposing something that was protruding from the wall but of the same gray metal. Almost hiding what he had discovered from the

Einstein's Bones

others and from the camera, he worked on it until he uncovered a large oblong loop. He stared at it for a moment and then shouted out, "Hey everybody, I think I've got a friggen door handle."

They all crowded around to see Josh's discovery. "So what makes you think it's a door handle?" asked Zeke. "I don't see no stinking door."

"And where's the door bell?" added Mike.

"What's this?" asked Karen pointing to a group of incised symbols above and to the left. "They look the same as the others we've found. Did you see it, Josh?"

"No, I don't know how, but I missed it."

Before there was any more discussion, Dick ordered everyone out of the trench so that Gene could dig out a more convenient area to work in. The hour consumed left the team time to eat and speculate. Was it really a door handle? If it was, what might be behind the door? Of all the guesses, a tomb was the most popular. "It's got to be the tomb of somebody important. What else could it be right here next to a cemetery?" supposed Zeke.

"How odd that sounds," said Lani.

"How odd what sounds?" asked Zeke.

"'Somebody important'. 'Somebody'. Like they were human. But I don't know what else you'd say. 'Somedino'? And yet, 'somebody' does fit in a way. I think we all feel the same way, like we're dealing with beings like ourselves. Thinking, caring, as intelligent as us. Maybe more so. Maybe beyond us – at least in metals anyway. And now they're gone. And until now, completely forgotten - unlike the Egyptians or the Maya. Now that we've found them, does this mean that they live again? That as long as a race is remembered it lives? And what about us? Will we leave anything behind that we are remembered by? Someday, the sun will die out and - - - and destroy the earth leaving nothing. Nothing of us and nothing of them - again."

"You better stop before we all get too optimistic," Zeke replied.

"By that time we will have colonized space," said Mike.

"You really think we'll be around that long?" doubted Colin.

"Not like what we are now, but in some form," replied Mike.

"You'd like to hope so," added John, "or at least leave something behind to be remembered by out there. If not, you just wonder what's the point. It makes me want to believe in something greater than ourselves. I wish I could."

"Before you all start thinking that what we are doing is just a waste of time, we do have some work to do," said Dick. "Let's go find out if it really is a door."

Back in the trench, Dick and three others carefully cleaned the area around the handle. After more debris was cleared off, they studied the wall with both their eyes and fingers, feeling for something, anything different. A foot to the right of the handle Karen's fingers felt a very slight edge. Two inches further to the right there was another. She moved her fingers up and down. "Dick," she said, "come over and feel this." He felt the same area. "Does it almost feel like a strip of tape to you?"

"It does."

They followed the tape with their fingers up several feet until it stopped and turned to the left at a right angle continuing another three feet horizontally then turning down again at another right angle. Down about seven feet it turned to the right and then up to meet where Karen had first felt it. A rectangle three feet wide and seven feet high, with a short tab two inches below the handle.

Einstein's Bones

"Sure as hell looks like a door to me," said John. "Taped shut? Taped shut with dino duct tape. Are we gonna take a pull and see if it comes off?"

"Not a good idea just now," advised Dick. "If it is a door and there is something inside of this, it's been sealed in there for sixty million years. There's always the possibility that there might be something dangerous in there. Microbes or gas, no way to tell. No reason to take any chances. We'll have to seal it off first. All we can do now is wait."

Einstein's Bones

Chapter 13

That night it was John's turn to spend his two nights in town - once again with Mike. As on their last foray into town, Mike kept up a one sided non-stop conversation, interrupted only by slurps of Pepsi, mouth-fulls of chips and frequent belches. "Did you ever see that movie?" he asked.

"If you mean *Forbidden Planet*, yes, a couple of times at least," replied John.

"Do you remember what Dr. Morbius found? I'll bet we've got the same thing here. Krell steel and the Krell lab."

"Mike, you might be right. Just don't put that Krell head set on." John decided to change the subject. "So how are you and your English girl friend getting on?" he asked, regretting his choice.

"She really likes me. Haven't you noticed the way she looks at me? And such a pretty smile. What do you think? What have you heard? Has she said anything to you? And her accent – it's so English."

"That might be because she's from England, ya think?" John was not the camp gossip, but it was impossible not to hear what was said when Mike was out of ear-shot. Kathy Stokes was trying to be polite, but her patience was wearing thin. She half expected that if Mike didn't stop bothering her, he would soon have a pick sticking out of the middle of his forehead. Pretty smile? As long as she didn't open her mouth and let the world see her teeth. But yes, she was a nice girl. He wasn't going to burst Mike's bubble. He probably couldn't anyway. He'd let Kathy do that. And if she did pin him with a pick, at least he'd be shut up. Yet, John did feel some sympathy for Mike, especially as everyone else in camp went out of their way to pick on him. "Yes, she does have a nice smile."

Einstein's Bones

"I'm going to ask her to come to town with me the next time it's our turn, if you don't mind switching with someone."

"I don't mind, but I wouldn't do that if I were you. Dick wouldn't like that," he replied, knowing Dick couldn't care less about who was sleeping with whom.

"I'm going to ask her anyway," he replied and proceeded to talk about Kathy Stokes the rest of the way into town and into the motel, making John's escape to Margaret's all the more urgent.

Ten minutes after dropping Mike off, John was at her door with a bottle of wine in one hand and a bag of dirty laundry in the other. John followed Margaret into the living room and glanced at several books and some literature on her coffee table. "What's all that?" he asked.

"My sister and her Bible banging husband just left. They are bound and determined to save me before I go to hell. I'm a divorced woman and, oh God, I'm seeing a divorced man. And you! My God! They think that you're almost beyond redemption – blaspheming all over the place. They just can't believe that you really think all those bones from the flood you've been digging up could be as old as you and your Satan worshiping friends think they are. But they do want to at least try to save your poor misguided soul. Give them a chance, and they'll get a hold of you and never let go. You were lucky the last time. I didn't tell them that you'd be here tonight and I would never tell her you'd be staying the night. But I think they've got that figured out anyway, especially the way I hurried them out. I wouldn't be surprised if she drives by tonight just to see if your truck is in the driveway. And then later on to see for how long."

John chuckled. "Satan worshiper, huh? Yeah, that's me alright. Whatever. It doesn't bother you does it – me staying here and causing trouble between you and your sis?"

Einstein's Bones

"No. Too bad you never knew her before she married her husband and he got her into that religion of his. She was a real slut."

"If they want to try and convert me, let 'em. It's been tried before. They might have a better chance with Dick, though. He's about a third of the way there already. I don't know how often he reads it, but he keeps a Bible by his bed. But that's OK. But for Christ sake, don't let them near him."

"According to them, he's the great Satan. So, what's new out there at the ranch?"

"You should come out tomorrow and see for yourself before they bubble wrap it. Big, big, big find. Looks like we've found a door on that thing I told you about, but we're not going to open it till a bunch of bio-hazard guys come out and seal up the door area like they seal up those bubble boys. Dick figures it'll be a couple of weeks before it's all set up and test results come back. So we just have to wait."

She didn't seem surprised. "I thought you'd find a door."

"Oh, and I almost forgot. Some metallurgist was out all day trying to figure out what that thing is made of. He poked at it, tried drilling it, went over it with some really weird looking equipment, poured some kind of acid on it and even went over it with a Geiger counter. He couldn't touch it. Doesn't have a clue what it is. Mikie thinks it's Krell steel"

"Krell steel?"

"Don't get me started, and whatever you do, don't ask him. At least it's not radioactive. So what do you hear about what's going on at Dale's? Do you know if the Skunk has found anything?"

"I don't know any more than you do. I just see them working there. I know Dale's there a lot, but he's not saying anything to us. Ever since he invited that guy out here he's distanced himself from the rest of the family, which is fine with me. Oh, I almost forgot, I

Einstein's Bones

saw Dale and Shunk at the Mint having a drink with your back-hoe operator."

"Really! He was supposed to keep his big mouth shut but then nobody – especially Dick – thought he really would. But that's a little much, but then he can't really tell them all that much anyway. Nevertheless, I'd better let Dick know."

"So what does that Allen woman do out there all day? Why a cultural anthropologist?"

"To look for culture, I guess. She's always looking at small artifacts and noting how the bodies – if that's the right word – are laid out. Takes a real close look at teeth, measures a lot and takes a lot of notes. But she doesn't do anything all that different from anybody else. She and Dick spend a lot of time in his trailer at night – writing a book I guess. They're both always writing."

"And you, too," she added.

"I have to keep track of what I photograph, and hell, I might get a book published out of this, too. Why not? We can take the millions I'm gonna make and escape to where ever you want. Did I say we? I guess I did. If your sister says it's OK."

"I'm bound for hell already anyway. Why don't you open that bottle of wine and I'll toss your dirty clothes in the washer."

John went to the kitchen and returned with a cork screw. He need not have bothered. The wine had a twist-off cap. He unscrewed the cap, poured two glasses and worried that Margaret might think that he was cheap. He sat down on the sofa and leafed through the literature on the coffee table. God's Plan for You. Evolution – Fact or Fiction? In His Image. He thought that at least some of the art work was fair.

"I'm going to have to wash everything twice," said Margaret when she returned to the living room. "Do you make it a habit of rolling in the dirt? And please be a little more careful when you eat. Try to get at least half of your food into your mouth."

"My apologies," he replied sheepishly. He looked down at one of the pamphlets he was holding in his hand. "So how often does she bring you this shit?"

"A couple of times a month maybe. It just gets tossed."

"Makes you wonder."

"What?"

"Did our late friends out there think at all like we do? Did they have any religion? Did they pass out this crap, too?"

"From what I've seen, they must have had some kind of religion," she replied.

He picked out the pamphlet, In His Image and studied it for a moment. "If there is a god, would there be just one god, just one creation? Would one god have created us in his image and a different god create them in his? Or was there some other god that didn't care what his creations looked like? Maybe one god created it all and then looked at them and decided to give it another try. But then why do I ask these questions in the first place when I completely believe in evolution? I wonder if old Einstein asked the same questions. I don't know if any of this is going to make anyone alter their belief set, but it's sure gonna change the rules of the game and set the world buzzing. So, what do you think?"

"Nice wine."

"No, really. Or don't you want to talk about it?"

"This is a good way to ruin a beautiful relationship," she started cautiously. "Then again if we're going to go anywhere in the future, we might as well find out now and not later. I'm not at all like my sister, but I do believe in God in my own way. I don't go to church – haven't since I was a girl. And I believe that He or She does have some sort of plan, but don't ask me what it is. I don't

Einstein's Bones

know. I do believe in evolution. Maybe that's part of the plan. It doesn't bother me that you are agnostic, as long as you don't totally deny that at least the possibility exists or get on the band wagon to have "In God We Trust" removed from our money. Then again, I like you just the way you are."

"You can count on me not to jump on any band wagons." He paused. "So you want to try politics for a while? How did you vote in the last election?" She told him. "Seems like we'll just cancel each other out. I think it's better that way. My one try at marriage and we agreed on just about everything. And where did it get me but divorce court. I wonder if those dino guys had anything like Republicans and Democrats?"

"And divorce courts," she added.

"So would you like to spend the day at the dig with me?" he asked Margaret when he woke up the following morning.

"Sure. I've never spent a whole day out there. I can learn how you get so damn filthy. Are they all pigs like you?"

"Believe it or not, some are worse, much worse."

They dressed and ate quickly then headed towards the motel. "Oh, I forgot to tell you, we gotta pick up Mike."

"Were you afraid I wouldn't come if I would have known I'd have to share a ride with Mike?"

"You haven't been with him like I have. And remember, don't ask him anything about the Krell or about his love life."

When Mike entered the van, Margaret took one look at his shirt which was spotted with his morning's breakfast and turned back to John. "Yes, you're all the same."

When he got to the dig, John immediately approached Dick and told him what Margaret had seen at the Mint.

Einstein's Bones

"I guess I'm not surprised," Dick replied. "At least it should really get Carl's panties all wet."

"Did you hear of anything going on at his site?" asked John.

"No, why?"

"I'm not sure. Seems a lot more active over there. More trucks and vans. I think you ought to go over and take a look for yourself."

"What for? There's nothing I can do about it. I can't see anything more from the road than you did and I'm not about to go walking up there and ask him – any more than he'd come in here and ask me."

John returned to his photography and for a while Margaret stayed by his side, taking pictures, carrying some of his equipment, and taking notes. There were several new remains, more jewelry, and two more 'pets'. She then drifted off to observe Barbara Allen at her work.

"So what is it that you are looking for," she asked Barbara.

"Clues to how they might have lived and interacted with one another. Their art, and we have some of that. Their religion and laws, and we have some notions of that from the way they are buried. What might be unique to them and what might be universal in all higher societies. This is a unique opportunity to find out what culture, civilization and what humanity mean."

"Don't you do most of your work with live subjects, like living with some isolated tribe in Borneo?"

"That's part of it. More for others, though. But I've done my part."

"Have you found out anything here yet?"

"Some very interesting things, yes, but too early to be definitive. I can tell without looking at the fossils if we are dealing with a male or a female. Slight differences in the way the bodies are laid out, but the simplest way is that only the males have any jewelry, and most of the 'pets' are with females. What it all means we might never know, but at least we know that a distinction was made."

Margaret noted how clean and neatly pressed Barbara's khaki field shirt was, and Kathy's, too. "You'll probably find out that the male of the species was as much a slob as he is now."

"Boys will be boys," said Barbara with a laugh.

"You drove in with Mike this morning?" asked Kathy.

"Yes, and he does have quite the crush on you."

"I was afraid you'd tell me that."

Margaret spent over an hour with Barbara and Kathy and then went about looking over the shoulders of everyone else – including Karen. After a half an hour with Dick, it was time for lunch in the bunkhouse. She gave it a quick inspection and signaled her tentative approval. "You've got this place looking pretty good – compared to what it looked like before."

"Margaret," Collin called out, "do you want a ham or turkey sandwich? Beer?"

"Turkey and a beer."

After he passed out the food, Collin turned on the radio. For a few minutes there was music - until 12:30pm and the news. Eating stopped. Talking stopped. And drinking beer stopped when they heard the lead story: "There has been an astounding find in Wyoming. World famous paleontologist Carl Shunk today announced the discovery of a race of civilized dinosaurs."

Chapter 14

"A world famous piece of shit is more like it," blurted Karen.

"Shh! Quiet!" ordered Dick.

The details from the forty second sound bite were sketchy at best. Some pottery had been found, some metallic odds and ends, bits of what looked like some kind of plastic, and what Shunk claimed were earrings.

"It sounds like he's found a garbage dump," said Josh. I always wondered just how long plastic would last, but sixty million years?"

"Krell plastic," added Zeke with a laugh. "But it seems like a big jump in faith for him to think he's found a race of civilized dinosaurs."

"Garbage dump or not, he's got something," added Colin. "But earrings in a garbage dump? Maybe, but they do sound very much out of place."

"And why would he assume they are earrings in the first place?" asked Karen. "That doesn't make any sense at all."

"None of it makes any sense except for the fact that Dale must have told him most of what we've found here. And he knows about our big box. Dale has seen the earrings, right, Karen?" asked Dick.

"Yes, sure he has."

"Could the Skunk have seen them too? Does Dale have a key to that space we rented?"

"He did, but you've got that key now, Dick."

"I think you better change those locks right now regardless. And while you're there, Karen, take an inventory, too."

"You don't think . . . ?" she asked.

Einstein's Bones

"I wouldn't put it past him," replied Dick as Karen headed for her pickup. "You need anybody to help you out?"

"No, I can manage it myself."

"I don't get it," said John. "The Skunk's been out here for how long and he's already making a big announcement? And what's he really got? Squat. Not a Sapienasaur anyway. If he'd of found one you'd think he would have announced that, too. So why not wait until he finds one or at least finds something to rival what we've got here. After all, compared to what we've found, he doesn't have all that much. And we're keeping quiet. I just don't get it.

"The son-of-a-bitch wants to steal the show. He wants to be the one remembered for the discovery. I doubt he'll be able to pull it off, but if nothing else, right now he's the center of attention," replied Dick.

"But he's got shit. If that's all he finds he's gonna look like a fool."

"We can only hope. He's doing it on the come, hoping he'll find more and with any luck a Sapienasaur or two. After all, there's nothing to say he won't"

"So what are you gonna do, Dick? You gonna make a big announcement, too?" asked John.

"I don't know. Diane, what do you think the National Geographic's going to say?"

"I'll give them a call and see what they think. I'm almost surprised they haven't called me already. What do you want me tell them from you?"

"It's up to them. I know we can't wait until the end of the summer like we planned, but I'd like a few days to get organized anyway. And I would think you'd like a little time, too. We'll have to keep our fingers crossed that in the meantime the Skunk and his crew don't stumble onto some god-damn lost city or something."

Einstein's Bones

Diane pulled out her satellite phone and called Washington. After a few minutes she took the phone from her ear and returned it to her bag. "Day after tomorrow – in time for the evening news," she told Dick. "They want us to uplink the footage we have now and they want some of the usual interview footage. They'd like it if we could open that door, too."

Dick rolled his eyes. "That's going to have to wait."

After lunch Dick and Diane adjourned to Dick's trailer while the rest of the crew resumed their work on the fossils and the camera crew headed down to their van to transmit their videos. All the while a field radio was kept tuned to the local news station, which broadcast no more details of what the Skunk was up to.

"Enjoying yourself?" John asked Margaret.

"I might just go back to school and get a degree in paleontology myself," she replied. "Not that I don't enjoy being a teacher."

"Maybe you could teach paleontology," said John.

Margaret continued, "I always thought that digging up bones was boring, but this is far from that. You never know what you're going to find. I wish we could open that door right now."

"You and everybody else. So how was your little chat with Karen this morning? You two seemed to be getting pretty chummy."

"You guys are lucky to have her out here – as long as you can keep your eyes off of her. And she seems to be very interested in the two of us."

"How so?"

"Maybe she's just nosey. She asked if you were hands off."

"And am I?" he said with a smile,

"You had better be," she replied as she stroked his upper arm.

Einstein's Bones

Dick and Diane emerged from the trailer after two hours carrying several sheets of paper in their hands. 'Dick and Diane – Jack and Diane' thought John as they approached him.

"I guess you look clean enough," Diane told John.

"I should – Margaret washed everything twice. Why?"

"Diane's going to interview you on camera," replied Dick.

"What the hell for? I've already told her everything. I don't think there's anything more I could say."

Diane handed John a sheet of paper. "I just want to get what you've already told me on tape. We might not even use it. It will take only a few minutes."

John read the questions. They were the same as everyone else had asked many times before. 'What was he doing when he found it? Did he recognize it for what it was? How long had he hunted the area? Did he have any background in paleontology?'

"Well, let's get it over with." They were about to begin the interview when a large van with a red biohazard symbol on its side pulled into the parking area. "Saved by the bell."

"Are you ready?" asked Diane.

While Dick conferred with two men in white suits who arrived in the van, Diane began her interview. "I'm standing here with John Steiner, the man who made this astounding discovery. Tell us, John, how you found it."

Suddenly he was nervous. "Give me a second." He waived the camera off. "You'll cut that won't you?" He took a deep breath. "Don't laugh, Margaret. OK, I'm ready." In less than fifteen minutes he related everything he had told her before, starting with an antelope hunt and ending with flying out to Wyoming with Dick. "Was that OK?"

"You'll never be a movie star," said Margaret with a laugh.

"Was it really that bad?"

Einstein's Bones

"You did just fine," said Diane. "And I'm not much of an interviewer either."

John picked up his camera equipment and turned towards the gray metal box. The two men in white suits were laying out framing for the containment area. An hour later the framing was complete and they brought up three long rolls of what looked like ordinary plastic sheets. By five that afternoon an area six feet on either side of the door had been sealed off, an area that contained several pieces of test equipment. "We'll pull off the seals in the morning," Dick told them all.

At the same time as the bio-hazard van left, Karen was parking her truck. She closed the cab door and slowly walked towards Dick, biting her lower lip the entire way. Dick did not like the expression on her face. "You got the locks and the security alarm codes changed, didn't you?" She had. "And?" he asked.

"Those earrings I brought back to the lab to finish cleaning – they're gone."

"You're absolutely certain?"

"I remember exactly where I left them, and no, they're not there."

"Has John photographed them yet?"

"I'm afraid the photos he took won't be any help. There was only a little gold showing then, not enough to tell at all what they were. He was going to do them tonight when he went back to town."

"John?"

"That was the plan. Would Shunk really steal them out of our lab?"

"My brother would," said Margaret. "I'm sorry I didn't warn you about him more strongly. I'd talk to him, but I don't think it would do any good. Maybe if I talked to my father about it we can get them back."

"I..," Dick hesitated. "I don't think you should do that – at least wait. We're all here as the guests of your father and by extension, his family. We start accusing your brother and we might not be quite so welcome. I'm just curious as to how he might have known they hadn't been photographed yet."

"I left them under my magnifying lamp," responded Karen.

"Then it had to be Shunk who took them and Dale who let him in. Who else but the Skunk would have guessed that they hadn't been photographed? I knew he was a snake, another Marsh, but I never thought he'd go that low. Well, he's got them now and we can't prove a damn thing. The security system at the lab is reset, right Karen?" she nodded. "I doubt he'll try anything more, but we'll have to make sure that everything is fully documented and photographed before we leave anything there without someone standing over it."

"Marsh?" asked Margaret.

"O. C. Marsh and Edward Cope, two rival paleontologists from the 1870's," replied Dick. "They hated each other, and Marsh stole bones from Cope, unless you're a disciple of Marsh, and then it's the other way around."

John's return to town began with Margaret apologizing for her brother. "Don't blame yourself," said John. "How could you have known?"

"I should have. More than once he's gotten into trouble and my father's always bailed him out."

"For stealing?"

"Yes. A car once when he was in high school."

"People change."

"I hoped he had, but it doesn't look that way, does it?"

"And then there was the time . . ." She stopped, remembering that Mike was in the back seat of the van.

Einstein's Bones

John dropped Mike off at the motel and then stopped at a convenience store for a newspaper. There on the front page was a picture of the Skunk holding up the pair of earrings – the pair that Karen had started cleaning two nights before. He showed it to Margaret. "I'm going to call that bastard and chew him a new ass hole," she said. "At least he was too ashamed to get himself in the picture."

"I think Dick wants you to forget it."

"I don't give a damn."

When they reached her home, Margaret went right to the phone without the customary removal of her shoes. John heard only one side of a very one sided conversation. "You prick, you stole those earrings, didn't you. Don't even try to deny it, ass hole. Don't think of calling me your sister again. Maybe Carol can save your worthless ass, but you can go straight to hell for all I care. No, don't bother with that bull shit. I wouldn't believe one damn thing you said. Goodbye and drop dead." She slammed down the phone and looked at John. "Was I too nice?"

"You really sweet talked him, that's for sure," he replied. "Remind me never to piss you off. How about a drink?"

"How about making it a double."

John made his a double, too. He needed it. The local news came on at 10:00pm and the Skunk and his big discovery were the lead story with a live reporter on the scene. She might have been there for the 6 o'clock evening news too, but Margaret and John had missed that. At least John and Margaret got a laugh out of it. The reporter, Cindi something-or-other started her report with, "I'm here with world renowned paleontologist Carl Shunk. It's dark now, but earlier it was much lighter."

Margaret burst out laughing. "What an idiot. Next thing you know she'll tell us that in a few hours it will get light again."

Einstein's Bones

When John stopped laughing he made an excuse for the reporter. "I'm sure if she'd have thought about it she wouldn't have said it. Poor thing. It's a live report and people say stupid things. She'll never live it down though."

The station devoted all the time from the opening of the news to the first commercial break to the story, most of it an interview with the Skunk. He had the gall to tell the camera that he had had his eye on the area for several years but never suspected what he might find, especially that he would find evidence of a race of sapient dinosaurs. He showed the earrings and claimed that they had been found by one of his assistants whom he was careful not to name. He did not explain why he thought they were earrings. Yes, they did look like earrings, but they could be any number of things. Even Dick and Karen were not completely convinced that they were.

What footage that did not feature Shunk closed in on what did indeed look like broken pottery, some concentrations of what might be the remains of something metallic, though to John they looked to be nothing more than patches of red dirt, and five or six clumps resembling a melted down Styrofoam cup. There were no fossils of any Sapienasaurs, but there were several fossils of much smaller creatures, accompanied by Shunk's explanation that, being they were found in what was certainly a dump, they could only be dino leftovers.

Shunk was careful not to reveal that he knew exactly what the fossils he hoped to find might look like, only guessing that their anatomical structure should be significantly distinct from all other known dinosaurs and that he expected they would possess a large cranial cavity. There was no hint that he had already had a peek at them in Dick's lab.

"He looks like he's got a case of the fantods and he's going to pee in his pants," said Margaret.

Einstein's Bones

"Fantods? What do you mean?"

"You know he wants to describe them. You know he wants to name them. You know he'd give anything to show off one of what Dick's got right now. But he can't do any of that, can he. All he can do is hold it in and hope he hits pay dirt before Dick goes public, which he has to know can't be too many days from now."

"I still think he's an idiot for doing this now, but then if he didn't and Dick announced before the old Skunk does, the Skunk wouldn't even make the funny pages. Still, unless he finds something a whole lot better in the next day or two he's gonna look pretty damn silly," said John.

The news segment ended with one of the anchors asking Shunk what he expected to find with further excavation. "We have a garbage dump, so there must be the remains of some habitation near by. That's what I'm looking for. Of course what I ultimately hope to find are the fossilized remains of its inhabitants." He was asked if he had a name for them as yet. Already knowing the name that John had given them, he replied, "No, I won't do that until I find one."

"How about *Skunkasaurus*? He's sure to attach his name to one if he's lucky enough to find one," said John.

"All that and no mention at all about another dig only a few miles away," added Margaret. "You guys have kept that secret well – except for Dale and the back-hoe operator. You suppose Shunk's paid him off so nobody knows Shunk's not the only bone digger around here?"

"Does this news repeat later so we can make a DVD?"

"Not until an hour or two after midnight and I'd rather be doing something else then. Why not just burn it off their web site. Let's do that now. Then we can do the other thing I had in mind."

Einstein's Bones

John couldn't sleep that night. There was nothing he could do that would change anything and no matter how much TV he watched, what happened would happen. But he got up at 1:30am and turned on one of the all news channels. There was nothing new. No new discoveries, just more of what he and Margaret had seen earlier. The only additions were interviews of the Skunk answering mostly the same questions, but from different reporters. Only one question added anything. When asked about his rivalry with Dick Johnson, Shunk revealed that he knew that Johnson was doing something nearby but claimed he had no idea of what and speculated only that he might be conducting a field exercise. Asked if he thought it unusual that they would both be working in the same area, Shunk replied that it was coincidence and nothing more.

John felt a tap on his shoulder. "Anything new?" asked Margaret. "Are you going to stay up all night?"

"Only that Shunk said he knows we're here. Covering his ass I suppose. He'd look really silly if he didn't admit it."

"Are you coming back to bed any time soon? You only have a couple of hours left." She led him back into the bedroom where he managed to get a couple of hours of sleep.

Einstein's Bones

Chapter 15

Waking at dawn, John felt surprisingly fresh. He knew he'd pay for his all night TV watching later that evening. "Would ya like to come out again today?" he asked Margaret who was already frying bacon and eggs. He wasn't sure she heard him the first time. "I said, do you have time for a quick one?"

"No and no."

"Too much Mike for ya?"

"Going shopping with Carol, and yes, that too."

He walked into the kitchen and took his plate. "Sorry I'm gonna miss the shopping. I'd like to know what your sis has to say about your wicked ways. Say, how'd ya like to take Mikie with you?"

"Only if you want me to take that plate away and feed it to the cats."

"Tempting. But I wouldn't do that to you." He wolfed down his breakfast and kissed her goodbye. "See you in a week?"

"No, I'll be out there tomorrow. Love you."

It was the first time that either one of them had said that. He did not hesitate with his reply. "I love you, too," and gave her another, longer kiss, then drove off to pick up Mike.

"Some contrast," he muttered to himself as he pulled into the motel's parking lot where Mike was standing waiting for him with one hand in a bag of potato chips. Mike climbed into the passenger seat. "Where's Margaret? Everything OK with the two of you?"

"We're just fine, maybe more so."

"Oh, really." Mike shoved the bag of chips at John. "Have some," he mumbled, his mouth stuffed with chips.

"No thanks. Is that your breakfast? Don't you ever stop eating those things?"

Einstein's Bones

"Sure you don't want some? Did you see what was on the news last night?"

"I watched a little of it," replied John. "From what I saw, there wasn't anything more than what we heard on the radio."

"Did you watch that Bible channel?" asked Mike.

"No, I didn't even know there was one here. So what did they have to say?"

"One of them was saying he thought the whole thing was fake, but all the others said it was a sure confirmation of the flood. Just one more piece of evidence that God destroyed all the wicked humans. But when those guys see what we've got, they're going to have to come up with something new."

"Wrong. No they won't. They'll see it just like they see it now, only they'll add that not only did God destroy all the sinners, but he got rid of a race of devils while he was at it, too. You could lead those guys by the hand through space and time and show them and still they'd never change their minds. If you think that you can get two of them to ever do so, that's two more than ever will. And please try not to talk with your mouth full, for Christ sake."

Mike shook the bag at John. "Last chance." There were only a few left. John grabbed the last handful and prayed that Mike didn't have another bag in his back pack.

At the Skunk's site, things had changed. Before, when they had slowed down, it was to get a better look at what the Skunk might be up to. Now John slowed down because he had to - if he wanted to avoid running into the numerous trucks, cars, and vans parked along the road – vehicles that had found no place to park where Shunk and his crew did. "What a fucking zoo," said John. "Now I know why Dick wanted to keep a lid on everything."

In contrast, nothing could be seen of Dick's site from the dusty county road. The rutted road into the ranch looked a little more used than it normally would, but one had to drive at least half way in before any activity could be seen and then only the parked vehicles. "Some difference," said John as he pulled up to the gate. "You'd never know we existed. That will change soon enough, I suppose." Mike got out and worked the gate. He almost had the hang of it now, though he still looked clumsy. After he closed the gate behind them, Mike got back in and fumbling through his back pack, took out a large jar of peanuts.

"Want some?" he asked. John shook his head in the negative whereupon Mike put the jar to his lips and swallowed a mouthful, spilling numerous nuts on the seat and floor of the van, all of which he picked up and popped into his mouth.

"You got any idea how much dirt and cow shit is down there?" asked John.

"Five second rule," Mike replied.

"Whatever."

They parked in their normal spot and walked to the site, John carrying his photo gear and Mike his back pack and his almost empty jar of peanuts. At least now when they dribbled out of his mouth he didn't pick them up. With his mouth full of his last gulp, Mike spotted Kathy. "I'm going to go ask her," he said as he walked her way. John couldn't hear what was said, seeing only that she let him say no more than a few words before she turned and walked away. Mike started to follow, but was stopped short when Kathy turned and gave him an uninviting look.

"I hope he's learned something," said John as he approached Dick.

"Who learned what?" asked Dick.

"Mikie there thinks Barbara's assistant is in love with him."

"I know. She's already mentioned it to me. I'm going to have to have a talk with him."

Einstein's Bones

"So what's the plan for today?" asked John.

"Just keep doing what you have been doing. When that bio hazard squadron gets here, they'll remove that seal and start taking their samples. Diane wants you to be sure to get some good ones of that, not that you wouldn't know that anyway. Right now Barb and I are going back to the lab with the Geographic. We won't be back for a while. While I'm gone, Karen's in charge."

"You don't want to be here when we take the tape off the door?"

"There's not going to be much for me to see when they do, and Diane wants to shoot footage of what's back in town. She wants to be ready by 4:00pm tomorrow. I'm not going to miss anything by not staying here."

"Have you heard what's going on over at the Skunk's? It looks like it's turned into a three ring circus. Cars parked all over the place. You'll have to slow down and be careful that somebody doesn't recognize you," said John.

"Well, let them. It might be interesting." With that, Dick took the van keys and he and Barbara, along with the Geographic crew, left for the lab.

Passing the Skunk site without incident, they arrived at the lab in forty five minutes. As soon as the lights were set up and the camera ready, Dick took Diane on a tour of what they had found and removed from the site. He started with their first find, the one that everyone called Einstein, pointing out his large cranial capacity, the sclerotic plate, and several other significant bones. He pointed to the pollex on the left manus. "You will notice that like the human thumb, it is opposable." He pointed to the hallux. "Again, unique to this species of dinosaur. On all other known specimens, this digit points backwards like on a chicken. But here, it points forward, not dissimilar to the human big toe."

"What conclusions have you come to?" she asked from her script.

"I think we can safely assume that they had and used hands much like we do and walked not all that differently – on their hind legs, upright and erect. From the size of their brain case they may have been just as intelligent, if not more so." Dick then showed the camera the medallion which had been placed on the rib cage - taking care to point out the mysterious symbols, some of the rings and several pairs of earrings, failing to mention that one pair was missing.

"You have no hesitation in stating that they are earrings. How can you be sure of that?" she asked.

"We can't be absolutely certain that they are unless we find hard evidence. However, as they were found adjacent to the temporal fenestra where ears would normally be, it seems the logical conclusion."

"You colleague, Dr. Shunk, announced a spectacular find several days ago. Are these two finds related?"

"We're not colleagues, but yes, I think they are. They must be. I think that we might be working at opposite ends of something very large and that as he has also found a pair of – from what I can tell – a pair of earrings which are almost identical to a pair that we found two weeks ago. I'd say that confirms it. Can we stop for a minute?" After the camera was turned off, he resumed. "Even though that bastard stole them, he really is on to something, something that by itself would be more than spectacular. He's working in a garbage dump and I'm working in a cemetery. I don't think we should speculate on camera, but the big question is what lies between us. The way the Skunk's mind works, I suppose he's sure some great lost city has to be only a shovel-full away and that he's going to go down in history as, well, who knows what. And he might just find it. But don't ask me any of that on camera. Let's go with what we have now and if you want to speculate at all, why don't we confine it to what might be inside that big gray cube – though I really don't want to go there either."

The camera started up again and Diane asked Dick about the inscriptions found on the medallion, several of the rings, and above the door.

"So far, we have identified about thirty five unique symbols. Several of them are repeated in the same sequence on the various pieces of jewelry. It's not my field, but they do have more the look of an alphabet than say some system of hieroglyphic or idiographic writing."

Though she knew the answer before she asked the question, she said, "Can it be translated?"

"No. Even if it were a known language, there are too few examples. And then you have to remember that not only is it an unknown language, but that it is non-human as well. Were we given a truck load of their books – assuming they had such things – we still couldn't decipher it. I am afraid that whatever they may have written will remain just meaningless symbols and the knowledge they left behind is forever lost. What we might learn if we could is useless to speculate."

Diane turned to Barbara for her opinion. "Yes, it does fire one's imagination. We were able to retrieve the written words of Egypt from the Rosetta Stone. However, had it not contained the Greek translation, we still would not know it, no more than we know Linear A, the writings of the Minoans. Even with the Greek side by side with the Egyptian, it was a most daunting task. Yes, I'm quite certain it would be foolish to hope for anything. But that does not exclude us from learning a great deal about these beings. Just as we learn much about human cultures from the way they care for their dead, so too are we learning about these creatures. They took great care of their dead and must have had some kind of religious belief system. One symbol, the symbol on the medallion occurs again and again, much like the Christian cross or the Star of David. Though we shall never be able to understand their written word, I am certain that, in time, we shall learn a great deal about them."

    Diane turned back to Dick. "Do you want to say anything about why you and Shunk are both out here?"

    "No, he's the one who needs to explain that, and he's already done it. Let's just go with what I've said before, starting with coming out here last fall with John."

    By 1:30, Diane had enough. "Do you want to do anything live tomorrow?" she asked.

    "No, not especially. Go ahead and make the big announcement with what you've got. I'm sure I'll have my share of stupid questions to answer live later. You'll have to help me keep those idiots out of my hair. Whatever you do, don't tell them exactly where we are, though I know they'll find out soon enough anyway. Time to head back."

    Even though there were seventeen coffins at least partially excavated and several times that number of red flags where the GPR had indicated that there might be something below the surface, after he photographed the bio-hazard men removing the seal from the door and taking samples of the air that escaped, there was nothing particularly new in the field for John to photograph. He had set up a mini studio in Dick's trailer where he had a 4x5 sheet film camera for detailed photographs of small objects. He was behind in that work and as Dick had ordered that nothing leave the site without being first fully documented, he decided to catch-up on that work after lunch. He was busy setting up specimens, adjusting his lighting, and loading film holders when at 2:30 the trailer door opened. He looked up from his work expecting to see Dick. It was Karen.

"I'm sorry, I thought Dick would be here," she said, knowing full well that Dick hadn't yet returned from town. "I'm not interrupting you am I? How about a beer?" She approached carrying a bottle in each hand. She opened them and handed one to John, taking a sip from the other. "That looks interesting," she said moving closer. "Which earring is that one? Is that the one Colin found yesterday?"

John glanced at his notes. "No, this is one of yours from last week."

"Really? I don't remember it." She moved closer to John and his copy stand for a better look. "Oh, yes, that's right, I remember it now." She turned and faced John. "I like your work. Do you do portraits too?"

"Yes, I've done them, you know that, but not for a while."

"Would you mind doing me?" she asked as she slightly tilted her head, brushed back her hair, and slowly moved closer still. She put her hand on the side of his waist and moved it slowly back and forth, looking at him with wide and lusting eyes. "We could find someplace near-by where no one would bother us," she said as she pressed her body against his. She looked up at him and could see that he was looking at her in the same way - that he was looking at her nearly exposed breasts and her swelling nipples. "Or you could do me right here if you want." She took his hand and moved it to her breast. He instinctively squeezed and remembered how full and firm it felt. She pulled his hand down to her inner thigh applying pressure as she slowly moved it up and down and in a circle. "It feels good, doesn't it?" It did. So smooth, so soft. She took her hand away and began to run her fingers through his hair as she began

Einstein's Bones

to pull his head closer to her lips and with her other hand began loosening her shorts. "It's been too long. Just fuck me now," she said as she began slipping her khaki shorts down her long smooth legs.

Trembling, John barely remembered what he and Margaret had told each other that morning. As Karen let her shorts fall to the floor of the trailer, he gently pushed her away.

"You want to do it that way?" she asked. "You can have me any way you want."

"No," he said firmly. "Not anyway."

"It's not like you've never done me before and I seem to recall that you liked it. I did."

"That was a long time ago," said John, "and things are different."

"You mean with you and the farmer's daughter? Have you told her about us?"

John didn't answer.

"You haven't, have you."

"And I won't," replied John.

She drew near to him again and started rubbing his chest. "I know how much you like this." She looked down. "And I can see you want to. We were so good together."

John pushed her away again.

"Karen, are you in there?" came a voice along with a knock at the door. "Dick's back and wants to see you."

"Give me a minute," she replied. She pulled John closer. "Just do it, do it now."

John pushed her back harder this time. "You better go. Dick might come in here looking for you."

"Do it," she repeated.

"No."

Einstein's Bones

She looked at him for a moment slightly surprised and then slowly lifted her shorts back up. "Later then," she said as she rubbed his chest once more and then walked to the door.

When Karen reached Dick, he asked, "Did he come?"

"The guy from bio hazard? Oh, yes, they were here at about nine. They left a little after lunch. When they removed the tape they said some air was released from inside and they took their samples. They told me they would have the results back in a week or so."

"Did they find out anything while they were here?"

"So far, so good. Just a lot of very hot stale air so far. That tape was interesting, though. They tried to cut it but couldn't. Otherwise, nothing exciting happening here at all. Are we ready to go for tomorrow? "

"Snyder's got all she needs. They'll release a kit to the media for the evening news and save their good stuff for some kind of special the night after. That'll give us a day or two of peace."

After Karen left the trailer, John had poured bottled water on a towel and wiped off his hands and forehead. He spoke to an empty trailer. "You better be sure of what the hell you want." He leaned his back against the copy stand and finished his beer. When he finished, he looked back at the earring he had been working on before Karen walked through the door. A few adjustments, and it was ready for the camera, but he just stared at it. "That was just too fucking close," he said as he closed his eyes and lightly bit down on his lower lip. He stood and thought. "Christ." He reopened his eyes. "Don't be an idiot." He looked back at his camera and adjusted the focus, slipped in a film holder and removed the dark slide. "Think a little, will ya?" He pushed in the cable release, returned the dark slide and flipped over the holder for a second exposure. "Ok, let's get back to work." Four more exposures and

Einstein's Bones

he was ready for the next specimen, a ring which he set in a small ball of clay. He readjusted his lighting and turned on the radio. "Just like it never happened."

Five hours of work, and he was nearly caught up. He began putting everything back in order when the news on the radio stopped him. Another Shunk discovery, and this time not just garbage or a stolen earring. This time a statue, a small statue, a broken statue, but a statue of a Sapienasaur.

John hurried to find Dick. "Did you hear about Shunk's latest?" he asked.

"Yes, Diane just got a call a couple of minutes ago. They're sending the video. We were just about to go down to the fifth wheel to watch."

Diane had a small TV hooked up to a recorder and the satellite dish on top of the trailer. "It's all downloaded. Everybody here?" she said as she pushed the play button. It was a short video which began with Carl Shunk's smug, smiling face. After several self-congratulating remarks drooled out of his smirking lips, he directed the camera to a spot on the ground where one of his minions was diligently chipping surrounding rock from his precious find while another brushed away the debris. The object of his pride was dark brown, a figure standing upright with its arms at its sides and looking straight ahead and broken into at least four pieces. "I wonder if it's something they just threw out?" said Diane. The camera moved in closer.

"It's a God-damn gargoyle," said John. "I wonder how long ago the first one was found. Does this change anything with us?"

"No, we'll go ahead for tomorrow as planned," replied Diane.

Chapter 16

In bed earlier than usual, John had trouble getting to sleep. There was the usual noise of a poker game and bull session to contend with and the thought of what Shunk had found. At least the Skunk hadn't given John's discovery a name. His name, Sapienasaur, seemed safe for tomorrow - as long as the Skunk didn't find something more than just a piece of garbage before then. And were the Gargoyles of Notre Dame their direct descendants? Maybe.

If that had been all that was on his mind, John might have peacefully drifted off to sleep. No, it was all about what almost happened in Dick's trailer. Was he sure he was in love with Margaret, or was that just a tamer version of the lust he had felt for Karen? And what about Karen? Did she care anything at all for him, had she cared for him all this time, or was she just having her little fun? She had slept with Dale hadn't she, or at least she wanted everyone to think she had. And she did have her reputation. But then what did John want? All his logic pointed to Margaret. He knew that nothing with Karen could ever last. But what did logic have to do with it? Oh, God, why did she have to look like that, why had he ever slept with her in the first place and how did he ever stop himself from doing again what would have been so easy and every other man's dream fuck. In the morning, things might look more clear.

Thursday morning started like any other in the field with everyone gathering in the old bunk house for breakfast. Kathy made the mistake of leaving an open chair to her right which Mike quickly occupied. "He's as big a fool as I am," thought John. Karen entered and made no effort to sit in the open chair next to John. She paid no more special attention to him than she had since she arrived in

Einstein's Bones

Wyoming - as though yesterday had never happened and meant nothing to her. Or was she making a special effort to hide it. He remembered that Margaret was coming to the site later. "God I hope Karen doesn't say something to her," he thought. "Well, if she does, she does. Hope she doesn't make it out to be something it wasn't. How can she? And if she says anything about what happened a long time ago?"

Throughout the morning, the field radio was kept tuned to the news. Nothing new, only speculation from Shunk that statues like the one he had found were probably the basis for several ancient myths.

"Interesting," said John to Colin as he photographed a skull Colin was working on. "I was thinking the same exact thing. I think the Skunk is right – for once. But I wonder how his whole 'birds are dinosaurs' bit is going to fit in. As far as I could tell, I didn't see any feathers on his little statue, and we haven't found any impressions of them here."

"I can't say. But then there are a lot of mammals that aren't exactly covered in hair, either. Too, bad we don't have some DNA, or a photo or two."

Margaret arrived at noon carrying a picnic basket. "I thought I'd be here for the big celebration. So where are all the cameras and reporters?" she said. To John she looked so sweet and almost innocent.

"I don't know if there's gonna be any big whoop or not. I suppose so. Dick ain't very keen on having a horde of reporters out here. And no live reports – at least tonight – we hope. They're just gonna use some of the stuff they filmed before. So what ya got in the basket?"

Einstein's Bones

"Some sandwiches and a nice bottle of wine. You haven't eaten yet have you?"

"Nope. You need any glasses?"

"Are paper cups OK?"

They walked a few yards beyond the edge of the site, far enough away not to be overheard, but not far enough to be out of sight or ear-shot in case someone wanted John to photograph something. John sat facing south lost in a view of rolling foothills that seemed to go on forever. From a distance, the hills looked gentle, not presenting any challenge to a traveler on foot or horseback. But up close they were an endless series of hills and ravines, steep ridges and deep draws that made John wonder how anyone ever got anyplace before roads and automobiles. To the east it was the same – stretching two hundred miles to the Black Hills and then another two hundred miles past that to the Missouri River – before the land began to level out. Mile after mile. Desolate, yet strangely beautiful and fascinating, every draw hiding some secret, something new behind every ridge, seemingly untouched by time or man. To the west were the Big Horn Mountains rising majestically out of the brown foothills. They looked like they were on top of him even though the nearest peak was fifty miles away. He wished their cool and fresh air would come down off of the slopes and refresh the hot and dry hill where he sat.

John's eyes kept pulling him into those distant places and back to distant times. He could see buffalo coming over one ridge, a band of Indians on another, and a troop of cavalry about to be ambushed in a draw below. He looked up and a contrail brought him back to the present. Where did the passengers come from and where were they going? Probably from New York or Chicago and on their way to California - a jet full of travelers by now too bored to bother to look down. Who were they and did they even know anyone was below them as they drank their gin and tonics at 30,000 feet? He caught a glint of the sun from the silver body of the jet and followed its vapor trail until it fell apart in the clear blue sky. "Christ, that's a long way up there. I wonder where they're going."

"Are you OK? You seem distant," said Margaret as she handed him a cup of wine.

"I'm fine."

"Something's on your mind. Is it us? Something about your work? Or don't you want to talk about it?"

"A little bit of both I guess. I look out and can't help thinking about the past – long before any of this was here. What was it like? No mountains over there and we'd be sitting on the edge of some great big inland sea."

"What about us, or is that what you don't want to talk about?"

"What do you want to happen with us?" he replied.

"So you don't want to talk about it?"

"Not right now anyway."

"Was it that I said I loved you?" She waited for a reply. "Ok, I'll just shut up."

"No, it's not that. I have to be sure."

"That I love you? Or sure that you love me?"

He took a sip of wine and then took a bite into his sandwich. "I want to do it right this time. I don't want to get hurt, and more than that I don't want to hurt you."

"Do you want to break this off now? Is that what you're trying to say?"

"No, no, not that at all." He held her hand and looked deeply into her eyes. "I want to make you happy and don't know . . . . well, just give me a little time. I do love you."

She brushed his hair and kissed his cheek. "No rush," she said softly.

"Now what's everybody gonna say if they see us neckin' out here?"

"Just tell them I couldn't help it," she answered.

John's face brightened up and he forgot about any ideas – if really he had any at all - of telling Margaret about Karen. He was sitting next to the best female friend he had ever had and was almost certain that he was in love with her. "So, sweet pea, are you disappointed we don't have some big party going on? Well, just between you and me, I think some of us might get a little hammered tonight. I saw a couple of new bottles of good stuff in Dick's trailer and if the press starts hanging around here soon everybody's gonna figure it's their last chance to act stupid. Hmm, I don't think there's anybody here from the WCTU, so ya best stick around and enjoy the fun."

"WCTU?"

"Women's Christian Temperance Union."

They finished lunch, washed off their hands with a damp cloth from her basket, and for the next hour John resumed his field work with Margaret at his side. "How'd ya like to help me out in the darkroom?" he asked her in his best imitation of a lecherous voice.

"I don't know? Can I trust you?" she asked with a smile. "Do you really have a darkroom out here?"

"Sort of. More like a black bag and developing tank. Come on, I'll show ya - that is if you trust being alone in the trailer with me."

He took her by the hand to Dick's trailer and showed her the 4x5 view camera and what he called his dark room which was nothing more than a large black changing bag, a black plastic tank large enough to hold a dozen 4x5 negatives, and three bottles of chemicals he kept in his own special refrigerator which also contained his supply of film.

"That's all you need?" she asked. "I thought you'd have some special room to do all this. Do you do color?"

"Just black and white here. Now that we've got running water, it's not a problem. Color's too temperature sensitive. I save that for back at the lab in town."

He gathered up six film holders, a dozen stainless steel film hangers, and the developing tank, unzipped the changing bag and put everything inside. He zipped it up again and stuck his arms through the bag's sleeves and began loading the tank. "Don't do that," he said as she began kissing the back of his neck and massaging his chest. "Do you want me to wreck this whole batch – or stain my pants?"

"I wouldn't want that. You do that just by touch? Load the film I mean," she said as she moved away.

"Just by touch. I thought you'd know I was pretty good with my hands by now." He pulled his arms out, unzipped the changing bag, pulled out the loaded tank, poured in the developer, waited ten minutes, poured it out and replaced it with the stop bath, waited another minute, and then poured in the fixer.

"Now I know where that God awful smell on your hands comes from," she said. "Doesn't that bother you?"

"To a photographer, it's like perfume. Too bad it's gonna be obsolete soon." He took six more film holders and another dry tank and repeated the procedure.

"How many more of those do you have to do?"

"A couple more batches after this. I'll be done in about an hour."

"Now what could we do by ourselves in here for an hour?"

"Wash the film and then hang it to up dry, that's what - unless you got a 'Do Not Disturb' sign in your purse."

"You're just no fun, are you?"

John finished developing the last tank and put the film in the wash. "We've got a few hours till the news. You want to help me with some specimens? It's kinda boring."

"It can't be any more boring than watching you develop film."

This time the woman at his side actually showed an interest in what he was doing, suggesting slight changes in the positioning of the specimen, and changes – for the better – in his lighting. They worked together until the trailer door opened without a knock first. It was Karen. She walked the few steps to where John and Margaret stood in front of the camera. "Some nice little setup you love birds have here. I trust I didn't interrupt anything or did I? Oh yes, Dick says it's time for the big show – unless you have something else in mind." She smiled and walked back to the door. She stopped, turned around and smiled again. "We can get by without you if you want to stay here for a while. I won't tell. Nobody's going to bother you." She smiled again and walked through the door, leaving John and Margaret to make three more exposures and then put things back in order.

"Kind of a snotty bitch isn't she," said Margaret. "Is she always like that? Dale got tired of her pretty fast."

"Did he say anything to you about her?"

"That she was more of a tease than anything else, but that he did sleep with her once. He said she treated him like just a piece of meat. With Dale it's usually the other way around." She looked at John with a teasing smile. "You know, if I were you I'd stay away from her."

"I'll keep that in mind. Let's finish this up."

Einstein's Bones

They walked the short distance to the bunk house where everyone was gathered and were greeted by the same coy smile from Karen followed by, "What took you two so long?"

Whether seated or standing, everyone's hand had either a beer or a plastic cup filled with Dick's good stuff, either Wild Turkey or Jameson Reserve. "How soon?" asked Margaret.

"In about two minutes," replied Dick as he sipped his whiskey. "Anybody need a refill?"

The last empty cup was filled just as the news began. Crowded around a small TV, they watched as the evening news began with, "Another stunning discovery in Wyoming," after which the sound was drowned out by the cheers of those watching.

Dick called for quiet, but it was useless and didn't matter as everyone knew what Dick had to say anyway. "Hey, that's me," said Mike who was no more than an indistinct figure in the background. "Great shot," said someone as the camera panned over the remains of Einstein. "Yes!" shouted John as he barely heard Dick announce to the world the name Sapienasaur. Some one else added, "I'd like to see the Skunk's face now," and then, "there you are," from Margaret as she pointed to John on the screen.

In five minutes it was over. "Ok everybody. We still have some work to do before anybody starts partying. Besides, somebody's got to be in shape to do the grilling."

"So when's the Geographic special?" asked Josh.

"Not for a while," answered Diane. "They want to see us open the big box – maybe live."

"Live?" asked John. "A little risky, isn't it? What if there's nothing in it like what happened with that special where they opened up Al Capone's secret room?"

"I don't think that'll happen, but if it does, we certainly have more than enough footage to make up for it," replied Diane.

Einstein's Bones

John finished his drink and returned his attention to Margaret. "You do want to stick around for a while, don't ya? We're gonna have a bonfire and grill some steaks." She agreed.

Half an hour later, John lit the coals in two large grills. He grabbed a beer for himself and Margaret and the two of them settled into a couple of camp chairs. "Ya know," he began, "I've always dreamed of being famous. Never of being rich really, or an actor, or a baseball star, or anything like that. Something creative. Maybe a writer or something like that. Never thought I'd get my fifteen minutes of fame this way, not in photography and certainly not in paleontology. But here it is. My name's going to be remembered at least a little. When this is all written down I'll get my paragraph or two and a lot of photo credits. Maybe even a book under my own name. And it all just happened. I didn't go out and try. It just happened. It makes me feel good that what I almost tripped over is important – something that will make a mark. Something that will say I was here. Yeah, I just feel good." He looked at her in silence for a moment. "And it feels so good to love you."

Einstein's Bones

Chapter 17

It was two weeks before the tests on the air samples came back. There were some molds, some bacteria, and the air from the gray box was not in the same proportions as the air outside, but there was nothing that posed a health hazard, nothing that couldn't be found somewhere within a few mile of Sheridan. The air might smell terribly stale, but it was perfectly safe – and perfectly safe to remove the plastic shroud which had sealed off the door for the past two weeks.

In the two weeks between the announcement of the discoveries on Paul Newcomb's ranch and the removal of the plastic bubble, there had been no major new finds on his ranch. More burials, more jewelry and medallions, a few more of what were thought to be pets, and the remains of two very young Sapienasaurs, which were buried with all the care and dignity that was thought to be a human trait alone. The major change on the hill where they worked had been an ever increasing stream of reporters, starting with Cindi Bright from the local Sheridan TV station. No one had told her where to look for Dick and his crew. Her sharp eye had spotted Margaret in the background of a few seconds of footage and almost out of focus. In Sheridan, everybody knew the Newcombs, and where their ranch was.

Cindi Bright, along with her cameraman arrived the morning after the first news segment was broadcast. The two uninvited trespassers seemed uninhibited as they parked their van and headed for Dick.

"Do you want me to ask them to leave? I will," said Margaret who had spent the night in the fifth wheel, sleeping only two feet away from Karen.

"If you don't want them here, go ahead, it's your ranch, or your father's anyway," replied Dick. "But I suppose it won't do much good. They'll just keep coming back or pestering us in town. No, let them come."

"Isn't that the same gal who interviewed the Skunk?" said John. "Yeah, she's the one who said, 'it's dark now, but earlier today it was much lighter'. What was her name? Yeah, Cindi Not-So-Bright."

If she had sounded less than brilliant when interviewing Shunk, that perception was soon dissipated. She wasn't just a pretty face in front of the camera. Before the camera was turned on, she asked Dick what she would be allowed to film and went over a list of questions she intended to ask. She had to settle for less than she had hoped. No filming of any of the current field work, and no questions that had anything to do with Shunk. She had to stick to the five Ws, and film only what had been broadcast previously. She may have been disappointed, but was slightly compensated with the promise that if she followed the rules and kept the location to herself, after the Geographic, she would get the first rights to report on any new discoveries.

"I saw your interview with Shunk," said Dick after she had finished. "I hate to ask, but did you know what you said about it being dark but light earlier?"

"Not when I said it, but I sure heard about it later," she said with a laugh. "I don't think they'll ever let me forget."

Her promise to keep the location a secret didn't do much good. Private property or not, more reporters arrived the next day and the stream of cameras and microphones kept increasing to the point where Dick had to hire a guard at the ranch gate. The presence of any one reporter was limited to no more than four hours each day, which for Dick was four hours too many.

Einstein's Bones

During those two weeks John had nearly put what almost happened with Karen out of his mind or had at least shoved it into some dusty corner of his mind. Karen hadn't made any more advances and if she did, John was confident he would do the right thing, or at least he expected he would. Nevertheless, he was thankful that he was not tested. Had Margaret suspected anything from the way Karen had acted? If she had, she kept it to herself, not mentioning Karen either when she came to the site or when John spent his usual two nights in town with her.

There were a few new developments at the Skunk site, too. More broken statues and a lot more interviews. For every minute that Dick appeared on camera, Shunk got ten, which was the way Dick wanted it. There were a few new finds to show off, what Shunk claimed were tools. They might well have been, but no one on Dick's team could see them for anything more than fragments of petrified wood and rusty colored stones. Cretaceous hammers or egg beaters, or maybe something left behind by Coronado – who could tell? Whatever they might be, they did show that Mr. Shunk does have a vivid sense of imagination.

And then there was the little matter of the sale. Fossils on private property and what is found along with them are private property, to be disposed of as the owner sees fit. Usually the sale is to a museum or discreetly to some wealthy collector. Such transactions might be frowned upon by some, but they were common enough and had helped Shunk maintain a vacation home in Europe. But to see the earrings, the earrings that Karen had found, the earrings that Dale had stolen, those earrings, to see them up for auction on an internet site with the bidding starting in the six figures – that was a bit much even for the Skunk. It wasn't until then that Margaret realized just how much in debt her brother must be – just how desperate he was for fast cash. Either that or lose his ranch, the one his father had helped him buy. And how much of a cut was Shunk getting?

But today, with the bubble wrap gone from the door of the big gray box, all of that was forgotten. Today was the day of the grand opening, a prime time grand opening, scheduled for 8pm on the east coast, 6pm in Sheridan. To be precise, that's when the special would start, with the opening to take place half an hour later – live. To be sure that at least it would open, Dick, then Dick and Zeke, and Dick and Zeke and Collin had given the door a tug, but without results. When the handle was chained to a tractor, enough progress was made so that the door could be pulled open the rest of the way by a single individual. But who would have the honor?

The night before, Dick had suggested to Paul Newcomb, who would be there with the rest of his family – except for Dale – that Paul have the honor of opening the door. For some reason, he declined and was surprised that Dick himself did not want to do it either. It could have been false modesty that led him to ask John who was spending the night with Margaret.

What do you think, sweetie?" he asked Margaret, "should I do it?"

"As long as you don't wear those filthy jeans. I better get them in the wash now. Do you have a decent shirt?" He picked a clean flannel shirt out of the closet. "Why do you guys have to wear flannel shirts all the time? Boring. It's hot out there you know. Don't you have something nicer? Why not this blue shirt?" she said as she pulled it out and held it in front of him. John shook his head from side to side. "Some kind of guy thing?" she asked. He nodded yes as he stripped off his jeans and handed them to her. As she brought them to the washing machine, he grabbed a beer, picked up the phone, and dialed Charlie.

Einstein's Bones

"Hey good buddy," answered Charlie, "it's about time you called. We were beginning to think you had forgotten us."

"I've sent you e-mails, haven't I? Besides, I've been busy."

"Busy with Margaret I see."

"Huh?"

"Caller ID."

"Oh. Anyway, I just called to make sure you've gotten your Wyoming hunting license. No, I really wasn't calling about that. You know about the special tomorrow night, right? Starts at 7:00 tomorrow night your time. And guess who gets to take center stage and open that door?" John waited for Charlie's reply. "Yup, me, on live TV. No, I don't know why Dick doesn't want to do it." John waited again. "Just be sure to watch. Remember, 7:00pm." John listened again, and the conversation ended.

"Well," said Margaret, "you certainly burned up the phone lines, didn't you. Did you ask him how his wife was? How his kids were? How his work was going? No. You really are a fountain head of verbal communication aren't you."

"Yup."

"And he's your best friend?"

"Yup."

"Are you like that with everybody? Are you going to be like that with me?"

"Yup," he answered with a smile.

"Do you love me?"

"Yup."

She feigned disgust. "I give up."

John laughed. "Oh calm down. I know so many people who'll talk for hours on the phone and never say anything. My ex brother-in-law could chew my ear off for hours. He finally gave up and said my whole family was just the same."

"Your father wasn't like that."

"Maybe not with you, but he was with everybody else. It was, 'hello, what do you want, and goodbye'."

"Are you excited about tomorrow?"

"Yup." He paused and looked for her reaction. "I can't help but be excited. Like everybody else, I can't wait to find out what's behind that door. But nervous, too. What if there's nothing behind it, or I need help opening the door. I don't think I will, but I'd look like a real wimp if I couldn't. Or what if I trip and fall on my face. But what I'm really worried about is that I'll be expected to say something, something profound. I don't have a clue. And even if I do, if I do figure out what to say, what if I blow my lines like Neil Armstrong did."

"You'll do just fine. Just be yourself."

John spent the rest of the evening trying to come up with just the right words, bouncing one idea after another off Margaret. She tried a few, too, but nothing sounded quite right. He thought it might come to him in the morning, but it didn't. "Just stop worrying about it," she said as they drove to the site that morning. It will come to you."

They stopped briefly at the ranch gate and learned that only Dick, his team, the Newcomb family, and the Geographic would be allowed in that day. No other reporters, no special guests, none of the just curious. Just the way Dick wanted it. As the guard closed the gate behind them, John asked Margaret, "well, did you come up with anything yet?"

"You're on your own, babe."

The National Geographic began setting up at 3:00 that afternoon, three hours before air time. They adjusted their lighting and cameras and tested their satellite link to Washington. A gradual descent towards the door had been dug down and widened so that

John could be followed by the camera and the area around the door itself had been enlarged to allow more room for another camera. Several times John or someone else made a dry run from the top down to the door to make sure there were no blind spots. When the Geographic was satisfied they had their cameras just right, they tested John for sound, following him down the path, checking the levels with each step he would take until he reached the door. They had him pull on the handle a few times to make sure it would open, being careful not to open it to the point where he might see anything inside. They wanted John's reaction to be unrehearsed and spontaneous.

"Are you going to want me to say anything as I'm walking up to the door?" he asked.

"Only if you really feel the need," replied the reporter from the Geographic who would be introducing the action and then accompanying both John and Dick the whole way. "I'll do the talking at least until you take a look inside."

"That's a relief," said John looking at Margaret. "For a while I thought I'd have to make some silly remarks the whole way down."

"You still are going to have to say something really profound and meaningful when you peek inside," she teased. "Think of anything yet?"

"How about 'oh wow'."

"That'll make 'em all sit up and take notice."

The hour for the broadcast approached all too quickly for John's liking. Yes, just like everyone else he couldn't wait to see what was on the other side of the door and at the same time almost wished he hadn't accepted, that he had let someone else do it. It was Dick's dig, wasn't it? Or what about Karen? He wanted to ask her. The cameras would love her. Well, maybe a little too much. She hadn't changed from her usual attire. Maybe if she knew she was going to be on camera she'd make an exception. No, she wouldn't. And if Newcomb didn't want to do it and Dick didn't want to do it, who else? It was too late to make any changes anyway. He had to be the one. Suddenly it was a half hour until air time and then in what seemed like two minutes, the time had shrunk to fifteen. Still he hadn't thought of one damn thing to say. He sat by the edge of the ramp leading down to the door next to Margaret just as the special was about to begin and was drawing a blank. Still worse, his mouth began to dry up.

"A minute to live," he heard someone yell out. He took his place next to Dick at the top of the ramp. At least he wouldn't be walking down by himself. He wondered what kind of look he should wear on his face. Should he be dead serious, or try a half smile. "Just be yourself," he heard Margaret say as she dusted off the back side of his jeans with her hand. "You get so filthy so fast."

"Better stop that," he said. "It's almost air time."

She gave him a pat on the butt and moved out of the way of the camera. As the director counted down from ten, she blew him a kiss and the show started.

Before the three of them began their decent, the reporter asked Dick a few questions which were lost to John. He asked John something, and a voice outside of his body answered, 'yes'. It wasn't the same reporter, Diane Snyder, who had spent so much time at the site, but someone whom John had just met that morning. But he was the same reporter who had narrated the prerecorded portion of the special. As they walked down the ramp with the reporter conversing with Dick, a conversation that John was oblivious to, it suddenly came to John that he had already forgotten the reporter's name. "God, I'm gonna make a mess out of this," he thought to himself.

Einstein's Bones

John reached the door and the three of them paused for a few more words with Dick. All that John was aware of was a nod from Dick, the signal to open the door.

John slowly moved his fingers around the handle and gently gave it a tug. It could have been a case of nerves, but this time it didn't move so easily. He looked back at Dick for help and the two of them pulled together. As the door began to open slowly, Dick released his grip and left the job to John, who was vaguely aware of a conversation going on in the background. With a slight grating sound, it swung open, first a narrow crack, and then several inches. He could see nothing inside, but was overwhelmed by the smell of stale air. He pulled again, this time enough to put his head on the other side along with a flashlight.

It took time for John's eyes to adjust. At first he could see nothing. As his eyes became accustomed, he began to make out details. Strange and mysterious objects stared back at him. Statues, fantastic objects, and gold, everywhere gold. He remained silent, overcome with awe. The reporter and Dick must have become impatient. Finally, as if on cue, Dick asked, "Can you see anything?"

"Yes," replied John, "wonderful things."

Einstein's Bones

Chapter 18

The words had been Howard Carter's, but they fit. John wished that he had been able to come up with something original, something more extraordinary, something expressing even more astonishment, but with Dick feeding him the question Lord Carnarvon asked when King Tut's tomb was opened, "Yes, wonderful things" was all that he could think to say. Nevertheless he silently thanked Dick for the line.

After he had gazed in at the treasures long enough, objects staring back at him from another world, beyond the limits of time, John gave the others their turns. Dick peered inside and said nothing, just stared in amazement, while the reporter, whose name John now remembered to be Howard Blood, told his audience that in a few moments they too would have a look at what must be the wonderful sights inside. When he at last poked his head in, all he could say was, "this is absolutely incredible, incredible." He quickly stepped back and said, "we're going to open the door all the way now." This time Dick did not hesitate to assist John in pulling the door all the way back, and as soon as they did so, the crew from the Geographic quickly reset their lights and re-positioned their cameras.

Before those in front of their television sets had their first look, the Newcombs, starting with Paul and followed by Margaret took their turns. After they had seen beyond the door, it was the turn of the rest of Dick's crew. Finally, before satisfying the television viewers, Colin brought down a rope and strung it across the entrance. For now, no one would be allowed to venture beyond the door.

With the powerful TV lights illuminating the interior, the contents of the 'box' were being viewed by anyone in front of a television set – unless they just couldn't pull themselves away from wrestling night. Directly across from the door stood two large statues, life size versions of the broken fragments that Carl Shunk had found earlier, but this time unbroken and clad in gold, guarding what looked like another door. There were other statues, statues of strange and long extinct animals, and stone carvings of what may have been every day objects, and many other objects for which there was no ready explanation. Most interesting, was that the interior walls were made up of shelves which looked as if they contained books, perhaps thousands of books. And half way between the wall and the inner door was more shelving which also gave the impression of containing books. From a distance, everything in the room had the appearance of being in near perfect condition.

As the camera panned from one object to the next, Howard Blood said little more than telling his views that what they had opened must be something like a museum or an archive. Ten minutes later he began to ask questions, starting with John. "What were your first thoughts as you opened the door?"

John guessed he would be interviewed after he opened the door, but did not have an idea of what the questions would be. "At first I was afraid there would be nothing," he began, "but when I saw inside, it was all so hard to believe."

"Did you have any expectations?'

"Not really. We all had our guesses, but no one expected this. Most of us thought it would be some sort of tomb. Then again, maybe it is."

"Your first words, were they something that you had thought about?"

"I thought about something to say ever since I knew I would have the first look inside, but I drew a blank." He then went on to explain their origin.

Einstein's Bones

Blood turned to Dick next. "This is absolutely amazing. You must be very excited."

Dick thought for a moment and worried that the interview wouldn't be much better than the standard sports interview where the questions are typically 'what's it going to take to win?'. He simply answered "Yes".

"How soon will you be entering all the way?" Dick wasn't sure. "What do you think those objects on the shelves are?" Dick did not have any idea any more than anyone else. "What is going to be the course of action once you enter?"

"Everything will have to be fully documented before anything is removed."

"Will you continue with your current excavation work?"

"Yes, certainly, but not as actively I think."

"What is going to be the impact of this discovery?"

Dick wanted to tell them, 'How the hell do I know. You tell me'. "Right now," he replied, "that's difficult to say. We're looking at an advanced civilization created by another species millions of years ago. The debate has already started and I'll leave it to others to attach the meaning. Myself – if God created us I don't see why He couldn't have created them too."

"Have you found anything that indicates that they had religious belief?"

"Yes, we have. I would be more surprised if we hadn't."

An hour special was too short. If nothing had been behind the door it would have been too long. With what little time remained, Blood managed to ask Karen and Barbara questions, too. Underneath her reserved exterior, Barbara was beside herself, knowing just how much she might learn from what she had just seen – so much more than any fossils or the few buried relics could tell her. But with typical British reserve, her reply to one of Blood's questions was only, "We have so much to study." Then when the lights went dark, she started hugging and kissing everyone.

"My god," said John to Margaret, "I didn't think the English could do that."

John had one more night in town with Margaret. As usual, he'd have to take Mike, whose efforts with Kathy continued to be less than successful, back with him. "Why don't we go someplace nice tonight?" John asked Margaret. "I really feel like celebrating. Hell, let's even take Mikie along – if you can put up with him for a couple of hours. I kinda feel a little sorry for him."

She was feeling too good to say no. "He might be a pain, but he gets left out all the time and he looks so lonely. And I don't like the way the others pick on him. If you can put up with him for dinner, I can too."

The three of them arrived at the Sheridan Inn at 9:00pm. Before they had a chance to reach their table, they were bombarded with attention from their fellow diners. Everyone in the restaurant must have been watching the National Geographic Channel. Almost all of the questions were the same, 'When do we get to see it?'. John's only answer was, "that's up to Dr. Johnson."

John thought he'd never get to even start his meal, but after half an hour, the assault died down, only to begin again every time hungry new patrons arrived, and with the same question. "What price glory," he said to his table mates half way into his meal. "Now ya know what those movie stars have to put up with and why they get testy now and then. I bet your father's getting clobbered with calls. At least everybody's forgotten about the Skunk."

An enjoyable meal or not, John did appreciate one celebrity perk. The bill never came. When he asked the waiter, he was told that it had been taken care of. John left an especially generous tip.

Einstein's Bones

The way back offered the first peace and quiet of the day – except for Mike who wouldn't stop comparing what they had seen that day to either the Krell laboratory or King Tut's tomb, and who, as soon as they had entered the van had opened a fresh bag of chips. After they dropped him off at the motel, it was another ten minutes to Margaret's. "Ya just got to wonder about that boy," said John shaking his head.

From Margaret's driveway, they could hear the phone ringing. By the time they reached the door, it stopped and began ringing again. After she closed the door behind her, Margaret walked to the phone and checked the caller ID.

"Anybody you know?" asked John.

"No," she said without answering it. Two more rings and it stopped only to start again. It was a different caller and as before, one she did not recognize. She let it keep ringing until it quit. Instantly, it was followed by another. "Screw this," she said as she pulled the plug from the wall. "If somebody really needs me, they can dial my cell phone. Want a drink?" She checked her answering machine and laughed. "This old thing's got a two hour tape and it's full, all from today." She pulled the full tape out and replaced it with another, carrying the old tape with her into the kitchen. She reached into the liquor cabinet and began to make Manhattans. She looked down at the tape as if she were weighing it. "Well, if somebody died, they'll still be dead tomorrow." She took one more look at it and threw it into the garbage.

She brought two full glasses into the living room and sat beside John, then took her cell phone from her purse and took a look. "Glad I had this turned off. It's full, too. But friends anyway."

"Are you gonna call em back?"

"Tomorrow. You want to watch the TV?"

"Sure."

"The news?"

"Why not. I gotta see how handsome I am. Yum, where did you get these?" he asked as he popped an olive into his mouth. "I love olives stuffed with anchovies."

She pressed a few buttons on the remote and the screen was filled with images from the Newcomb ranch. Three minutes in, and there was John walking down the ramp to open the door. "God, I look awkward," he said.

"You look just fine."

"I hate my voice," he said as he heard the words he had spoken.

"You have a nice voice."

They watched for another ten minutes – until Carl Shunk was asked to comment. "Well, he certainly sounded gracious, didn't he," John remarked. "He won't sound so gracious if he stumbles onto anything better. I've seen enough. Let's watch a movie."

John picked up Mike before sunrise. "Where's Margaret?" Mike asked.

We took the phone off the hook last night, so she's gonna stay home all day and take calls until she can't stand it anymore. I don't envy her."

"I know," replied Mike as he stuffed a sweet roll into his mouth. "The motel phone didn't stop and neither did my cell phone. How many calls did you get on your cell phone?"

"I don't have one."

"Really?"

"Really."

It was a beautiful sunrise. Low clouds in the east caught the first rays of the sun just at the right angle, painting a horizon of rich reds mixed with deep blues and blacks. John had to stop and take photographs. "Red sky in the morning, sailors take warning," advised Mike.

"A little rain won't hurt anything today, and it'll keep the dust down. I think we're gonna be inside today anyway, at least Dick said something about getting started inside the box today."

"Oh, so he's not thinking outside the box?"

That was the first time Mike had ever said anything that made John laugh.

As they drove by the Skunk site, it seemed strangely empty. There were no cars parked along side the road, no media vans, no congestion of vehicles that normally would be parked within a hundred yards of where Shunk was digging. Those that John could see belonged to the Skunk and his team, still digging and hoping for something that would top Johnson.

All the cars, vans, and trucks that had left Shunk's site and more than twice that were now parked as close to the entrance of the Newcomb ranch as they could get. "Holy shit," was Mike's reaction. "I was afraid of this," was John's.

There were two guards at the gate now, and along with them was Zeke. "So what's the story?" John asked as he made his way through the traffic and drove up to the gate.

"It's been like this ever since you guys left last night. Everybody wants in and wants in right now. Dick's got a time limit on these guys and only when one comes out, can another go in."

They drove on. "A guy could make a pile of money taking tickets there if he wanted to," said Mike.

The site itself was not as crowded as John had feared. Beside the crew from the Geographic, there was the local news in the person of Cindi Bright, a network news team, and a handful of local dignitaries: town council members, the mayor of Sheridan, and several prominent businessmen and ranchers, all friends of Paul Newcomb, who was the only family member present.

"Are we going in today?" asked John.

"Yes," replied Dick, "as soon as the light gets better."

"Oh shit, here they come," said John as he spied a man with a microphone coming his way. John winced at the first question, wondering how many more times he would be asked the same question, and if he could ever come up with better, or at least different answers. "What I saw inside was impossible to believe, just wonderful." And then, "No, the words were Howard Carter's", and finally, "I had no idea what to expect." The reporter thanked him and moved on.

"You'll have to work on your answers," observed Karen, "and come up with some better ones."

"Why bother. If they come up with better questions, then I'm sure I'll come up with better answers."

"Where's your sweetie? I trust your little Maggie suitably rewarded you last night. If not, we do have some unfinished business, you know. We could take care of that tonight or anytime you want. Just let me know – any time." She smiled and gave him a wink and turned around.

John watched her hips sway as she seductively walked away – not having given him a chance to reply.

"What was that all about?" asked Mike.

""I don't know."

"I wish she'd look at me that way."

"No you don't." replied John with a wry smile. He absent mindedly grabbed a handful of corn chips from the bag that Mike offered him and the two of them walked towards the big gray box where, now that the light was good, everyone was gathering in anticipation.

Einstein's Bones

This morning, no one gave any particular thought as to who would be the first to enter. With the hand held video cameras and lights at the ready, Dick, with the help of Jeff pulled on the handle and opened the door once again. Dick stood at the threshold, moving his eyes from side to side, for what seemed like minutes but must have been no more than thirty seconds. He cautiously took three steps inside and stopped again and took another long look at the wonders inside. Two more steps and he turned around and beckoned the cameras to follow.

John was right behind the video cameras. He stood in awe, forgetting that he was in there to take pictures. He surveyed the contents of the room that he had only partially seen the day before. He looked at the others as they stared at the contents of a room that had been sealed for 65 million years. No one said anything, not even the reporter with the microphone in his hands. Their childlike faces were words enough.

Before anyone had entered the room, Dick had insisted more than once that nothing be touched. He saw the two life-sized statues guarding some inner door. He marveled at the many objects that filled the room. His eyes scanned the shelves filled with what looked to be books. He gazed at everything with a dream-like stare. Then silently and slowly he walked over to a pedestal which was to the immediate left of the door. It was made of some pinkish stone, about a meter in height and some twelve centimeters in diameter. He looked down, not at the pedestal, but at what lay on top of it. The object of his attention was the same gray color of the walls, about 13x10 centimeters in height and width and perhaps two centimeters thick. Absentmindedly, not remembering his own injunction, he reached out his index finger and brushed away a light covering of dust that partially hid more of the strange symbols he had seen before.

Einstein's Bones

"It is a book," he said softly, "a God damn book." He slowly picked it up and stared at it and then opened it, revealing not paper pages, but thin pages made out of some kind of metal, the same kind that had been used to seal the door, and every page engraved with some kind of writing. He turned another page and stared, and then another. "A book," he kept repeating. Lost in his thoughts, he reverently turned a few more pages before he closed it and returned it to the place from which it came. He brought up his eyes and surveyed the walls. "Books, hundreds of books, maybe thousands."

He began to come out of his dream state and remembered that he was not alone. He turned to the bright lights, still with a look of disbelief. "If only we could know what they say." Then, as reality returned, "ok, let's not touch anything - else."

For the next two hours, all who had gathered that morning on the side of that hill in the middle of Nowhere, Wyoming carefully wound their way through the outer room, stopping for a minute or ten at each object before they moved to the next, all the while closely watched by Dick or another member of his team. "Should we really be letting them do this," John asked Dick. "They could knock something over."

"I don't like it at all, but I think it's best we get it over with now."

Besides taking a turn standing guard, John snuck photos of the reactions on the visitor's faces. Years before he had seen an exhibition of the treasures of King Tut's tomb. He had stood with dropped jaw in front of the famous gold death mask. As he released the shutter, he wondered if he had looked that awe-struck back then and tried to remember what expressions the faces of the other visitors to King Tut had. He couldn't. Just like the visitors then, the visitors now were completely absorbed in what was in front of them, unaware of who might be standing by their side.

Einstein's Bones

The item closest to the book that Dick had unthinkingly opened looked like abstract sculpture. It was just slightly dusty, approximately 1.5 meters in height and carved of a white stone. Four of what looked to be branches came off from the main figure at irregular intervals. It certainly could have been something of practical use, but then again it might have been what it was taken for - abstract art.

The next item was more easily recognized, at least in part. Under a light coating of dust was a gold statue of some long extinct dinosaur. As to what the fierce looking creature was, not even Dick would venture a guess. "You have to remember, we've only scratched the surface. For every species we've found, there are at least ten we haven't," Dick had to constantly explain to the news crews and town dignitaries. The creature was about fifty centimeters in height and posed in a sitting position. It sat atop a black stone block which was again about one meter in height. The eyes of the creature were inlaid with either ruby or garnet, or some other clear red stone. And around its neck – a collar. Full size or not, it did not look like any pet to keep in the home of your average *Homo sapiens*.

It was the two golden guards, the gargoyles who had stood so faithfully by the inner door since nearly the beginning of time, which attracted the most attention. They both stood nearly two meters high which was about the height expected, judging from the remains found in the cemetery. They were expressionless and stiff reflecting the seriousness of their mission. Their pose almost Egyptian. They stood with one arm that fell to its side while the other, the arm closer to the door, held what looked like a baton diagonally across its chest. Covered completely in gold, they were unadorned by any other material or by any coloration - at least none that had stood the test of time. But they were not naked. A cape hung from their shoulders to the waist. From there to their feet, each leg was covered by loosely hanging gold mesh cloth, their feet in some kind of boot. The craftsmanship and the detail were exquisite.

As politely as he could, when two hours had passed, Dick asked his guests to leave. "We have a lot of people waiting at the gate," he told them. They reluctantly filed out, walked to their cars and vans, and drove back to the ranch gate. "Sure as hell not getting anything done today," said Dick as he watched the next group of reporters march in.

Einstein's Bones

Chapter 19

And on they came, and came, and kept coming, two news crews at a time, each limited to no more than two hours. Without exception, the big attractions were the two gargoyle-like guardians of the inner door and to a lesser degree, the book on the pedestal. With each new crew, Dick had to instruct them to touch nothing. Yes, he had opened the book, but steadfastly refused to do it again, apologizing for his mistake of opening it in the first place.

After that, the viewing habits of the news crews followed no particular pattern. One crew was entranced by a large vase standing on the floor. It stood over a meter high, decorated with bands of black, yellow, and green, somewhat garish, but an indication that its makers could see colors. Except for the colors, the pear shaped vase with its four handles was not unpleasing to the human eye. Another reporter was fascinated by a simple metal bar marked off in seven equally spaced indentations. His guess was that it was the Sapienasaur's equivalent of a yard stick.

And always the same questions starting with, "Is this a tomb?" and "What were your thoughts as you entered the room?" then, "What do you suppose is behind that inner door?"

Repetitive and dim-witted questions, all of them, except for one. As his camera videoed the shelves of books, the reporter's face took on a quizzical look. He walked up to them – as close as Dick would allow – put on his reading glasses, and stared. He then walked to the book on the pedestal, the one that Dick had opened, studied it for a moment and then returned to the books on the walls, carefully noting the symbols on each. "Could these be numbers?" he asked Dick.

Dick was skeptical. But then he hadn't looked that closely at the spines of any of the books, being too busy shepherding news crews and answering their questions. He looked again at the book on the pedestal and for the first time noticed what the reporter had seen, the symbol "|". He took a few steps and studied the first book in the upper left hand corner of the first shelf. There was the symbol "∨", and on the book to its right was "ⱽ". "I'll be damned, one two three." The next six volumes contained the symbols "Ⱡ", "ⱠⱠ", "ⱠⱠⱠ", "ⱠⱠⱠⱠ", "⋈", and then "||". Dick thought for a moment. "Base eight – eight digits on their hands – makes sense." He paused. "Math, the universal language. Now if one of these books happens to be a math book – who knows." He continued down the line of books to the sixty-fourth, which was marked "|⋈⋈". The sixty-fifth was "|⋈|" "Maybe we can. Just maybe."

Dick resigned himself to losing the rest of that day and the next two to the media. "It's just better to get that shit out of the way," he said on more than one occasion. On the morning of the third day he was ready to resume serious work with only the interference of the National Geographic.

Not counting the shelves full of books, there were hundreds of items to catalog and photograph. First, each item received a number printed on an index card which Lani, wearing cotton gloves, placed next to each. Item number one was the book that Dick had carelessly opened and then the pedestal, upon which the book lay, became number two. The third entity cataloged looked like a very large, and for a human very awkward pestle, but without a mortar. The tall vase, the one with the green, yellow, and black bands, the one John thought so garish was number 78. The metal bar with the evenly spaced markings was number 216. The last numbers, numbers 526 and 527, went to the two tall statues, the gargoyles, or maybe representations of the devil himself, which guarded the still sealed inner door. Dick decided to number the books after everything else was removed. John couldn't help wondering where everything was to be removed to, but he need not have as Dick had already secured more space in town.

For four days, the cataloging and photographing went on without any interruptions from the media, which still swarmed at the gate, pissed off, complaining, and constantly begging for admittance. Their only peek at the ten to fifteen items that had been carefully wrapped and packed for transfer into town was when they passed out the front gate. Their cameras saw nothing, yet they taped anyway.

John's fifth day in the outer room began just the same as all the others. After a seven o'clock bowl of grape nuts flakes and a glass of orange juice followed by a smoke, he ambled over to Dick's trailer and removed a fresh box of 4x5 sheet film from his refrigerator, loaded two dozen film holders, and headed for what everyone now was calling the tomb. The first specimen to focus on that morning looked like an average size pumpkin with a long crank coming out the top and a latch on its side, suggesting that there was something inside of it. He had no idea what it was. It was tempting to release the latch for a quick peek, but that would be left to the team back at the lab in town. After his first exposure, Karen entered to begin her cataloging. "So where's everybody else?" he asked her.

"Dick sent Colin and Kathy into town to get some supplies. Everybody else is in a meeting in the bunkhouse."

"Doesn't he want us there, too?"

"No, he wants us to keep working." She removed a tape measure from her pack and began recording the exact position of the object John was working on and then started to write down some notes. "What do you think I should call it?" she asked.

"What's wrong with just calling it number 82?"

"So what's your guess? Looks kind of naughty to me."

"I don't see where you get that."

"You need to use your imagination a little more." She laughed. "I'll just bet these dudes were as horny as anybody. Want to take a peek inside and find out?"

"Jesus, no."

"You are just no fun. God but it's stuffy in here," she said as she pulled her t-shirt away from her chest several times, trying to circulate some air. "Dick's got to get some fans in here or something. And those hot lights of yours aren't helping things either."

John couldn't help seeing glistening sweat trickle down through her ample cleavage as she knelt down to take a measurement. He tried to avert his eyes, but it was hopeless. "Damn, no woman should look like that - but no harm in looking," he said to himself. He put his head under the focusing hood, moved the lens back and forth, and adjusted the swings and tilts. "That looks just about right," he said as it came into focus. He pulled his head out and slipped a film holder into the back of the camera, pulled out the dark slide, and released the shutter. Trying not to be obvious, he looked at Karen and wondered how a female paleontologist could be so incredibly attractive. Weren't they all supposed to look like weather beaten plain Janes and not something on the cover of Playboy?

"We really did have some hot times back then, didn't we," said Karen.

"Back when?" asked John.

"Don't be stupid, you know what I mean," she replied.

"Yeah, we did have some hot times."

"I miss it, do you?" she asked.

"I did for a while. Not any more."

Einstein's Bones

"Not since you started getting it on with Maggie?"

He looked her over with restrained desire. "If that's what you want to think." John tried to move his eyes back to his camera.

"It's really getting hot in here." She smiled seductively. "Do you mind if I take off my top?"

"Yes, I do."

"It's not like you haven't seen me naked before, and besides you've been eyeing my boobs for the last ten minutes." She smiled and moved her hands to her waist and in one quick motion pulled her t-shirt over her head revealing her perfectly formed breasts. "Now that didn't hurt, did it?"

"For Christ sake Karen, what if somebody walks in here?"

"All you guys make way too much out of a pair of boobs. You know in Europe they don't think anything of it."

"Well, this isn't Europe. Just put the t-shirt back on, will ya?"

"Does it really bother you that much or are you afraid that you won't be able to finish off what we started back in Dick's trailer? Or are you afraid to let down that prissy little miss goody two shoes that everybody knows you're sleeping with in town? You are screwing her, aren't you? You can't wear out your cock, you know. Don't worry, it's alright, I won't tell her. I haven't told her anything yet, have I? "

"Just put the shirt back on," he pleaded. "Somebody could walk in here any minute."

"If that's all you're worried about, we can always go for a little walk, but we've got that whole big other room between us and the door and we could hear anybody coming in. I just love the feel of two sweaty bodies sliding against each other – back and forth," she said as she moved her hands slowly over her body.

"Put the damn shirt on and shut up. Or do you want me to say something to Dick?"

She laughed. "Oh, excuse me. Am I being inappropriate? You won't do that. I could say a few things, too."

"Look, I'm not going to say that what happened in the past wasn't fun, but that was a long time ago and things have changed. It just ain't gonna happen again. So put the damn shirt on and get on with what you're supposed to be doing."

She covered her face with a false look of hurt, but refused to put her t-shirt back where it belonged. "You got any idea how long it's been since I got laid?"

"There's always Mikie."

"Yuck. I'd rather do it with the Skunk. Five minutes?"

"Karen, it just ain't gonna happen," he said as he heard foot steps entering the tomb.

Before Margaret rounded the corner of the inner room, Karen resumed a degree of modesty.

"What's the matter?" John asked Margaret, considerably worried that she might have heard something. "You don't look too good."

"I just got a call from my sister. Dad's in the hospital."

"Oh no, what happened?"

"Carol sounded pretty broken up," she replied in a faltering voice. "She says she thinks he's had a heart attack, but she really doesn't know. I was almost here when she called and they were just taking him away in the ambulance. So I've got to go back." She glanced disapprovingly in Karen's direction then turned her eyes back to John. "Here, I brought this out for you." She handed John a box with his favorite sandwiches and a bag of Oreo cookies. "I'll try and call you tonight if I can."

"No, why don't I go back with you. This can wait." With only a fleeting glance at Karen, John secured his gear and made a quick march to the bunk house, interrupting Dick's meeting at the half-way point.

As John relayed the news, no one looked more concerned than Dick. In the short time that he had known Paul Newcomb, they had become very friendly. Dick admired Newcomb's intelligence and warmth, his fairness and honesty, and Dick especially appreciated his generosity, without which none of what Dick and his team were doing would be possible. "Would you think it alright if I go back to town, too?" Dick asked. Margaret said no, she didn't think it would be good for her father to have too many visitors especially since she didn't know what condition he was in. "Then tell him I will be praying for him and for you."

"Thank you. I'll tell him," replied Margaret, who, with John at her side then hurried back to her Chevy Tahoe.

"So what exactly did your sister say," John asked as they passed through the gate.

"Not much. She sounded so frightened, the way she did when mom died. She said Jason went over to dad's house to pick something up and found him collapsed on the kitchen floor unconscious and called an ambulance and then called her. She sounded pretty broken up. He's had one heart attack already."

"Did he regain consciousness?" he asked. He could see tears beginning to roll from her eyes. "Would you like me to drive?"

"No," she replied staring straight ahead. "I'll be alright. From what she said, it doesn't sound like he had, but I'm not sure. Maybe you better drive."

They stopped near where Shunk was continuing his dig, but was now mostly left to himself, without any media to worry about. "Where did they take him?" John asked.

"Sheridan Memorial," she said as she put her hands to her face with her fingers spread apart. ""Do you know where that is?"

"No."

"Just stay on 330. It's about two miles past Main Street – on 5th."

"I got it." He looked over at Margaret, wishing there was something he could do, something he could say, anything that might comfort her, but he knew from experience that at times like this it was almost impossible to touch another person's inner soul. There was nothing he could do to dry her eyes or calm her fears. "I love you, Margaret." It was the first time he had ever said that without her saying it first. He touched her shoulder for a moment. "Your dad's a great guy." The road was too rough for one handed driving. "And we all think that way, not just me or Dick. Everybody feels that way." She tried to say something, but his words only made her bury her face deeper in her hand and begin to sob. "Don't think the worst," he said trying as best he could to comfort her. "We don't know. Let's hope it's not as serious as your sister made it sound."

She pulled back her hands and wiped each eye in turn. "Oh God, I've been so afraid of this ever since the first one. I don't want him to die."

Sheridan Memorial Hospital had been a fixture in town for more than one hundred years, but it looked as new as any. John stopped Margaret's SUV at the front entrance. Margaret jumped out, said she'd meet him inside, and ran to the doors. John drove around to the back and parked.

She was not waiting for him. Margaret had already gone to her father's room in the Cardiac Care Unit. When John joined her she and Carol were holding hands and looking at their father who lay motionless on his bed, attached to an IV, oxygen, something on the tip of his finger, and a monitor. With Carol was her husband

Jason, who was reciting a prayer, and a nurse. "It doesn't look good," said Margaret as she put her arms around John for comfort. "Very bad."

"Is Dale coming?" asked John.

"Carol says he left here half an hour ago and in a hurry."

John didn't ask why. All that he could do was be there for Margaret. They stayed at the hospital until 6:00pm, never far from Paul Newcomb's private room, conferring occasionally with his doctors and praying that they would see the still figure on the bed open his eyes. It didn't happen.

"Margaret, do you want me to stay with you tonight?" John asked as they walked out of the hospital.

"Yes, I'd like that," she softly replied.

He asked for her cell phone to update Dick who listened attentively as John described Newcomb's condition and then asked, "If it's alright with you, I'd like to stay with Margaret tonight."

"You might as well," replied Dick. "We've been shut down."

"What," said John in disbelief.

"That's right, we just got shut down. The sheriff and some lawyer of your girl friend's brother kicked us out."

"That co . . ." John caught himself. "How the hell can he do that? What about all the stuff and our own equipment? What about all that?"

"All I can tell you is that we got orders to pack up our gear and leave everything we've found here."

"What about what's in town? What about that?"

"All we can do is take out our own equipment and leave behind everything else."

"What are you doing right now?" John asked.

"Packing up and getting ready to leave. I'll call you at Margaret's when we get back to town."

John folded the cell phone and handed it back to Margaret. "What was that all about?" she asked.

"Seems as though your brother booted us off the ranch."

"You're kidding?"

"I wish I were. But Dick isn't one for practical jokes."

"That fucking bastard," she blurted out.

"Can he do that?" John asked.

"I don't know. I think so. I'm not sure." She paused. "Oh hell, I remember after dad had his first heart attack he and Dale signed some papers. I think they gave Dale power of attorney if dad was ever incapacitated. I should have paid more attention, but really didn't think that much about it then. I'm so sorry."

"Don't be. It's not your fault. You can't help what your brother does."

"I know. Do you want me to talk to him?" she asked.

"If you think it might do any good. But right now you've got more than enough to worry about. Why don't you wait a while?"

"What about all your equipment?"

"Don't worry about it, Dick said he taking care of it."

Instead of driving back to Margaret's they followed Carol and Jason to their house for prayers. Not being religious and knowing that Carol and her husband were well aware of John's lack of faith, he felt awkward when he was asked to form a circle, bow his head, and join hands as Carol asked for God's intervention in the life of Paul Newcomb and for Him to forgive Paul of all his sins. "We ask you, Lord, to forgive our father for not putting all his trust in You, knowing that his affliction is Your way of pointing him to the true path."

John felt an urge to object, but held his tongue. He couldn't believe that any god would give anyone a heart attack no matter how much he had sinned. John had a hard enough time believing in any god let alone a vengeful one. And if God really did exist, why would He intervene when so many others needed His help. But he kept his head bowed and continued to hold hands. At worst, it couldn't hurt and it might be some comfort to Margaret.

When the prayer session ended, Carol went into the kitchen and returned with a tray of Triscuts and cheese. "Did you know what Dale did?" Margaret asked her sister.

"You mean about shutting down that affront to God?"

"You knew about it?"

"Yes, I asked Dale to do it," replied Carol.

"You what?" Margaret asked. "How could you do such a thing?"

"What was happening on your father's ranch was blasphemy, and God has sent him a message," said Jason.

"I asked Carol, not you," said Margaret.

"He's right, it's the Lords will," said Carol.

John squirmed as Margaret replied, "You're out of your fucking mind. God is punishing our father? That's just crazy. And you really think Dale is doing this to carry out some grand fucking design of God? You know damn well what he's going to do. You know or you sure as hell ought to know that all he's going to give a shit about is what's in it for him."

"It won't help to take the Lord's name in vain," said Carol.

"Amen," added her husband.

"You can take that amen and shove it up your ass, dear brother-in-law." Margaret turned to John. "Let's go."

John said nothing as he got into the passenger seat of Margaret's Tahoe. He watched as Margaret bent over and placed her forearms against the steering wheel and then straighten up. All of the sadness had passed from her face, replaced by red anger, something John had never seen before but was glad to see now. "That Bible banging bitch. What do I have to do, write off my entire family? I am so, so sorry. I could have expected that from Dale, but not from Carol. I am so sorry."

"You can't help who your relatives are," said John.

"No, but how could she?"

"I've always thought that people always believed that they are doing the right thing, no matter how wrong the rest of us might think it is. I'm sure your sister thinks she did the right thing, too. If I believed in God the way she does, who knows, maybe I'd of done the same thing."

"And my brother? Strike me dead if he believes in anything other than himself," she said as she turned the key in the ignition. "I know that all he can see right now is money."

"So I guess there's an exception to every rule."

"Do you feel like anything?" Margaret asked as they walked inside her home.

"No, not really. Would you like me to read to you?" John had made a habit of reading to Margaret in bed most every night. He was well into *Nature Girl* by Carl Hiaasen, having reached the point in the story the last time he had stayed with Margaret where Honey Santana begins her ill-fated eco-tour. "Come sit here," John said tenderly as he put his palm down on the seat beside him.

"Do you want anything to eat or drink first?" she asked.

"Maybe if you could just bring me a glass of water."

She put the glass with the customary three cubes of ice on the end table within easy reach of his right hand then curled up on his left side with her head on his shoulder saying little as he opened the book with the yellow dust cover and began reading in his slow voice, trying as best he could to give each character their own distinctive voice and personality. He read well, something that he had inherited from his father, except when he got to an expletive that was any stronger than a "hell" or a "damn", which in this book was often. When he got to those words, words he had been taught never to say in mixed company, he always hesitated and his voice always seemed to fall out of character. Margaret had tried to make him feel less self-conscious about those words, but it never worked. She laughed a little inside each time he began to hesitate, having a good idea which word would come next.

After two chapters, the doorbell rang. It was Dick. "I've got all your stuff in the van. You want it here?" Dick asked.

John looked at Margaret who nodded approval. "Guess so."

"How's your father?" asked Dick.

"We haven't heard any more since John called you. I am so sorry about all this. What are you going to do?" said Margaret.

"Get drunk and then go home," replied Dick

Fifteen minutes later, everything that John had brought with him to Wyoming was in Margaret's study. Most importantly, all of his film and all of his memory cards were with it.

"And you?" asked Dick as he prepared to leave.

Once again John turned to Margaret who returned his questioning look with a smile. John held out his hand to Dick. "I guess I'll stay here at least for a while. Give everybody my best. It's been the greatest experience in my life – job wise anyway."

He returned to the sofa with Margaret and began reading where he had left off. She curled up close again. "So what's the greatest thing in your life – not work wise?"

"Do you really have to ask? Now let me read to you."

Einstein's Bones

Chapter 20

For the first time since he had arrived in Wyoming, John awoke late, past 7:00am. That was unusual, and it was his full first day off since he began his work in Wyoming, though he had never thought about taking any time off other than his two nights with Margaret three times every month. But what was a day off? There would be no thrill of each new discovery, no new sights that no man had ever seen, no losing himself in time, or rather that strange feeling that he got every time he entered the outer chamber, that feeling that time did not exist, that its past occupants had departed leaving behind their treasures just the day before. And yes, he had to admit that he missed being a treasure hunter discovering hordes of gold and priceless statues. He would miss it all. And then there was Karen. How in hell could he think about her when Margaret was lying just a few inches away? Would he miss her? She had no doubt boosted his ego – two women with him in mind. And of all the men at the camp, was he the one that Karen was really after? It inflated his ego even more that he had been able to fend her off. He silently thanked her that she had not tried more than twice. But what did he really know. Was she after him because of their past, because maybe she had already been with all the others, or was there some other reason? All the others – all the others except for Mike? Maybe she's slept with him, too. No, if she had, Mikie would have told the entire state of Wyoming.

He felt a soft warm hand on his bare shoulder. "What are you thinking about?" asked Margaret.

"About your dad and what I'm gonna do now. Like I want to go to Australia or something. When do you want to go and see your father?"

Einstein's Bones

"When my brother and sister aren't there. About ten. You sorry she's gone?"

"Who, your sister?"

"Miss Peterson. Karen."

"Why do you ask me that? I never thought about it."

"You never thought about her? Never looked? She sure was giving you the look yesterday."

"I never noticed. I think she gives everybody that look. Yeah, I suppose I might have looked at her a couple of times, but all the guys looked at her, too."

"She certainly did advertise," Margaret noted.

"That she did."

"Has she slept with anyone - other than my brother, that is?" She hesitated. "I have to ask, and if you say you have, it will hurt, but I have to know. I'll only ask once, and tell me the truth, have you been sleeping with her. I think I can live with it if you have."

"No. Maybe if I didn't have you I would have, but I do have you and I haven't, and she's gone. End of story."

"I'm sorry, I had to ask."

Had John just lied to Margaret? In the strictest sense, no, but only on a point of grammar. But another minute alone with that woman in the outer chamber and it might have turned into a lie. Would he have admitted it? Probably not. And he wasn't going to tell Margaret anything about the trailer or what had happened yesterday morning or especially what happened a couple of years ago. Hell, he'd never ask Margaret about her past, would he? Now Karen was gone. Out of sight and mostly out of mind.

But Karen would never be out of his mind as long as he kept it a big secret. And then what if someone else told Margaret? But who would do that? Karen was gone and John was sure she was the only one who knew. Damn, it didn't matter; it would just keep eating at him.

"Darling," he began slowly, "it is true I have not been sleeping with her." He drew a deep breath. "But, right after Phyllis and I broke up, well, Karen and I did have a short relationship. It didn't amount to anything, and she means nothing to me now. You are what matters to me and I won't let anything or anybody come between us. I'm sorry."

"There's nothing to be sorry about – as long as it was long ago and as long as it stays that way. I don't know why, but I thought there was something between the two of you. Maybe just the way you seemed to be nervous around her. I don't want to know any details and I won't bring it up ever again. But I am glad she's gone." She looked at him lovingly and gave him a kiss.

"Thank you," he responded. He felt much better but still wished he could go back in time and erase what he now so much regretted.

John's criminations were interrupted by the telephone. Margaret rolled over and answered. "It's for you," she said. "It's your brother."

"Kinda early for you, isn't it. What's up?" said John as he put the phone to his ear.

"You tell me. What the hell's going on out there? I got a call from Dick last night."

"What did he tell you?" asked John.

"He sounded pretty shit faced and told me the dig was over – that he got kicked out. I'm hoping you can tell me why."

"That's all you got out of him?" John asked.

"Like I said, he was pretty drunk. So what happened?"

Einstein's Bones

John told him what he knew for certain – about Newcomb's heart attack, the power of attorney and about Margaret's sister telling Dale that the excavations were an affront to God.

"That's a bunch of bull shit. There's got to be more to it than that."

"I can't say for sure, only a good guess," replied John.

"So tell me."

"I could be wrong," John began, "but I don't think so. You do know that Shunk's been out here, right? Maybe you didn't know he was doing his work on Dale Newcomb's land. He's the son of Paul Newcomb who owns the land Dick's been working on."

"Yes, I know all that," replied his brother.

"My guess is that Dick got booted off so the Skunk could move in so he and the son could start cashing in. He's done that with some of the stuff they found on their own already. Yeah, and the earrings, too. Did I tell you about that, about how they stole them? That's what I think and that's what Margaret thinks. The thing I can't figure out is how the Skunk thinks he's gonna get away with it. The whole world knows it's Dick's discovery. How's the Skunk gonna move in without the whole bone digging world coming down on his head? The guy has at least some self respect doesn't he? I mean if he goes somewhere and makes a big deal presentation about 'his' dig, aren't they just gonna boo him off the podium? It sounds so stupid."

"This Dale guy, what's he like?"

"He likes the money," replied John.

"I always knew Shunk was low. This Dale guy could always claim that he and Dick had some dispute they couldn't resolve or something and Mr. Innocent Shunk just happened to be convenient, standing around with his thumb up his ass with nothing to do. Call it all Dale's idea. Knowing Shunk, he'll think of some good excuse for taking over and he probably will get away with it."

"You know more about him than I do. What do you think he'll do?" asked John.

"For sure he'll make a pile of money auctioning off to the highest bidding museums, and no doubt he'll turn it into a three ring media event. But as much as I can't stomach the guy, he does do good work."

"Small comfort."

"Yeah. How are you taking it? What are you going to do?"

"I'll survive. For now, I'm taking a vacation."

Almost as an afterthought, John's brother asked how Margaret was doing.

"Here, why don't you ask her yourself?" John replied.

John passed the receiver back to Margaret and heard only one side of the conversation. Margaret said she was holding her own, that her father was in rough shape, thanked Willy for his concern and ended the call.

"Do me a favor, and let's not talk about any of this for a while or I could start beating on things," said John as Margaret hung up the phone.

"What would you like for breakfast?" asked Margaret.

As planned, Margaret and John arrived at the hospital near ten. Other than a short conversation with the doctor, they were by themselves. Paul Newcomb continued to lie still on his bed with tubes attached to more places than John could imagine. The good news was that he was still alive. The bad news was that the doctors had just discovered that he had swelling in his skull, probably caused by his fall in the kitchen. If it continued, he'd need surgery. They stayed until noon, when Margaret said what John was thinking. "I can't believe the doctors didn't figure that out before this," then, "I can't take this. Let's go before they get here."

      Dale Newcomb was feeling good, very good. For the first time in his life things were really going his way – at last. Sure, a few things in the past had turned out OK. His father had helped him buy his own ranch by giving him the down payment, but then he'd gotten stuck with the rest of the debt. And yes, he had made some money from what little Carl Shunk had dug up on his property, but after giving Shunk his share it was only enough to get him almost caught up with his back payments on the ranch but did little for his house, child support, his pick-ups, his ATVs and assorted other toys.

      Dale's father. Always the big deal lecture whenever he helped out his son in some small way. So what if he had done some of the same crazy things that all kids do. OK, so maybe he shouldn't have borrowed that car for a joy ride, but did his father have to treat him like some kind of criminal? And why the big stink about Janet Hill? It was just as much her fault, wasn't it? Dale was willing to bet that his father had been bailed out once or twice by his father, too. So why was the old man always on Dale's case?

      Well, no more. No more getting kicked in the ass every time he deviated from that ridiculously narrow path that his father had laid down. No more having to please an old man who could never be pleased – at least by him. The ranch was going to be his, the ranch with all its treasures, the ranch that Carl Shunk was now working at. There were two other ranches – one for Margaret and one for Carol – with nothing on them but cows. He hadn't thought much about it when his father had told them two years ago who would end up with what, but now, now Dale Newcomb was feeling very good.

But for a while, he was going to have to be patient. If he started selling off everything now – as long as his father was alive - he would have to split it with his sisters. So, he'd wait, wait for his father to die.

Carl Shunk wasn't in any hurry either. The money would come, but for the present he had the job of being a paleontologist to do and a reputation to repair. He might not be able to fool all in his profession; he doubted he would be able to fool more than a handful, but he could at least make a good attempt at fooling the general public to whom he was the archetypical bone digger. So he carefully protested any impropriety, any secret deal with Dale, any hint that he was anything but an innocent bystander who had been called in to rescue a dig that was going horribly wrong. So let Dick and his allies piss and moan. As long as Shunk could get the public on his side, what did he care? And what better way to do that than bring the media into the dig full throttle – for a price anyway? After all, wasn't the supposed disagreement between Dick and Dale the fact that Dick had limited media access?

John didn't see the changes. He refused any suggestion that he even drive by the site for a quick look. But he couldn't help but see something every time he turned on the news. What had been a relatively low key dig with controlled access was now turning into a close approximation of a P.T. Barnum side show with an endless stream of visitors, lights and cameras occupying every square inch of ground that wasn't being excavated and interview after nauseating interview with Carl Shunk. It was a wonder that he had any time at all to direct the work he was supposed to be doing or to sit down and write some of his self-serving articles for magazines or even begin writing the first of what he knew would be many books.

All of which is not to say that he too was not in awe of the discovery that he inherited. He too had stood in stunned silence the first time he entered the outer chamber. And he was not without a sense of responsibility for doing the best job that he knew how to do – before he decided which museums would be paying him the highest prices. And for the public there was a show of humility. "I am truly grateful for the work Dr. Johnson has done before me and regret that unresolved issues resulted in his departure," he told one reporter. "It was unfortunate, but these things happen."

Two weeks had passed since Paul Newcomb had taken an ambulance ride to the hospital. Two weeks with no improvement despite one operation on his heart and another on his brain. And for most of that time Carl Shunk continued, despite the crush of the press, to carry on with the careful documentation and removal of the artifacts in the outer chamber.

Two weeks, and Dale Newcomb was getting impatient. Maybe an evening bottle of Scotch with Carl would help.

"So when the fuck are we going to see some fucking money?" asked an unannounced visitor to what was now Shunk's site. "Let's go to your trailer," said Dale Newcomb.

Once inside, Dale pulled out a bottle and poured out three fingers for each of them. "So when the fuck are we going to see the fucking money?"

"Just how bad do you need it?" asked Carl as he downed his three fingers in two swallows. "We can't go selling off all this as soon as we take it out of the ground, you know. It's going to take some time."

Dale refilled their glasses. "Just how much friggin time? If I had all the fucking time in the world, you wouldn't be here. I could have called in some other schmuck. Shit. That god damn old man. Thought he was doing me a big fucking favor with that ranch. What the fuck does he know?" He laughed. "Nothing now. He just lies there waiting to die." He finished off his second drink and grabbed the bottle again. "And my bitch sisters. As long as the old man's around they think they're gonna get their cut, too. Well, fuck them. Ain't there some way we can move some of this junk without those bitches finding out?"

"I don't know how. Johnson knows what we've got, and with all the reporters hanging around it wouldn't be easy. At least with what's in the outer chamber."

"Fuck the shit that's in the outer chamber. Christ, you haven't even opened the other door yet. It's got to be full of good crap. Who the hell's gonna know what we take out of there? You've got some friends who buy that shit and can keep their fucking mouths shut, right?"

"Some," replied Shunk as he brought the bottle to his glass.

"Well, start calling."

"It's risky. I've got a reputation you know. So what's in it for me?"

"Half. Fuck the reputation bull shit. They all call you the skunk anyway."

"Half?" said Shunk, his speech beginning to slur. "I'll drink to that. Hit me again."

"So how soon?"

Gimme a couple a days . . . to talk to . . . a couple a guys and let me clear out . . . . . . some of . . . of the clowns hanging around here. You gotta keep yer damn mouth shut . . . ya know."

"You're gonna be one rich asshole," said Dale showing much less effect from the Scotch. "Ya know, the only thing that worries me about this whole fucking thing is what if that door is the last seal?"

"What the hell are you talking about?" asked Shunk.

Einstein's Bones

"The fucking seventh seal, Mr. Skunk. The last seal. What if that's it? Shit, you know what that means? The whole fucking world's gonna come down on us, just like in the book."

"What book?" Shunk asked with a blank face.

"*Revelations*, you stupid shit."

"You believe that crap? You said your sister . . . was . . . some kinda Bible banger."

"You haven't heard?" Dale Newcomb took another hard swallow and looked hard into Shunk's glassy eyes. "The first six have already been opened."

"Yeah, and who opened 'em?" Shunk asked mockingly.

"Don't fuckin' argue with me. Why you have to question everything I'm telling you? You can see it all for yourself on the web. Shit, it's been comin' for a long time. End times. I mean really fucking end times. That's why we gotta get what we need to survive now. All those fuckers from the East are gonna come here cause they ain't gonna have any food in the cities and they'll be rioting and killing each other for what's left and then they're gonna all come here and take what we got and just you wait and it's gonna happen and when it does I'm gonna be ready. We gotta sell that crap fast so we can stock up on what we need. You got a gun?"

"You're fucking crazy," mumbled Shunk as he refilled their glasses.

"If I'd a known you liked to drink I'd a gotten a bigger bottle. You think I'm crazy? You'll see. Trust me. They're gonna come."

"What ya gonna . . . do . . about the old man?" asked Shunk.

"Pull the fucking plug, that's what. Ya got any beer?" Shunk motioned over to the refrigerator in his trailer. Dale Newcomb got up slowly, balancing himself with the back of his chair and retrieved four beers. "Thanks. Ya know why it gets so cold here at night after it's been so fucking hot during the day?"

Einstein's Bones

Shunk showed no response. "I'll tell you why. I'll bet you didn't know this. It's fucking true. I bet you didn't know it but the sun's gravity pulls the heat away at night. I'll bet you didn't know that. It's true and the sun pushes the heat back in in the morning. I'll bet you fucking didn't know that."

Had Carl Shunk been only mildly drunk he might have asked himself what kind of idiot he was dealing with. As it was, he wasn't in any condition to question anything the moron he was drinking with had to say, even when Dale Newcomb informed him that the faster two cars were going in a head-on collision, the safer it was, or that all of that moon landing stuff was all a fake. The last thing he remembered being told before he passed out was that JFK was still alive and living in France.

When Carl Shunk woke up the next morning, he wondered how in hell he had made it to his bed and wondered where Dale Newcomb was – if he had actually tried to drive back home. The second question was answered when his cell phone rang. Still lying in his bed, slowly and almost painfully he unfolded his phone and said, "Who's this?"

"Did you start making those calls yet?"

"Jesus, is that you Dale? Where the hell are you? Home? How'd you get there? No, I just got up. Give me a while, will ya? I need some time to clear my head. I'll call you when I've got something." Shunk folded his phone and with a quarter turn put his feet on the floor and put his head between his hands. "Jesus. And I thought I liked to drink," he said out loud to an empty trailer. He looked down at his watch. "Jesus Christ, the guy calls me at eight in the fucking morning after last night and asks that bull shit. He's gonna have to wait."

Einstein's Bones

But Dale Newcomb didn't have to wait – at least not for Carl Shunk. Ten minutes later Dale's phone rang. It was the hospital – and time for a decision.

Einstein's Bones

Chapter 21

  Except for a slightly fuzzy feeling and a god awful taste in his mouth, Dale Newcomb felt surprisingly good when he awoke at 7:00am, considering he had had more than half a bottle of Scotch and four beers the night before. He knew of but one cure. There was no Vodka in the cabinet above the sink, but there was a nearly full bottle of gin. He opened the refrigerator and pulled out a can of V8. "What the hell," he said as he mixed it with a healthy slug of gin. "All the fucking same." He pushed a few buttons on his radio for his favorite station – an early morning drive time talk show with a few classic rock tunes thrown in. "Shit, those guys are right on," he said hearing more confirmation about the end times coming from the speakers. "If those dopes would only listen to what these guys are telling 'em." He looked across the kitchen table at a sweater. "I wonder when that stupid bitch is gonna come back and get it."
  He dismissed his call to Shunk. "At least it'll get the fucker moving." He thought he'd call again some time after lunch, but he instinctively reached for the phone to make sure that Shunk knew that Dale Newcomb was a man who expected action. Lucky for Shunk, Dale's own phone rang first. It was his sister, Margaret.
  "So, what? You're speaking to me now? What do you want?" He listened for a minute. "Yeah, how bad?" He listened again. "And you need me for what? OK, I'll get there when I fucking get there," and hung up. "Bitch." He got up and refilled his glass bringing it into the living room where he turned on the TV. It was judge something-or-other. "About fucking time," he mumbled.
  Carol had gone to the hospital early. She always did. Yes, it was before normal visiting hours, but no one in the town of Sheridan was going to put up barriers to any of the Newcomb family and besides, Carol knew most all of the staff and had even managed

Einstein's Bones

to convert one of them the year before and thought she was close to converting another. Carol did not like the look on the face of Nurse Sarah Nonte as she walked up to the desk in the ward where her father was being kept. Sarah was Carol's latest project – very friendly, but so far not sold. "My father?" Carol asked hesitatingly.

"I was about to call you. His doctor has been in with your father for a while and it does not look very good," said Sarah. "I think you should call Margaret and Dale."

"Is he, ah . . ?" Carol couldn't bring herself to finish the question.

"He's alive, if that's what you're asking."

"But?"

"I really should have you speak with the doctor."

"Sarah, tell me."

Sarah Nonte hesitated. "He's not responding to anything. He doesn't have much time left. I think you should call your brother and sister," she said and then added, "Please don't say that I mentioned any of this."

Carol opened her cell phone and called Margaret, and then turned back to Sarah. "She'll be here in fifteen minutes."

"What about your brother?"

"I'll let her call him." Carol turned at the sound of footsteps behind her. It was her father's doctor who asked for a private conversation. "No," she replied, "let's wait for my sister."

As she said she would, Margaret arrived in fifteen minutes accompanied by John. They had just cleared the breakfast table when Carol called. When Margaret had put down the receiver, she said only, "The call I was afraid of. We better go now."

At the hospital, the sisters came together, hugged, and then began sobbing. It was all John could do to keep from joining them, but he did not want to intrude on a family moment. "Is Jason here?" Margaret asked.

"No, he's at work. I'll call him later. I didn't call Dale. Can you?"

She did. "Well, that wasn't pleasant," Margaret said after she hung up with her brother.

"He is coming, isn't he? Did he say when?"

"Yes, when he feels like it," replied Margaret.

"The doctor wants to talk to us," said Carol.

Margaret turned to John. "Do you want to come?"

"No," he replied. "I think it's better if it's just the two of you," he said as he watched Margaret and Carol approach the doctor and then go off to a private room.

They returned a half hour later, subdued, but in control. "Did Dale come yet?" asked Margaret.

"No, not yet. How are you doing?" said John.

They embraced in a tight hug. "I think I'm OK," replied Margaret. "The doctor told us all his brain activity has ceased and there's nothing they can do. The only reason he's alive is all the life support he's on. He'd never want that. He told me that many times and he put it in a living will." She drew her breath. "But I don't know. I thought I'd be up to this when the time came."

"And Carol?" he asked.

"She's for ending it now, too. I never thought she'd say that. Tell me, what do you think?"

"It's not up to me, dear. All I can say is that when my mother and father died nobody prolonged it and that was the way they wanted it. It was the right thing to do – for them anyway. I suppose you'll want to wait for your brother. Are the doctors going to go along with whatever you decide?"

"Yes," she replied.

Einstein's Bones

There was nothing more to do but wait for Dale. "Maybe you should give him another call," John suggested.

"I've called him once. If I call him again he'll just get angry and make us wait even longer." So they sat by Paul Newcomb's bed, joined now by Jason, waiting for Dale.

Dale Newcomb watched as two former lovers argued in front of the judge over who got custody of the dog. "Fuck this," he said and called Carl Shunk. "You are not going to fucking believe this," he told an irritated Carl Shunk, "but it looks like the old man's ready to tip over, so you don't have to worry about your buddies or any of that secret shit we were talking about last night. It's gonna be all mine soon enough anyway, so forget all that shit we talked about. And we can go back to the same split we worked out before when we were diggin' on my other place. That's the way it's gonna be. Later." He switched channels, found a Japanese game show, and opened a beer. "They can fucking wait."

Margaret with John, and Carol with Jason waited until 11:30 before a half smirking Dale sauntered into Paul Newcomb's room. "Well here I am," he announced.

Dale sat spitting tobacco juice into a styrofoam coffee cup as Margaret and Carol explained the situation. "So, what the hell do you need me for?" he asked.

"We thought you might like to be a part of this family," replied Margaret.

"Part of this family? When did you ever treat me as part of this family? When was the last time I ever heard anything from the two of you or from that old man that was anything but telling me what a piece of shit I am? Well, you know what you can do with all that family crap, don't you? If you want to pull the plug, go ahead. It's no loss to me. Do whatever the hell you want. Go ahead, I won't stop you."

"I had hoped for something a little better," said Margaret.
"God will not forget this," added Carol.
"Yeah, right," replied Dale as he spit into his cup. "Let's just get this over with."
Margaret asked John to find the doctor. Ten minutes later the doctor returned and entered Paul Newcomb's room. John left and went outside the hospital for a smoke. Nearly finished with his cigarette, Dale passed by.
"You can go back in now and all hold hands and have a good fucking cry," Dale said without stopping.
John crushed out his smoke and hurried back to find Margaret holding one of her father's hands, Carol holding the other and Jason with his arm resting on Carol's shoulder – and the doctor standing nearby. All the life support, all the tubes, all the wires were gone. John felt guilty that he had left – even for those few short minutes – yet, he thought he had done the right thing. He wasn't sure. He bent down and kissed Margaret's forehead. No one said a word. The only sounds in the room were Paul Newcomb's increasingly uneven and labored breathing.
It was not a long wait and then he was gone. First Carol and then Margaret gently kissed their father's forehead. John put his arms around Margaret. "No, I need to be alone for a while," she said. She left the room to find a private place to let her emotions go. The doctor said a few words of sympathy and then asked what the family wanted to do next.
"He wanted a green funeral," replied Carol. "I've already talked with Barb Olson. Do you know her?" The doctor did. "It's been arranged. We'd like the funeral the day after tomorrow." Carol and the doctor discussed the transfer of the mortal remains of Paul Newcomb and then, before she left, she once again kissed her father's forehead. "Goodbye dad, I love you so very much." In the

hallway, they waited until Margaret returned, her face drawn and her eyes red.

John had never been to a green funeral and did not know what to expect, but it was not any different from any other funeral except that the body was not filled with embalming fluids and the coffin was a simple pine box. Paul Newcomb was buried on his ranch next to his wife, Mary and about a mile from where John had made his discovery. That evening, Margaret and Carol were to join their estranged brother for the reading of Paul Newcomb's will.

The reading of Paul Newcomb's will was supposed to begin at 7:30 that evening, but not unexpectedly, Dale Newcomb had not arrived. So Margaret, her sister, and her brother-in-law waited in the lawyer's outer office still dressed as they had been for their father's funeral. When Dale arrived twenty minutes late, he was dressed in dirty blue jeans and a worn flannel shirt – and obviously drunk. With a smile on his face he said, "Well, let's get this over with."

After the customary, "I, Paul Henry Newcomb, being of sound mind," and so forth, came the division of his assets. Paul Henry Newcomb died a very wealthy man, having accumulated much more than his offspring realized. Besides the ranches, there were stocks, bonds, properties in Wyoming, properties in Florida and New York, and a considerable amount of cash tucked away in half a dozen banks. The first to receive the benefits of his sizable wealth were several charities and then lesser sums for two nephews who were serving over-seas in the military. Dale Newcomb couldn't hide his smile as the lawyer began to read the meat of the will, "and to my daughter Carol I leave," and the lawyer listed the ranch west of Gillette, some stock and bonds and cash. "To my son

Dale," was followed by a listing of much the same. Too drunk to pay close attention, Dale heard the words "stocks", "bonds", "ranch", and "Sheridan" and smiled. It was all his, the ranch and all the treasures on it. The lawyer continued to read. "And finally to my daughter, Margaret I leave," and once again there were stocks, and bonds, and more money than she would ever know what to do with, and lastly, "my Sheridan ranch."

Dale shook his head and half straightened out of his slouch. "What was that? I thought I just heard that the old man left that ranch to me, and now two paragraphs later he leaves it to Missy? What, did he leave it to both of us? Read that again." A second reading said the same thing. "You mean he did leave it to both of us?"

"No," replied the lawyer.

"What the fuck's going on here? I thought you just read that he left that ranch to me."

The lawyer re-read the paragraph beginning with, "To my son Dale." Yes, it did say "Sheridan", and it did contain the word "ranch", but what the will stated was that Dale Newcomb's ranch, the one that his father had helped him buy, the one that Carl Shunk had first worked on and found nothing worth anything to Dale, would now be Dale's free and clear.

"What the fuck is all that? The will pays off my ranch? Big fucking deal. The old ranch goes to Missy? Bull shit. That's not what that old fool told me. You think she's gonna get away with that? Bull shit."

"Your father left you a very comfortable estate," the lawyer pointed out.

"Jesus fucking H. Christ," were Dale's last words as he rose from his chair and stormed out of the office.

Einstein's Bones

The lawyer regained his composure and finished with a few minor points.

"Are there going to be any problems?" asked Margaret.

"No," was the lawyer's reply. "That ranch is yours, and as long as he wasn't excluded from a fair distribution, there is nothing he can do about it."

Margaret returned home to a waiting John somewhat shaken. "What's the matter?" asked John. "Were there problems?"

"Just Dale," she replied. "He comes late and drunk and acts like a real asshole, and gets really pissed."

"About what?"

"He didn't get the ranch," replied Margaret as she began to relax. "He sits there and says F this and F that and starts calling me Missy. He knows how much I hate that. Some brother. I don't know what he's got to bitch about. He got plenty."

"So who got the ranch?"

"I did," she replied as it finally occurred to her what that meant. "I think you should give our friend Dick a call."

Einstein's Bones

Chapter 22

Unlike John Steiner, Professor Richard Johnson had followed the events in Wyoming closely, if only to pounce upon some flaw in the work of his rival, Carl Shunk and be able to prove to the world, the world of paleontology at least, that he, Richard Johnson, the better paleontologist, had been grievously wronged. And with inside information he followed the doings of Carl Shunk more closely than most people imagined.

Though he worked for and with Carl Shunk and respected his abilities, Darrel Beckman had no love for him. He thought Shunk self-centered, arrogant, condescending, and was fed up with Shunk's attitude towards his assistants that the mere pleasure of working with the great Carl Shunk was more than enough reward for the extraordinary amount of work he asked of them. Darrel Beckman wanted a change. For the moment, Carl Shunk was where the action was. But that might change.

Darrel Beckman loved to read spy novels. A secret agent, in his dreams, that's what he wanted to be. And that's what he felt he was every time he sent Richard Johnson a report of what the Skunk was up to, with the anticipation that his present overlord would get cut down to size and that he, Darrel Beckman might become not only one of Richard Johnson's loyal paladins, but perhaps be rewarded in other ways, too.

Interesting as they might be, most of Beckman's reports were of little practical use to Dick, stating what had been cataloged and removed, where a particular item had been sent – which was the same facility that Dick had used – and what new finds had been made, of which there very few. If there was something in those reports with which Dick Johnson could hang Carl Shunk, it was precious little except for several small artifacts going off to one eastern museum or another for a hefty price and some gossipy mention that Carl Shunk made a habit of sharing the bed in his trailer with a woman who was not his wife. No, if anything, the intelligence Dick received showed that while Shunk might not be as scrupulous as Dick, the Skunk was following standard procedures and in general doing what any competent paleontologist was supposed to do. That is, until Dick received Darrel Beckman's last report, an admonition that Carl Shunk and Dale Newcomb were about to open the inner door and start a massive – and secret - selling spree. Dick didn't know and he didn't care how Beckman had found out and he knew that there would be nothing illegal about it. But it could destroy Shunk's reputation once and for all. So, Richard Johnson sat in his office in Minneapolis watching and waiting. When he learned that Paul Newcomb had died, he knew the selling would begin.

  He might have nailed the son-of-a-bitch with that, but all of that was forgotten when Dick Johnson received a call from John telling him to come back to Wyoming and finish what he had started. Revenge might be sweet, but this was better. Darrel Beckman called later with the same news adding only that the Skunk was busy packing up along with more than a hint that Beckman would be more than happy to switch sides. "We'll see," was all that Dick would tell him.

  Dick and Colin Yeager flew into Sheridan the next day and immediately drove to what was now Margaret's ranch where they found John and Darrel waiting. By noon the Skunk had cleared out, not remaining to greet Dick's return. Gone were Carl Shunk and the rest of his team except for Beckman. Gone were Shunk's trailers and equipment.

Dick surveyed the scene. A few beer cans here – a bag full of garbage there – but in general, remarkably orderly. "Were there any problems?" Dick asked John.

"Like what?"

"Any vandalism – fossil smashing? Anything like that?"

"You mean like what Marsh did to Cope? No, none of that."

"Thank God. Any other problems?"

"Not really. Just in case I brought out a copy of the will to show to the Skunk, but I guess Dale must have already told the Skunk what the score was. I would have thought the Skunk and Dale would have made a mess of things, but Darrel here says the Skunk was pretty cool about it and kept Dale from going nuts. That, and from what I hear, Dale was too drunk to do much of anything anyway. So, when I got here this morning, Shunk was pretty much packed up." John pulled a set of keys from his pocket. "He gave me these. He was kinda snotty about it and said something like 'you don't have to count it, it's all there'. And then he left. Oh, sorry, but he didn't tell me to say 'hi' to you. And I almost forgot, he did say something about a few items that were already packed off to some museum."

Dick glanced at Darrel. "Yeah, I know about that." He began walking towards the tomb. "Have you been inside yet?"

"Yes. It's pretty much cleaned out except for the books and the two Gargoyles standing by the inner door."

"Did they open it?"

"No, at least I don't think so. And Darrel says no."

"Let's go see for ourselves," said Dick. "Oh, by the way, where's Shunk now? I didn't see any sign of him or his crew at the other site when I drove in."

Darrel answered. "It seems as though he and Dale had a big falling out just as Shunk was packing up. I guess Shunk told Dale

that he was getting too greedy and from what I overheard, Dale said the same to Shunk. Bottom line, Dale kicked him off his ranch, too."
"Just like that?" asked Dick.
"Yup, just like that."
"So sad to see the bastard gone – gone for good, I hope," replied Dick.

Walking into the outer chamber felt like walking into an empty house with no chairs, no couches, no pictures on the walls, no lamps. There were only the books and the two lone and silent guardians of the inner door which Dick quickly confronted. "Now why did they leave these, I wonder?"
"Darrel says they tried, but they were too heavy," replied John. "He says they were gonna move 'em in a day or two when they got some heavier equipment in here. So when we gonna go to work?"
"Soon as we can."
"Everybody coming back?"
"Yeah, and a couple more undergrads, too. Even Barb and her assistant should be here in a couple of weeks."
John bit his lip thinking about Karen's return and how Margaret might react. "Are we gonna open it soon?"
"Don't know. Might save it for next season. Lots of other stuff to do."
Dick had a last look around. He bent down and picked up a cigarette butt. "Pigs!" he said as he put the butt in his pocket. "Keys?" John handed the lab keys to Dick. "I think Colin and I are going to have a look at the lab. We'll be back later. Does the bunk house look livable?" John nodded yes. "We'll stay there tonight, then. I'll pick up something in town for dinner. Chinese OK with you?"

Back on the road to Sheridan, Colin asked Dick, "What are you going to do with that Darrel guy?"

Dick laughed. "What do you think I should do with him?"

"Get rid of him."

"And why's that?"

"I don't trust him. If he'll spy for you, he's just as likely to spy on you."

"You might well be right. But not just yet. He might come in handy and he might know a few things he hasn't told me about yet. But keep a close eye on him anyway."

By the time Dick and his team re-assembled they were not prepared for the onslaught that followed. The low key so favored by Dick was impossible. The circus master Carl Shunk was gone, but the audience remained and if nothing else, increased. The media was there – they had never left. And the requests to see the wonders of the tomb – if that was what it really was – poured in from every corner of the world – from academics, from museums, from politicians and from just plain ordinary people who nearly always claimed that they were in one way or another related to someone at the dig or knew someone who was of some importance. Or people Colin or Zeke or John had known in grade school – and the girls who had refused to go out with them in high school. And then there were those who had not the slightest training in paleontology or any related field but who were more than willing to work at the site, usually for modest wages or none at all. All wanted to see with their own eyes what they had seen only on television and in print; all clamoring to see what treasures lay behind the inner door.

The decision to let them come or try as best he could to keep them away was not Dick's alone. Margaret owned the ranch now, and everyone knew it. She changed her phone number twice yet it

Einstein's Bones

still rang continuously. Her cell phone was little better. The situation forced John into a decision he thought he would never make – to buy a cell phone, one of those irritating intrusions into private lives and constant distraction when other things - more important things – needed to be done. So he bought two, one for him and one for Margaret, both in his name with the understanding that no calls out would be made to anyone who might in any way be suspected of giving out the number to the madding crowd. He went so far as to drive to Billings to make sure that their phones had out-of-state area codes. But he figured it wouldn't last. And the e-mail. Hell, he just deleted everything.

Both Margaret and Dick made the decisions as to who would see what and when, and at least for the time being, not to charge admission as Shunk had done. Their first decision was that no one would be admitted to the site itself until the inner door was opened. Until then only those artifacts in the lab were to be open to the public which required that the lab be organized and made secure. That took two weeks. By appointment only, the first visitors were academics and politicians, politicians who had not visited the tomb while Carl Shunk had been the master of ceremonies. The Governor of Wyoming, the senators, state legislators, and academics from across North America, from Europe, from Asia. They all came and always their reaction was the same. Awe and wonder – an almost religious experience. As the small groups slowly walked from one exhibit to the next they seldom said a word, their mouths open, but no words coming out. And just like John when he saw the wonders of the tomb for the first time, most felt as if they were intruding into a sacred space, a place where they had no right to be, as if in some small way they were part of the desecration of a holy site. Then there was the sensation that time did not exist or stood still, that the 'hands' that had crafted the exquisite objects had finished their labors only the day before, not sixty odd million years ago. What a wonder – the mortal creatures of the planet Earth. The academics, the politicians, the ordinary people. The hundreds who came twenty at a time, their reactions were all the same.

Another decision had to be made. What of the remainder of the summer? While the lab was the most popular – though not most visited – museum in the world, Dick's team, with several additions continued the work of finding and extracting more of the remains of the Sapienasaurs – leaving the tomb alone. But soon Dick and most of his students would return to the University of Minnesota. With two weeks left, should they open the inner door which the ancient gargoyles still guarded?

Dick would have preferred to have waited, waited for the start of the next season, waited for a time when he could have the entire season to properly examine and care for what treasures might lay sealed behind the inner door, but he too was curious, he too had an almost uncontrollable sense of anticipation. If it were up to him alone he might have waited, but the pressures to see what was on the other side were intense. So, open it he would on the second day of September.

The last night of August, John and Margaret sat and watched TV. John had to admit that he was getting bored with his job at the lab as part-time photographer and tour guide though he was still spending most of his time at the site photographing every new bone that came back into the light of day. When his cell phone rang and Dick was at the other end telling him his decision, John could not conceal his excitement.

"You look like you just won the lottery," said Margaret as John handed her his phone.

"It's Dick. He wants to talk to you."

Einstein's Bones

"What, another problem with some disappointed big shot who didn't get in today?"

"No. Here, talk to him."

Margaret listened. "Yes, that's fine with me. Day after tomorrow?" she said. And then, "Me? You want me to do it? Are you sure about that? Are there going to be a ton of people there? Yeah, just how many?" She listened more. "And TV, too? I'm going to have to think about it. How soon do you have to know?" She handed the phone back to John. "He wants me to open the inner door."

"Fantastic. Who better? It's gonna make you famous."

"But what am I going to wear?" she asked.

"Jesus, your big shot at immortality and that's what you're worried about?"

"I'm serious."

"How about a low cut tank top and really short cut-offs?"

"Like Karen?" she asked.

"Good grief. So just wear some jeans and that red and black flannel shirt I like. You know the one."

The following morning John was at the site photographing what at first glance looked to be a deformed Sapienasaur. Its skull was slightly misshapen and appeared to have been fractured and then healed. Two digits from the left 'hand' were missing. Further, three of its ribs at one time had been broken. Laid upon its breast was another gold medallion of the usual size and shape, but instead of the standard insignia of right angles inside of a triangle in front of a sunburst, this medallion had two crossed what looked like swords, two swords that looked similar to the ones carried by medieval knights. Were these the remains of a warrior? Perhaps. Later, John spent a few minutes checking out camera angles for the big event, watched the National Geographic set up, and watched as the students set up crowd control barriers.

He returned home at 7:30 and was almost immediately asked by Margaret what he thought of the more than half a dozen outfits she had bought that afternoon for the big event. "What do you think of this one?" she asked as she modeled a blue pants suit with a white blouse. "Do you like it?"

"Yeah, it's fine."

"You don't like it, do you?" She stripped down to her bra and panties.

"Now that I do like."

She retrieved a gray blouse, white jacket, and black skirt and modeled that. "So, what do you think of this?"

"Nice."

"You're no help at all." Again she stripped down to her underwear.

"Oh, really nice. I could really get into this."

Her next outfit was a simple light salmon colored dress. "Honey, you know I'm not even close to being any kind of fashion expert. Remember, you're not going to the opera or the inaugural ball. They all look nice, especially on you."

She looked at him with a feigned expression of disgust. "I guess I'll have to ask my sister."

"Hey, the show was just getting good, don't stop now."

The morning of September 2nd was a beautiful morning. The sky was clear, it was seventy degrees, and there was a light wind blowing off the mountains to the west. Margaret arrived wearing blue jeans and a red and black checked flannel shirt. A few of the one hundred invited guests were already present either talking among themselves, with Dick or one of his team, or wandering about the site taking photographs and all anxiously waiting for noon when Margaret would open the inner door.

Dick had made several changes - first for the benefit of the site and also for the guests. First, he had set up barriers around all of the places where there was active digging, enough to keep the guests at a distance, but at the same time not obtrusive enough to keep them from taking pictures. The brush and grasses were cut back, just in case someone unfamiliar with the high plains of Wyoming might step too close to a prairie rattler so common to the area. In front of the tomb more barriers were in place, the kind of crowd restraints one sees at a movie theater. Inside were more of the same. And lest the creature comforts of the guests be forgotten, two large canopies shaded several tables well stocked with coffee, juices, and assorted pastries. Later, a luncheon would be served. Last but not least, Dick ordered extra portable toilets.

By 10:30am, all who had been invited and accepted Dick's invitation were present. Out of professional courtesy, or maybe to rub it in, Dick had invited Carl Shunk knowing he would decline. Among those present were Margaret's sister, Carol, with her husband, numerous politicians, both local and national, local businessmen and friends of the late Paul Newcomb, noted paleontologists from around the globe, and two Hollywood actors – both particular favorites of Margaret. Notably absent were large numbers of the media – the National Geographic having exclusive rights to the day's events - and the one person who had made all of it possible, Paul Newcomb. As for his wasted son Dale, for all his sisters knew, he was sitting at home watching court TV and getting plastered.

"Oh God," whispered Margaret to John moments before they were to enter the tomb. "I'm so nervous I'm afraid I'll wet my pants. Why don't you do it instead?"

John gave her a peck on her cheek. "I had my moment of glory. Now it's your turn. I know how you feel. I felt the same way. Everybody feels the same way. Once everything starts, you'll feel fine. Oh yeah, don't forget to say something brilliant."

They entered the outer chamber followed by Dick, Barbara Allen, Karen and the first twenty of the one hundred guests. Margaret walked up to the inner door and as the lights were turned on, she lightly touched the handle hoping that she would be able to pull it open by herself. At exactly noon, when the reporter from the National Geographic began the broadcast, she instantly forgot her fears and could only wish her father could be there and see with her what lay beyond. She watched as Dick and Barbara pulled away the seal and felt a slight rush of hot, stale air. When they finished she grasped the handle and began to pull, but hesitated and looked back at Dick as if to ask if it was all right for her to go ahead. He nodded and she pulled harder, easily opening the ancient door and then, with a flash light in her right hand, she took her first look.

"What do you see?" asked the reporter.

"I'm not sure at all."

Chapter 23

No, it was definitely not a tomb. With the door fully open, Dick followed Margaret and took a few steps inside, then was followed by the television cameras. What they entered into resembled a small class room – a miniature lecture hall, with permanent seating to the left of the door facing to the right where two simple gray squared blocks stood on the floor - one large, about a meter in height and the other a third of that and both about twenty centimeters on a side. Three of the walls of the room were the same gray shade that dominated everything. At first glance the back wall – about one meter behind the third and last row of seating, looked solid black. No one ventured in more than those first few steps.

John was disappointed – hell, he was more than disappointed, just as he figured everyone else was. He had read Howard Carter's *The Tomb of Tutankhamen* and expected something similar to what Carter had seen in Tut's sepulcher – shrines covered in gold concealing more shrines and then, finally the king's nested coffins, the last made of solid gold. And all around it more exquisite treasures – some kind of treasures anyway. But what was this? Nothing more than some meeting room for the long vanished staff of a museum? For the moment, John forgot about how important and revolutionary what had been found up to this point had been.

Along with Margaret, John left what he had heretofore referred to as a tomb to make way for others to have their disappointing looks inside. "Well, shit," John said as they made their way outside to the waiting tables. "I sure don't feel like drinking any of that champagne now." He grabbed two beers from a tub full of ice and handed one to Margaret. "All that hype, and for what? I almost wish we had left it for the Skunk and let him be the one to make a fool of himself."

"You really should hear yourself talking," she shot back. "You guys make the greatest discovery of all time, get yourselves famous and now you have the nerve to get distraught just because you didn't find something even more impressive? Just what the heck did you want? I'm fine with it and I'm the one who opened the door to what you seem to think is a big nothing. If anyone's got a right to feel let down or embarrassed it's me, not you. And I feel just fine. Can't you be satisfied with what you've already found?"

John sat and contemplated what he considered a big failure. "I'm sorry, you're right. I was just expecting so much more. Kinda like when I was in high school and wanted a car for graduation and all I got was a crummy pen and pencil set. Well, it really was a nice set and I still have it which is more than I can say for any car I might have gotten."

A few minutes later they were joined by two more beer drinkers, Karen and Zeke. John did not notice Margaret's disapproving look as Karen sat next to him and held his upper arm. But then he hardly noticed Karen's touching him either. "Well, what do you think, Mr. Steiner? Bummer, huh? Disappointed?" John raised the bottle, knocked back his beer and forced out a belch. "Yeah, me too," she said. "But then on the bright side it looks like we've got a lot less work to do than we thought we would. And hey, at least all those . . ," she looked around and lowered her voice, "all those assholes from the press might leave us alone."

"I suppose you could say that," replied John.

"You know," she continued slowly, "it doesn't make all that much sense. There's got to be more to it. A lot more. If it was just some kind of meeting room or class room, why go to all the trouble of sealing it? And why the two goons guarding the door? Maybe there's something in those blocks on the floor or something under them. Just got to be something more to it." Karen spied one of the Hollywood actors who had been invited. "Oh hot, I just have to meet him." She rose. "Now don't get too jealous."

As Margaret turned to speak, John feared some scathing comment about Karen, some renewal of her suspicions. "You know, I think she's right. Think about it. Why all the fuss with the seals and the statues? When is Dick going to really get in there?"

"I overheard him say something about waiting till everybody cleared out, or tomorrow morning. But I suspect if the crowd clears out quick, he might go in later this afternoon or evening. I guess I better check with him. Hungry?" John got up and brought back two plates and two more beers. "They sure didn't interview you for very long."

"It was long enough for me," she replied.

Late that afternoon, with all of the food eaten and most of the alcohol drunk, all of the guests were gone. At 5:30, Dick called a short meeting. After expressing some disappointment with their recent discovery, he reminded his team that there was still a lot of work to do, both in the field and in the lab. In the morning, they'd go in to the lecture room for a closer look.

Back home, Margaret made a batch of Manhattans. "Here," she said as she handed him a double. "You'll feel better."

"Oh, I'm fine. Don't worry about it. How about I put a couple of steaks on the grill? We'll make like we found all the treasures in the world." He went to the bookshelf, found his CD of Beethoven's 7th, and loaded it in the player. "And after dinner I'll make love to you like I never have before."

"You mean you're going to get it right this time?"

"Can't exactly say that, but I'm gonna keep trying until I do."

"As a teacher, you know, I'm going to make you do it untill you get it right, no matter how many times it takes," she replied with a laugh.

The next morning brought a gentle rain and with it a fresh smell and a sense of renewal. It also brought muck and the 'mud rule", for which John kept a clean pair of shoes in his truck.

There was no fanfare, no lights and cameras, no ceremonies, no Grand March from *Aida* playing in the back of John's mind as he followed Dick into the inner chamber the morning of September 3rd. At first there were just Dick and John, Karen and Colin casually strolling in for a look around. Facing the two square objects near the right wall were twenty four seats in three tiers. Dick was the first to try one out. "Ouch. If you've got a bad back, this won't help one bit," he said as he vainly squirmed to find a comfortable position. John and the others followed, gently dropping into the cold, hard seats.

"With a little padding these might not be all that bad," said Colin.

"Old Einstein must have had one hell of a hard ass," added Karen. "I hope I can get out of this thing." She wiggled her hip suggestively. "Help me get out of this, will you John?"

"It's not all that difficult." But he gave her his hand anyway, regretting it as she conveniently lost her balance and fell into him chest first. She said nothing, but her eyes told John that she was still very much available.

Dick rose and the four of them went to the back wall. What yesterday from the entrance appeared to be a solid black mass was in fact made up of thousands of individual wafer like objects stored edgewise. Dick put on a pair of cotton gloves and pulled one out. "Fascinating," he said as he slowly turned it over in his hands. It was black, square, about eight centimeters on a side and no more than a centimeter thick – about the size of a thin piece of toast. On one side, three centimeters from the edge, was a shallow slot about five millimeters in width. The other side was perfectly flat. On its edge were more of the same numbers which had been found on the books. "I think we've got something very important here, but I'll be damned if I know what."

"Like some kind of computer chip, maybe?" asked Colin.

Dick carefully returned it to its proper place. The others could almost hear him thinking. He slowly stepped back and scanned the wall. "Damn," he whispered. "Let's take a look at those blocks."

The larger of the two, the one about a meter high, looked as though it might have served as a lectern had the Sapienasaurs been a little shorter. But it had to be something else. It was encased in a close fitting shroud which was made from the same ubiquitous material that so much else was made from. The top was not as flat as first thought. There were the outlines of two squares, the same shape and size as the mysterious objects on the back wall. By contrast, there were no irregularities on the smaller block which was also covered.

"Let's see what's under there," said Dick.

Dick put his cotton gloves back on and Colin did the same. Together, they pushed up on the sides. "Slippery little devil," said Dick. "Karen, go back to my trailer. I've got a box of rubber surgical gloves next to my computer."

"Yes boss."

Five minutes later she returned with the box along with all of the rest of Dick's team. Dick and Colin donned the gloves. "God, I hate these things. Ready?" said Dick.

Four hands slowly pushed up on the shroud. The closeness of the fit and the partial vacuum created made for slow going. It

Einstein's Bones

took ten minutes to reveal a solid black object perfectly smooth on the sides, with no writing or any other marks, except on the top, on which had been placed two of the same kind of squares found on the back wall. On the edges, they were marked " I " and " V ". "Number one and number two," said Karen. Hidden under number two was a slot with a ridge which exactly matched the slots on the squares.

"This ain't no ordinary lecture room," said John.

"No shit," said Josh. "What ya think, boss? Should we stick one in and see what happens? There's only one way to put 'em in, and what with the numbers, they want us to put that one in first."

"Are we gonna?" asked Zeke.

"Let's wait," replied Dick. "Let's take a look at that other block first." He and Colin put on a fresh set of rubber gloves. This time the shroud came off quickly. The smaller block looked much the same as its larger companion with the same slot on top, but with no squares on top of it. But on one side, about a third of the way down and recessed about three centimeters was a square knob, about two centimeters on each side. Below that was a rectangular opening approximately 11x20 centimeters and four centimeters deep containing a very ordinary looking crank with a socket which looked a perfect fit for the square knob above it. And if there was any doubt as to which way the crank was to be turned, a circular arrow surrounding the knob indicated clock-wise.

There was nothing else in the small auditorium. No statues, no decorations of any kind, only the seats, the black chips on the back wall, and the two black blocks with slots on their tops.

"A computer with a zillion terabytes. That's what it is," announced Mike. He went to the back wall and re-examined the computer chips. "You've got number one and two there, and here's number three," he said pointing to the chip in the upper left hand corner of the wall. "What are we waiting for? Put number one in the slot and see what happens."

"Hold your horses, Mike," advised Dick. "Before we do anything I think it's best we find those boys from the Geographic. They're back in town and probably tipping back a few. Anyway, it's not going to help our funding if we go ahead without them. John, round them up when you go back to town tonight, will you?"

"They won't be hard to find. I know where they like to hang out. I hope this thing – what ever it is – still works. I don't want to let them down again."

"Sure it'll work. Have faith. After only sixty million years, why wouldn't it? But on the off chance that it does – well, I don't know what. Even if it doesn't, it's still fantastic. In the meantime, we've got the rest of the day to get some work done," Dick said as he led the team out.

John still enjoyed watching Karen work – not so much for her professional abilities, but for the way she moved, the way she smelled even from a distance, and the way her body presented a picture of raw sexuality. On the other hand, he hoped that she had gotten the message that nothing was going to happen between the two of them. As he watched, he heard a voice behind him.

"Margaret's not going to like that – the way you're looking at her," warned Colin, "but if you want to do her, just fuck her and get it over with and out of your system. It's no secret she's been dripping for you all summer. You know you want to do her."

"Sometimes, but you forget who I've been living with all summer? The owner, maybe?"

"So who's gonna tell her?"

"Somebody would."

"And screw all of this up?" said Colin. "Ah come on. I don't think so."

"Well why don't you take care of her?"

"Oh, I surely would if I surely could. I get the big wood every time she walks by. It's a shame you're not taking advantage of that fine, fine stuff."

"Well," said John as he walked away, "I'll let you know just how fine - fine it is if I ever do."

John returned to town earlier than usual. First, as it would be his last night with Margaret for a while, he wanted to take her to dinner. Second, he had to round up the crew from the National Geographic. They wouldn't be too hard to find. The chances of their being at the hotel were slim, but John had spent enough off time with them to know where they were likely to be in the early hours of the evening, especially if there was nothing important on tomorrow's plate. His first stop was the Mint. John was mildly surprised that they were not at their favorite watering hole. He walked across the street to the Rainbow. Sitting at the bar were Howard Blood, the man who had held the microphone the day before and his videographer, Ben Alvord.

"So why aren't you guys at the Mint? They kick your sorry asses out?" John asked as he took a seat next to them.

"Get this boy a – a red beer, right?" John nodded. "Well," said Howard, "variety is the spice of life. We are gonna have us a grand old time tonight. Why don't you come along for the ride?"

"Nope, can't tonight. Taking Margaret out. Where's the rest of your crew?"

"Hell if I know. Come on, call the old lady and tell her something important came up and you just gotta take care of it."

John thanked the bartender for the beer. "Well, as a matter of fact, some thing did come up."

"Yeah, what? Ya find some new secret chamber with all kinds of goodies?"

"Something like that. I would suggest that you boys don't get too shit-faced so you can get back to the site real early tomorrow morning, or you might miss it."

"Miss what?"

"Can't tell you any more here. Just get that crew of yours together, sober 'em up, and be there bright and early."

"You're not shittin' me are you?"

"Have I ever?" John finished his beer. "Be there or the Geographic's gonna have you lookin' for a new job." John got off his stool. "See you tomorrow – early."

For the evening out, Margaret made use of one of her new outfits. "God, you look so beautiful," John said as Margaret handed him his favorite drink.

"How'd things go today?" she asked. "Everybody recovered from the big let-down?"

"Yup. I'll tell ya all about it after I get cleaned up. What time did you say you wanted to be at that steak house?"

"In about an hour."

John put down his drink. "I think I'll take that shower now. You got anything going on tomorrow? Can you come out to the ranch in the morning?"

"School starts day after tomorrow, and I have some teachers' meetings I'm supposed to go to, but I think I can get out of them if it's really that important. Is it?"

"I think so. I'll tell you after I'm all cleaned up. Why don't you join me, and I'll tell you while we wash each other."

"John! I'm not getting all undone. Go take your shower."

"Well, I tried."

After standing under the hot water and watching the day's dirt swirl down the drain, John stepped out and looked around.

"Margaret. I need a towel." She brought in a freshly washed towel and snapped him on his backside. "Ouch."

"Now get your ass moving and tell me what's going on," she teased.

Wasting little time, he dried off, dressed, returned to his drink which Margaret had topped off, and proceeded to tell her what had happened that day, excluding of course his conversation with Colin.

"I knew it. Didn't I tell you there'd be something more to it," she said. Yes, I do want to be there. Any ideas at all what it is?"

"Not really. Mikie thinks it's some kind of computer. Could be. He very well could be right – for once. But then, really the chances of it working are about nil anyway, so the chances of finding out are next to zip. You think your sis would want to be there? She seems a lot less upset and open minded about all this lately, especially after what your brother did."

"I'll give her a call right now." Margaret reached in her purse and took out her cell phone. Carol did want to be there and so did her husband. She made another call to her school's principal. "There, done," she said after she hung up. "All taken care of."

They sat back and relaxed on the couch. "You know, I think your sister might be changing her mind about some things. For a while I got the impression that she thought we were all in league with the devil. And now she wants to be there. We might just make an evolutionist out of her yet."

"Maybe you're right. I was talking with her before you came home, mostly girl talk, but she did say something like 'I'll still believe in God, regardless'."

"Nobody's telling her not to. If the Pope can believe in evolution, so can she."

Einstein's Bones

John and Margaret arrived at the restaurant, were quickly seated, ordered a bottle of wine to go with their prime rib, and enjoyed their meal – until John spotted a familiar face walk in. "What the hell is he doing back here? He was supposed to be long gone, back in his cage at UW." It was Carl Shunk.

Einstein's Bones

Chapter 24

Dick wasn't concerned when he learned from John the following morning that Shunk was back. "Hell, I suppose he's doing some clean-up work on Dale's place. Who knows? Forget about him. I really don't care what he's doing."

With the lights and cameras in place, Dick and his team filed into the lecture room which now contained a supply of pillows. John handed Margaret one. "You're gonna need this," he said as they took seats together in the second row.

With hot lights blazing, Dick strode to the lectern and took chip number one in his gloved hand. He looked it over for a moment and then held it over the slot. "Everybody ready?"

"A video game, that's what it is," quipped Mike as he consumed a handful of chips.

Dick rolled his eyes. "Got to be one in every crowd. Well, if there are no other asinine comments, let's see what – if anything – happens." As he spoke he inserted the black square into the slot. Halfway in, he felt it seat firmly. Nothing – and then almost magically a faint glimmering appeared in front of the lectern.

"Douse the lights," someone shouted.

And then there it was in front of them – an image, almost life-like, almost real, almost as if it could be reached for and touched and then perhaps return the touch, an image of a creature unseen by any man or any other set of eyes for sixty five million years. "Jesus Christ," said John. "My God," said someone else and yet another said, "Holy shit." Everyone was saying something, something to express their amazement and wonder, until Dick commanded silence. Even Mike stopped eating his chips. In the darkened and now silent room those first glimmerings were transformed into a

Einstein's Bones

nearly concrete holographic projection, a full-size likeness of a Sapienasaur. As expected from the fossilized remains it was about the height of an average man, only slightly shorter than the awed professor of paleontology who stood behind it. Its bare skin was a mottled yellowish brown with no hair and not a hint of feathers, looking exactly like the gargoyles who stood on guard outside the room, a cross between a man and a reptile with eyes facing forward and a mildly protruding snout with two small holes for nostrils. Hanging from its small, pointed, and lobe-less ears were two beautiful earrings, unlike any they had previously excavated. From its narrow shoulders and extending half way down its slightly scaly legs hung a loose fitting white tunic with stripes of green, purple, and orange. Its arms were bare.

"No sense of style at all," said Mike.

"Shut up."

Einstein's cousin – or was it Einstein himself - was not the only image being projected into the room. Einstein was facing the image of another lectern, or rather another holographic projector which was itself projecting another image, an image which slowly began to fade out. When it did, the Sapienasaur in the striped tunic pulled a chip from the projector and inserted it into the slot in the top of a smaller block, the same kind of block that in the lecture room contained the crank and knob. The Sapienasaur then removed a crank from the side of the image of the block, coupled it to the square knob, and gave it twenty clock-wise turns, each turn taking about two seconds. When the Sapienasaur finished, it removed the chip from the smaller block and reinserted it into the larger. The holograph now re-appeared, much brighter than before. A projector and a re-charger.

Einstein's Bones

A few seconds after the Sapienasaur had made his presentation, his image went dark. Before any of the stunned audience could react, the image of another Sapienasaur appeared, this time by himself and directly facing his awestruck audience. John suppressed the urge to reach out and touch him; he looked so alive and as real as anyone else in the room.

The creature stood for a few seconds with his arms by his side and then slowly raised one arm with a closed fist. He extended one digit. That action was accompanied by the first sounds to be uttered by him in sixty five million years. It was high pitched and somewhat grating to the human ear. As John heard it, he felt like a knife had been thrust into his chest, not only by the force of the sound itself, but also by the thrill of hearing the speaker articulate it.

The word spoken sounded like a high pitched 'EICH'. As the Sapienasaur spoke the word, the symbol for the number 'one' appeared to his right. To his left, there materialized two other symbols. The Sapienasaur then extended a second digit which was accompanied by another high pitched word which sounded like 'ISHTOC'. At the same time, the symbol for the number 'two' was projected to his right and three symbols were projected to his left. This was followed by the raising of a third digit, with the accompanying sounds and images.

As he raised a forth digit, the image faded out, leaving the audience in semi-darkness for what seemed an eternity. Everyone was too lost in his own thoughts to perform the obvious function.

Finally, in the still silent room, Dick got up from his seat and said just, "Lights." He went to the projector, removed the chip, and then placed it in the smaller recharging unit. After affixing the crank he attempted to turn it with one hand just as the Sapienasaur had done, and then he tried with both. With two hands on the handle it began to turn, but not nearly at the rate as had been seen in the short

Einstein's Bones

demonstration. He called for Zeke's assistance, and the two of them were able to turn it at nearly the required rate.

Dick was no weakling. John had arm wrestled him a few times and knew. Either the recharge unit was stiff from countless millennia of disuse, or the previous owners were incredibly strong. After they gave the chip the required twenty turns, they returned the chip to the projector.

The lecture resumed just slightly back from where it had left off, with the lecturer raising his forth digit. The numbers five, six, seven, and eight were all demonstrated using the Sapienasaur's digits. Several of the words spoken to accompany the numbers were less like words and more like whistles and chirps. Instead of the sounds being able to be represented by the letters of the Roman alphabet, they would more easily have been represented by musical notation.

After the number eight, which was the limit of the number of digits that the creature possessed, he continued with his counting using projections of miniatures of his fellow beings. As he spoke the word for nine, eight of his small companions appeared in one row to his right with one underneath. Below that were the symbols for the number nine. Again, the letters for the word nine materialized to his left. 'Ten' followed the same pattern – a row of eight figures above a row of two which was above the symbols for the number ten. Once again, the Sapienasaur's letters for the word 'ten' appeared to his left.

He continued counting. Eleven, twelve, and so on until he reached the number sixty four. At that point, he crossed his arms over his chest, made a slight bow with his head as if to say that he was finished, and the holograph quickly faded out.

Einstein's Bones

The audience sat for a moment in silence and the lights were turned back on. "Did you guys get that on tape?" Dick asked the crew from the Geographic.

They checked their equipment. "Got it," replied Howard. "Wish we had been live."

Everyone understood what they had just witnessed - lesson number one in how to speak dinosaur. And what could have been a better way to begin than to start off with mathematics, the most universal of all languages.

"Maybe we ought to do it again from the start. This time with the lights out when you put the chip in," suggested Howard.

Dick returned the chip to the charger. "I hope it works more than once." With the lights out from the start, they saw the show for a second time, and this time without any interruption.

"Well, what the hell can you say?" asked Zeke, rubbing his hands over his face as the lights were turned back on. "Sixty five million years and it still works. Unfucking believable. Oops, sorry. You didn't tape that, did you? And the wall back there is just full of those things. We all thought this was some kinda big nothing. Christ, were we ever wrong. It's impossible to comprehend just how important, how beyond belief this all is. And we haven't even scratched the surface. All those questions we thought we'd never be able to answer, not even make a good guess at. It's all right here and God knows what else. We might have to start thinking about a new field to work in, at least when it comes to dinosaurs. Just unfucking believable. Oh, sorry again."

"I'm not going to worry about that," replied Jeff Basarus. "So do we take a look at the other one?"

"If you folks don't mind waiting," replied Howard, "much as we'd all like to see it now, I want to give Washington a call. No doubt they'll want to do a live, probably tomorrow night. Can you wait, Dick?"

To the accompaniment of loud groans, Dick agreed. "But if they don't go tomorrow night, I'm going to go ahead without them."

"Recovering from her excitement, Margaret spoke up. "I'd like to invite a few guests – no more than we have seating for here – if that's all right with you, Dick."

"It's your call – your ranch. How could I refuse? How can we ever thank you enough?"

She was slightly embarrassed. "No, thank you."

"We're going to have to get some language experts in here," suggested Lani Katiama.

"Right," replied Dick. "We'll need them soon, very soon." He glanced at the back wall. "When they come, they're going to have their work cut out for them."

"And all those books, too," added Mike. "All the secrets they must have. Just like the Krell."

"The Krell?" Margaret asked John in a whisper.

"You know. I told you about that. Mikie's big into sci-fi movies."

"Mr. Mike," replied Dick, "for once in your life you might be right. Until tomorrow night, then."

Six o'clock found Carl Shunk sitting at the bar drinking a double bourbon, his third. A buzzing in his pocket diverted his attention from his drink. "What the fuck is that," he muttered to himself as he tried to figure out where the buzzing was coming from. "Oh," he said as he realized it was an incoming call. He fumbled in his pocket and pulled out his cell phone. On the other end was a familiar voice. "Well, what ya got for me?" he asked his caller.

"I'm pretty sure I can nail him."

"Nail who? Oh yeah, him. You sure about that?"

"She sure wants to fuck him, and I know he wants to do her. Hell, everybody here wants to do her. She told me she almost got him twice already, but somebody's always got in the way, or he acted like he was too fucking good for her. So she's real pissed and wants to see him get his - and she can't stand his prissy bitch girlfriend anyway."

"Does she know why you're doing this?"

"No. She thinks I get off watching other people do it."

"Do ya?"

"So, what's in this for me?"

"I told ya already. Plenty. And you're sure it'll get Dish – Dick's ass out of there? She won't forgive him or some crap like that? He got any idea what you two are up to?" said Shunk.

"No. We've been real buddy buddy."

"Ok. Just fuckin' do it." Shunk folded his phone. "Hey, bartender, hit me again."

Dick had conveniently squirreled away a case of champagne, champagne he had planned to empty when all of the 'who's who' were celebrating the treasures behind the inner door. After the big flop, he had thought better. It now was the choice of drink for a smaller, but much happier celebration. There was a case of steaks, too. By six, both the champagne and steaks were gone.

"Are you OK to drive home?" John asked Margaret.

"I didn't drink anywhere near what you did. Remember, tomorrow's the first day of school and there's nothing worse than a classroom full of screaming kids when you have a hangover."

They walked to her Suburban. "What a day," he said as they embraced. "Hard to imagine one better."

"I can," she replied.

Her remark went over John's slightly fuzzy head. "I do love you, you know that, don't you?"

"Yes," she replied, "I do. Now don't do anything you'll regret tonight like lose all your money at cards."

"What, me play cards for money? No, of course I wouldn't do that." He kissed her softly. "Drive safely."

She entered her Suburban and turned the key, said, "I love you too," and drove away.

John walked back to the bunkhouse. "Cards?" someone asked him. "Sure," he replied.

It was the usual crowd, just the boys and, as more often than not, without the presence of the boss. Stakes were low and the beer was plentiful. An hour from midnight, John wasn't sure if he was ahead or behind, but either way it wasn't by much. After exhausting talk about their work, the conversation turned to the second most popular subject. "So, how's your sex life these days, Mikie? You getting' anywhere with your sweet little honey, Kathy?" asked Josh.

"I'm doing OK," he replied.

"So you mean you got your new Playboy?" chided Jeff.

"Just shut up."

"So you did, huh? Kathy's gonna be jealous."

"Yeah, like any of you guys are doing any better," said Mike.

"If you can't get into your English sweetie's pants, what about Karen? Oh, I'll just bet she'd have you hurtin' for a week. Lots of nice stuff in town, too. I keep hearing they're all hot for you. Ya just gotta keep those girls happy you know," said Josh.

"Leave him alone, will ya," said John. "Don't you guys ever get tired of riding him? I bet a buck."

"Speaking of riding, are you doing Karen yet?" asked Colin.

John wrinkled the corner of his mouth. "It's a buck to you, Zeke. Oh my, I do have to admit she is one fine looking lady."

"The whole camp's waiting for you to bang her," said Colin.

"How the hell does that shit get around, anyway? Everybody forget I'm taken?"

"Yeah," said Zeke, "but the way she's been panting after you. Only a queer could resist her, and nobody thinks you're one of them. Just a matter of time till you slip her the big wood. She'll thank ya."

"And you guys?" John replied. "How many of you have been with her. Come on, raise your hands. Well, looks like I'm playing with a bunch of fruits. Oh well, as long as your money's green."

"Really, so why haven't you done her?" asked Colin. "It could be set up you know and your Margaret wouldn't be any the wiser."

"Shit," replied John. "You pimping for her or what? Sure go ahead. Do what ever makes you happy. I don't care. What ever it takes to get you to shut up."

"You'll make her one happy lady."

"Whatever. Now can we get back to cards?"

The supply of chips and cold beer exhausted, the game ended two hours later. John counted his money. "Oh boy," he declared, "ain't I the big winner. Two whole bucks ahead." He took the last swallow of his beer and left the bunkhouse for one last call of nature. Nearly finished, he was joined by Mike.

"Thanks John."

"For what?"

"For getting them off my back."

"No problem."

"You really gonna do Karen?" asked Mike. "They all think you will."

Einstein's Bones

"Are you kidding? What a bunch of idiots."

Einstein's Bones

Chapter 25

"Ah, good morning, sunshine - glorious," John exclaimed as he stepped outside to greet the new day. He looked to the southeast and watched a small herd of antelope as they grazed on a ridge where he had often seen them and where he and Charlie had hunted them in the past. But he wasn't hunting now or thinking about it all that much as he watched them peacefully eat their morning meal. "Just beautiful."

"What's beautiful?" asked Mike who had just joined him.

"Look over yonder and behold the wonders of nature."

"All I see is a bunch of deer."

"Mikie, Mikie, Mikie. Thems is antelope, podner. You ain't from around these here parts, are you stranger? So Mike, where are you from, anyway? If you told me before, I forgot."

"Portland."

"Oregon or Maine?"

"Oregon."

"Nice town, I suppose. Never been there. Look at that." Below the herd, a lone coyote loped up the ridge toward the herd. "Watch this. Not something you're ever gonna see in Portland – Oregon." The coyote continued his approach toward his unconcerned potential prey. Thirty yards from his quarry, the coyote broke into a dead run, scattering the much faster antelope. Seconds later, the coyote gave up the hopeless chase.

"What was that all about?" asked Mike.

"I spose old Mr. Coyote was either trying to figure out if any of them might be sick, lame, or lazy, or maybe he was just havin' him a little fun."

"You ever shoot one?"

Einstein's Bones

"A coyote? No. If ya can't eat 'em, what's the point. Let's go get us some grub."

There was an air of anticipation in the camp that morning, but little work was being done. A little digging here and a little chipping there, as if no one wanted to soil their clothes before the live broadcast. John looked about for something different to do, something to get his mind away from the night's show. He approached Lani and Kathy who were working on a grave, but not very intently.

"You gals look bored," said John as he sat down and pointed one of his cameras at them. "I haven't gotten enough pictures of the two of you yet, and you know how the Geographic likes pictures of pretty girls. How about you making like you're really hard at it?" They changed gears and did the best they could. "That's more like it. Cut the smiles, you're supposed to be serious. Now stop laughing."

"Do you mind if I ask you something personal?" said Lani.

"Go ahead, but I won't guarantee an answer."

"How are you and Margaret doing?"

"Fine. Why?"

"Karen says a lot of things," said Lani.

"Does she now? About what?"

"About how she's going to break the two of you up."

"Now why would she want to do that?"

"You don't understand much about women, do you?"

"Not one damn thing."

"She wants to do it because she can," replied Lani. "She's like that. And because she's angry with you. She told Kathy she was going to get you in big trouble."

"How?" asked John.

Einstein's Bones

"Telling us all how she was going to sleep with you," said Kathy.

"Really," laughed John. "But . . . .," he said, catching himself before he told them of his surprise that Karen hadn't already informed them that long ago she had.

"That's what she said."

"Guess I'll have to keep the bunkhouse locked up at night," said John. "You're making this up, aren't you?"

"No, it's the truth. Be careful. Maybe nobody's said it before, but we all think you and Margaret make a nice couple, and Kathy here, Miss English Match-maker – Miss Emma, thinks the two of you should get married."

John looked at Kathy and smiled. "You think, huh? Well, I don't know about that. I've tried it once already and found out I'm not very good at it." John moved to his left to catch the backlighting on Kathy's hair. "Hold it. Perfect. I'm getting good at this. Course, it helps when ya have beautiful women to work with. You two ever think about posing for Playboy? Anyway, thanks for your concern. But not to worry, I can take care of myself." He took a few more photos. "I'm gonna send these off to my buddy Heff soon as I can. Thanks again," and he moved on to photograph Barbara as she was writing field notes.

Margaret and her sister, along with a few friends arrived at 4:00pm, an hour before the originally scheduled broadcast time. "How'd your first day back teaching go?" John asked Margaret.

"All the kids could talk about was the dinosaurs. Do you think maybe you and Dick could come to class some time and talk to them? Maybe bring some of the things you have found and show some of your pictures?"

"I'd love to. Can we make out in class?" She frowned. "Hold hands? OK, just kidding. I think Dick will come to your

Einstein's Bones

school if he can, but he's planning to leave here pretty soon, so you best ask him quick. I hope you didn't rush out here. They pushed the time back an hour."

"Good," she replied, "now I'll have more time to show my friends around."

In the fifth wheel trailer, the trailer which served as the women's dormitory, their home away from home, sat Karen, and across from her, Colin.

"You sure he'll show?" asked Karen.

"Sure I'm sure. That's what he said."

"What exactly did he say?"

"I don't remember exactly, just that I could go ahead and set it all up."

"Why you? Did he say why he wanted you to do it? Why hasn't he said anything about it to me?"

"I don't know. What am I, some kind of fucking mind reader? Maybe he's afraid somebody will start talking if they see you two together. I don't know. Maybe it's some kind of game with him. Like I said, he wants me to set it up. What's the fucking problem? You'll have your little fun, and you can do with Johnny boy whatever you want. So tomorrow night, or the night after when you're staying in town you can have your little revenge."

"And you?"

"It's never bothered me being the second one at a party. You will keep your word, won't you?"

"If I said I would, I will, much as I'm not looking forward to it."

"Who knows, babe, I might just surprise you. I've been saving it up for a long time."

"That's a relief. You'll get it over faster."

"No, I don't think so," replied Colin.
"What ever, Superman. Remember, he doesn't show and you go home with blue balls."
"He'll be there, and I'll be there right after."
"I can hardly control myself," she said with distain.

The audience took their seats – and pillows – in the lecture room ten minutes before air-time. At 6:00pm the broadcast began and moments later the lights were lowered for a repeat showing of the first disk – accompanied by a few screams from the first time viewers when the Sapienasaur made his appearance. When it finished, there was a pause for an interview with Dick and then a commercial break.
I always wondered what they did during a commercial break like on the Tonight Show," said Margaret above the buzz of the audience.
"That's when they talk dirty," replied John. He looked around the room, noting the expressions on the faces of Margaret's guests. "They sure all look like they've just seen a ghost. Then I guess they have. I wonder how many wet their pants."
"John," Margaret scolded. She took a look around for herself. "That's odd."
"What?"
"Karen sitting with Colin. I thought you told me she didn't have any time for him." John started to turn towards them. "Don't" snapped Margaret. "I don't like the way she's looking at us."
"Forget it. Hey, here we go," he replied as Dick stood at the ready with disk number two.
Disk two picked up where the first disk had left off. The Sapienasaur, now nicknamed 'Mr. Rogers' stood facing the audience. He – or was it a she, they had no idea – began by

Einstein's Bones

reiterating the number sixty four, followed by sixty five. He then skipped ahead to seventy two, followed by seventy three, then eighty, then eighty eight, ninety six, one hundred four, 112, then 120, to 128. After 129, he skipped ahead to 192, then 193, 256, 320, until he got to the number 512. Then he faded. After a brief pause to recharge the chip, Mr. Rogers proceeded with something more challenging. John thought to himself that if the audience didn't get it by now, they never would.

It was a lesson in addition. Again using his digits as tools for demonstration accompanied by the appropriate symbols, he spoke something sounding vaguely like "Eich in eich eng ishtoi". More than one in the audience could be heard to say, "One plus one equals two." The plus sign was a dash with an ascending tail, like an "L" turned 90 degrees counter clockwise. The equal sign was a simple dash. Then one plus two equals three, until Mr. Rogers reached eight plus eight equals sixteen.

Next on the program for the hopelessly challenged in math was a quick lesson in subtraction starting with two minus one equals one. The minus symbol was an "L" rotated 90 clockwise. Again several examples were given such as five minus two equals three. So far, so good. Everyone was paying attention and following along. Of course someone just had to say, "I wish he'd take this a bit slower, I'm not sure I'm getting all this," followed by a good laugh.

The last lessons, all in base eight, were multiplication and division. At the end of the sixteen minute disk, Mr. Rogers once again crossed his arms, made a slight bow, and then faded out.

"Let's get out of here," said John as the lights were turned back on. "Unless of course, you want to get pestered by Mr. Blood and his crew."

"No, I've had more than my share of that," responded Margaret. She looked at her friends who were still in a mild state of shock. "But I can't just leave them here." She rose and spoke to one of them. "Are you OK?" she asked the wide-eyed woman directly behind her.

The woman took a moment to reply, slowly closing her mouth that had been open ever since 'Mr. Rogers' first appeared to her. "My God, oh my God. I don't think I was ever so scared or ever so thrilled in all my life. I thought that thing was going to jump right into my lap." She looked down at her right hand which was still tightly gripping her husband's left. "I just never . . . it's so hard to believe." She tugged at her husband. "Honey, I need to get some air."

She and her husband rose and walked into the fresh air, followed by Margaret, John, and her other guests. As Margaret's friends regained their composure, John gave Margaret a nudge and pointed to the back of the pants of the husband of the woman Margaret had spoken to. Margaret giggled softly. "Yes, I see that."

"I figured some one would wet their pants," John sniggered. "Oh, shit, here comes Blood. Run for your life."

The reporter from the Geographic ignored Margaret and John and headed instead for her guests who actually seemed pleased by the attention and what would probably be the only chance they would ever have to appear on national television. Margaret gave them a little wave of her hand as if to say that she would be back with them soon.

Alone with John, Margaret turned to him with a serious look on her face. "What are you going to do once this is all over? What about us? And don't tell me you don't want to talk about it."

"Do we have to? Right now?"

"Yes, now."

Einstein's Bones

"You know I'm not leaving with all the others when they go back to the university. I'm gonna keep working at the lab. There's no end to the work I'm gonna have to do."

"Do you really love me?" she asked.

"You know I do."

"And what do two people do when they love each other? They make some kind of commitment."

"Darling, we've been through all this before."

"No, we haven't," she said with a touch of irritation. "You never really want to talk about it."

"Come on now. I tell you I love you, we share the same bed. Have I ever done anything wrong? Don't I make you happy?"

"You know that's not enough. What are you afraid of? Afraid of hurting me? Is that your excuse? More like afraid of hurting yourself, I think. I'm not asking you to marry me. God forbid I should do that and you should go through all that again. Poor you. What I'm asking you, what I need to know is, is there going to be a future for us or are you just going to pack up one day and be on your merry way?"

"Ah Christ," he replied. "We just get through with the most wonderful night in the whole history of the world and now you want me to give you some kind of commitment. Why now? Can't we just wait and see what happens and be sure?"

"Maybe you can wait. I won't. When you make up your mind let me know, but you better not wait long." She turned and walked away.

"What the hell was that all about?" said John to himself as he watched Margaret rejoin her friends. "Shit," he said as he walked towards the bunk house and a stiff drink.

"Mind if I join you?" asked Colin who entered the bunk house ten minutes later.

Einstein's Bones

"No, don't mind at all."

Colin went to the sink and grabbed a glass.

"Get some more ice too, will ya," said John.

Colin sat down and filled his glass with bourbon. "She didn't look too happy."

"Who?" said John as he motioned to Colin to refresh his glass.

"Margaret. Something happen?"

"You might say that, but I'll be damned if I know what or why."

"Women. They'll do it to you every time. So what did happen?"

"Just drink your drink and shut up."

"I took care of it for you," said Colin.

"Took care of what?"

"You know – Karen. I got it all fixed for tomorrow night, nine o'clock. All ya gotta do is be there. You know her room number?"

"Nope."

"Room 227. The door will be unlocked. Just walk right in. Oh man does she have the fucking hots for you. Make you forget all your troubles with Margaret."

"Just show up, huh?" John refilled their glasses. "That's mighty swell of ya. Sure, why not." John got up from the table with his drink in his hand and went in search of Margaret. She was gone.

Einstein's Bones

Chapter 26

John was up and outside the bunkhouse early the next morning, feeling nowhere as enthusiastic as he had felt the morning before – the result of an excess amount of bourbon and brooding over what had happened between Margaret and himself. Why did she have to go and spoil such a perfect day by asking him to do something that maybe – probably - he wanted to do anyway but didn't want or have the nerve to tell her? Sure, go ahead and tell her, tell her that he'd love her forever and that he'd be there at her side till the end of time. He felt that way, didn't he? Yes, he did, or at least he was pretty sure he did. And then when it ended he'd feel like a fool, just like the last time he told that to a woman and watched as the whole thing went to hell. Or keep his mouth shut? Margaret would understand, right? No, she'd made that clear enough. "What the hell," he said as he pulled up his zipper and headed back to the bunkhouse. "And there is always Karen."

At the breakfast table, John sat next to an unfamiliar face. "And who are you?" he asked the blond, blue eyed stranger seated next to him.

"You don't remember?"

"Sorry, I don't remember much from last night."

"Dan Kochanowski."

"Dan Kocha-what-ski?"

"Kochanowski, you know, just like the great Polish poet."

"Oh yeah, him. How could I ever forget? And I suppose you told me already, but I'll ask anyway, what are you doing here?"

"You really did tie one on last night didn't you. Sarah and I got here last night. We're the linguists that Dr. Johnson brought in from New Jersey. We're the ones who are going to try to make some kind of sense out of all those books and chips."

Einstein's Bones

"Good luck with that," replied John. "Sarah?"

"Sarah Cooper, we're from Princeton."

"Well, glad to make your acquaintance, Mr. Kocha-something or other." John rested his forehead in his left hand. "Don't worry, I'll get it right sooner or later. Princeton, huh? Sounds like we're getting pretty fancy around here. You ever been in the Wild West before?"

"No. Other than flying over on my way to LA, I've never been west of Chicago. But fear not, I'll try not to get scalped."

The next showing in the lecture room began shortly after 8:00am. The cameras from the Geographic were there to record the sights and sounds on the chips, but not live this time. In the middle of the second row sat Dan Kochanowski and Sarah Cooper. They made an odd looking pair – Dan blond, blue-eyed and at least six and a half feet tall, looking like a recruitment poster for the Polish army. Then Sarah, almost a foot and a half shorter. Mousy brown hair, slightly overweight, and wearing thick rimmed glasses that did nothing for her very plain looking face. John would have been mildly amused had he remembered that they were husband and wife, sitting there with note pads and recorders.

When the lights went down and Dick inserted the third disk – this one from the collection on the wall – John turned to watch their reactions, and prepared his ears for the loud piercing screams from Sarah that he was sure would follow. Instead, the two linguists stared ahead as if they were watching nothing more interesting than a lecture on the history of white bread. John turned back to the front of the room expecting that there must be some trouble with the projector and that 'Mr. Rogers' had failed to make his appearance. But there he was. John turned back to Dan and Sarah and wondered what it would take to get them excited.

Einstein's Bones

Today's first lesson continued with mathematics. It was getting more complicated. To the accompaniment of the vocalizations emanating from 'Mr. Rogers' – a conglomeration of squeaks, chirps, squawks, grunts, and other assorted high and low pitched birdlike calls – squares and square roots took up the whole of disk number three. When it finished with 'Mr. Rogers' making his customary bow, John looked back at the newcomers who were too busy writing notes and checking the gain on their recorders to notice John's puzzled look. "Oh well," he said softly. As he returned his head, he caught a slight smile from Karen and the hint of a wink. "Oh God," he muttered to himself as he shook his still fuzzy head.

"She's sure been giving us the look, hasn't she," said Mike who was sitting next to John.

"I haven't noticed," replied John.

Disk four began with basic geometry – points, lines, areas, and solids. Disk five was more geometry. Disk six was trigonometry. 'Mr. Rogers' drew a circle and then a line next to it that touched it at one and only one point and then said what must have been the dino equivalent of "tangent" which sounded like someone with bad table manners.

"Time for a break," said Dick when it ended.

"I'm all for that," responded Zeke. "I never was all that hot with math. This is starting to get way beyond me."

Carl Shunk sat at his motel room desk reading Newsweek's latest account of the happenings outside of Sheridan, Wyoming and waiting patiently for a call from Colin Yeager. Though not as severe as John's, he too was suffering from a hangover. When his cell phone finally rang, it was one of his assistants. "Get off the damn line," he barked, "I've got an important call coming." Colin's call followed five minutes later.

"Well," asked Shunk, "so what do you have for me?"

"It's all set for tonight. It's gonna be perfect."

"There're gonna do it?"

"You bet," beamed Colin. "Karen's staying in town tonight and our friend is paying her a visit at nine for sure."

"Pardon me for asking, but what makes you so sure he'll show?"

"Cause he said he would for one, and for another, seems like he and Margie had some big fucking fight last night."

"Excellent. What did they fight about?"

"I don't know. Who cares? Enough of a fight to get his mind off her and dip it in something else anyway. She'll boot those guys out faster than you can say 'what the fuck'. Now all I have to do is get his sweetie there while Johnny is dipping his wick. You want to call her, or do you want me to do it?"

"No, she'd recognize our voices. I'll have my assistant do it. He's good at that kind of thing," said Shunk. "And Karen still doesn't know why you're doing this?"

"Not a clue. She thinks all I want is to boink her, too."

"Sounds like you don't need anything from me."

"Don't forget," said Colin, "I can always shoot off my mouth and let Little Miss Margie know this was all your doing. Well, gotta go now, the second show is about to start."

Carl Shunk folded his phone and smiled.

Two more disks continued the math lessons. At the end of the eighth, 'Mr. Rogers' pick up a book identical to the ones in the outer chamber, opened it to the first page and pointed to several mathematical symbols. He closed it and showed his audience the number on its spine after which he pointed his reptilian finger to the door which led back to the outer chamber. He crossed his arms, bowed, and faded out.

"Did you catch that number?" asked Dick.

"I got it," replied Sarah. "If I got it right, it's number 280." She got up and showed her notes to Dick who took a moment to translate the symbols for himself.

"You're right," said Dick. "Zeke, put on a pair of gloves and see if you can bring me that book if it's out there."

Zeke left and quickly returned with the book that 'Mr. Rogers' had held. Dick opened it to the first page. "It's the same." He held it open for the Geographic camera. "Lani, you have a major in math, don't you?" She said yes. "Come over and tell me what you think."

She rose from her front row seat, put on a pair of cotton gloves and studied the first few pages of the book. "It's more trig, starting where he left off on the disk." She turned more pages. "I think I get it," she said tentatively. She turned to the middle of the book. "Hmm." She turned to the end. "Very interesting," she said slowly. "I don't know what this is, but if we follow along, we – or someone with more than I've got – we should be able to figure it out."

"John," said Dick, "get copying this so we can send it out."

"Will do."

"Lani, for now, see how far you can get." He looked at his team. "Let's stretch our legs a bit before we see any more."

They all rose from their seats except for Dan and Sarah who put their headphones on and wrote more notes.

"Those two must have iron asses," John told Mike. "I don't know how they can sit there in those god-awful seats without some kind of padding."

"I wonder what they look like when they're in bed together," replied Mike.

"Those two? That would be something to see. Talk about a mismatch – physically anyway. Those two in bed together? I wonder if they ever have."

"They are married after all."

John coughed up the water he was drinking. "Really? Who'd a thunk it? I can just see 'em there taking notes about each other. I wonder if they get excited then. But ya never know. They might be real wildcats. Looks like it's time to go back to school."

Math class was over. Disk number nine was reading and writing with 'Mr. Rogers' standing at the head of an oval table at which were seated twenty three much smaller Sapienasaurs, dressed the same as 'Mr. Rogers' but with only a single blue stripe going down the length of their tunics. Behind the teacher was a board with at least fifty symbols, the same symbols as were found on the medallions and had been projected during his previous demonstrations. In his right hand, the teacher held a pointer. He pointed to the first symbol in the upper left hand corner which was a square and said something like "enth". He pointed to the next, a right angle and said something resembling the call of a bass-throated eagle. Next was an upside down "T" with what sounded like a chirp with a "th" appended to the end.

Of the fifty eight symbols, only a handful of their sounds could be represented by letters in the Roman alphabet; the majority were various whistles, chirps, clucks, and growls. "I hope those two are really good," John said to himself.

The 'abc's' done, 'Mr. Rogers' pointed to a creature like himself and uttered a sound like "eritii" with several symbols appearing above it. Another, but slightly smaller Sapienasaur joined the first. "Eritin" or something like it, said the teacher. Still a third, but much smaller Sapienasaur entered the projection and 'Mr. Rogers' made a low chirping sound.

"Got to be man, woman, and child," said Mike.

"Quiet," ordered Dick as the disk faded out. "One more and that's it for today. He looked at the mass of disks at the back wall. "We sure as hell aren't going to watch all of those today – or in the next year."

Disk ten began with the same male and female – or was it female and male – but without the juvenile. They disrobed. There was nothing except for size that suggested any difference in their genders. The two figures then assumed the mating position common to most mammals and reptiles. 'Mr. Rogers' pointed to the first figure, the one on top and said, "eritii" and then to the second, saying, "eritin".

"This is kinky," said Karen. "Pornosaurs."

When the two dinosaurs finished mating, they stood. The male disappeared and the audience saw a time-lapse of the female as she got heavier and heavier, and then squatting and producing a live young. "Mr. Rogers' pointed to the baby and made a sound similar to the chirping sound he made for the juvenile, but with a higher pitch. All the while, his words were spelled out at the top of the projection. Of no little importance, the new born Sapienasaur had a light covering of yellow down.

"That's enough for today," said Dick as the disk faded to black.

John had to admit to himself that it was fun to watch the Sapienasaurs going at it with a passion he could only wish for. "What a stud."

"What did you say?" asked Mike.

"I said, what an incredible stud."

Einstein's Bones

Home from school, Margaret sat on her sofa sipping on a beer with her legs tucked under her, holding a private conversation with herself. "Should I have done that?" she asked. "Was I pushing things too far too fast? Maybe I should call him and tell him I'm sorry and I was wrong. But it's not like I was asking him to marry me, for Christ sake. Just tell me, John, where are we going. You needed a kick in the ass." She got up for another beer, forgetting that she had barely started the one she already had. "All right you win. I'll sit here like a good little girl and wait. Right, like I'm supposed to wait here for ever? Well, I guess my timing could have been better. I should have waited till he came home in a couple of days, and I could have said something after we made love. No, not then. Before. Well, I can't change that now, I already did it. I'll make it better. Or maybe I'll let him hang for a while."

As she was about to ask herself another question, the phone rang. She picked it up quickly, hoping it was John. "Hello," she answered before the phone had a chance to ring twice. The voice on the other end was unfamiliar. "Who's this?" she asked.

"A friend of yours. Do you want to know what your boy friend does in his spare time?"

"Who is this?"

"What does it matter? Like I said, if you want to know what your boyfriend is up to, be at the Holiday Inn, room 227 at 9:30. The door will be open. Enjoy."

"Who the hell is this?" she asked, but her only response was the dial tone. She put the phone down and thought for a moment and then dismissed the whole thing. "But who was it, and how did he get my number. I changed it only a couple of weeks ago," she said to herself. "If somebody thinks I'm going to fall for that shit, they must think I'm one really dumb bunny." She took another sip of her beer and thought about it again.

Einstein's Bones

In room 227 of the Holiday Inn, Karen looked through her things. A light brown teddy caught her eye. She picked it up and held it next to her naked body. "Now this is hot," she said. She put it back down. "No, and have him rip it to shreds? Maybe not." She sorted through her bag and found a pair of black lace panties. "I've got to get some use out of them," she said as she headed for the shower. "He is gonna be so fucked in more ways than one."

Twenty minutes later she stepped out of the shower, smoothed on a generous supply of scented body lotion and looked at the clock next to her bed. "Just about show time. Am I hot or am I hot." She looked in the mirror and slowly slid her hands from her ample breasts to her thighs. "Yes, hot." She pulled back the covers of her bed, touched the master light switch, laid her naked body face down, propped a pillow under her hips, and waited. Right on time, there was a knock on her door. "Come in, it's not locked," she answered. "Don't say a word, and don't turn on the lights. And leave the door unlocked. It's so much more exciting that way."

He opened the door slowly and could see her shadowy body lying naked on the bed, her round hips waiting anxiously for him. He felt a surge in his penis. He closed the door behind him, quickly undressed, and slowly crept toward the object of his desire. In the darkness, he reached out his hands and gently rubbed her back, moving slowly down to her hips and then, as she let out a low moan, to her thighs. How soft yet firm she was. How good she smelled. How hard he felt.

"Do it to me," she said. "Do it to me just like you saw him do it this morning. Do it hard. Just don't stop, and then you can do it again. You can do it all night, any way and anything you want."

He grabbed her hips and pulled them up towards his as he lowered himself on top of her. "You don't know how long I've waited for this," he nervously whispered in her ear.

Einstein's Bones

Chapter 27

"Who the hell," she shouted as she flipped on the lights. "Mikie? What the fuck are you doing here?"

"John said you wanted to see me," he stammered as he instantly jumped off her body.

She looked up and down at his naked body several times, and then stopped and stared at his johnson. "He did, did he?" she said as she continued to stare. "Wow." She reached out, held it in both hands, and slowly stroked it. "Looks like you can stay for a while."

John felt his arm explode as a Confederate bullet shattered bone just as he reached the rebel lines. He went forward anyway, ignoring the pain and leading his men on. He felt another bullet strike and heard someone call his name. It didn't matter. He continued to the lead the charge. He had to rescue Margaret who was being held captive in a house only a hundred yards in front of him. Again he heard the voice as he was struck by yet a third minie ball, but instead of moving forward into the swarm of lead, he opened his eyes to see Mike standing over his bunk bed. "What do you want?" he asked still more asleep than awake. "What the hell time is it anyway?"

"About four."

"What the hell is so damn important at four in the morning?" John closed his eyes and thought. "Oh yeah, I'll bet you're pissed."

"Can we go outside?" said Mike.

"Why not." John had visions of the fight scene from *The Big Country* where Gregory Peck and Charlton Heston duke it out before sunrise. He pulled on his jeans, buttoned up his flannel shirt and tied his shoes – without socks – and followed Mike into the cool early morning air.

"I figure you want to beat the crap out of me," said John with resignation. "I deserve it. That was pretty mean of me. Go ahead, but it won't be easy."

"Do you ever have that wrong. I want to thank you."

"Thank me? After what I just did to you?"

"I just had the best night in my whole life. She's insatiable. I'd still be there if I'd a been able to keep up with her – and that you wanted the truck back early."

"Who are we talking about? Karen?"

"Oh man, you wouldn't believe her. I'm all fucked out."

"You're telling me that I send you up there to her room as a joke and you end up screwing her brains out? So how did that happen?"

"Well, she had the door unlocked and the room all dark, I knock and she invites me in. She was expecting you, right?"

"That she was."

"Anyway, so I go over and start to do it and then the minute I open my mouth she almost screams wondering why I'm there and almost scares the shit out of me. But then she grabs my little buddy anyway and we go at it."

"Well son-of-a-bitch. My congratulations. All's well that ends well. Mikie my boy, sounds as though all your dreams have come true. You had a better night than I did for sure. But couldn't you have waited to tell me till at least the sun came up?"

"Well, there's more."

"What, she blew you till ya couldn't see straight?

"No, just about when we start going at it for a second time, your girl friend, Margaret comes busting in like she's real pissed and like she's expecting me to be you."

Einstein's Bones

"Margaret was there? My Margaret? You know why?"
"When she calmed down she said something about getting a call saying that you'd be there. She left pretty quick. And then later Colin shows up."
"Son-of-a-bitch. Pricks! This is starting to make some sense. So then did you have a threesome?" he asked with a laugh.
"She told him to get lost and he left."
"Was Margaret OK?"
"I think so. I got the feeling that she thought it was all somebody's idea of a sick joke."
"It was a lot more than that," said John. "And did Karen say anything about why everybody was trouping to her door?"
"No, all she wanted to do was fuck, fuck, fuck. And can she ever."
"Glad you had a good time anyway, Mikie my boy. I did try and pull a fast one on you, you know and for that I apologize. I knew she'd be sitting there and waiting in her little web for me. Really, it was her I wanted to have some fun with. Just don't say anything about this to anybody. I don't think Karen or Colin will. I'll have to have a talk with Margaret, but I'll leave those two to stew on it, if Karen ever stops smiling. Again, sorry. Any more? So are you gonna make an honest woman out of her now?"
"That's about all there is. Thanks again. Marry her?" Mike chuckled. "She's worn me out and she's not rich enough."
"Then let's go back and get some sleep – if you can."
It was difficult for John to get back to sleep. The more he thought about it, the angrier he got. Angry at himself for having used Mike that way and for not having told Colin and Karen to shove it in the first place. Angry at himself for not letting Margaret know just how much he really did care for her or why else would she have gone there in the first place. Mostly he was angry at Karen and Colin

for what they tried to do. He could figure out why Karen did it, but why Colin? What had John ever done to him? Was he after Margaret? It puzzled him. And he was just a little angry – no, more like annoyed – that Margaret would even think that he might be fooling around on her. But could he really blame her? Even if she did trust him, who wouldn't have gone to find out if the phone call had any truth behind it? She should have called him. More than anything, he hated not being trusted. He'd have to have that talk with her that he had avoided the day before. But for the moment, he was going to find out if he could drift off back to sleep and put himself back in that blue uniform.

If John did re-enter his dream, he didn't remember it. When he awoke two hours later, he looked over to where Mike was prone on his bed, wide awake, staring at the ceiling, and with a dreamy smile on his face. "That's one happy camper," John said to himself.

Two more linguists had joined the camp, Ming Jen, a Chinese exchange student, and Rose Keller. Both were the grad students of Dan and Sarah. This time John did remember who they were. They would be staying at the site with Dan and Sarah long after Dick and most of the rest of his team left for Minnesota.

With his season drawing to a close, Dick had little time to view many more of the disks. He would view them later on his PC in the comfort of his office in Minneapolis. Watching all those disks was the job for the language experts. Dick's job, and his team's job, was to finish the field work – to remove and care for the fossils that remained exposed in the ground. He left the position of projectionist to John, who was relieved that an electric motor had been attached to the charging unit.

That morning, John entered the inner chamber and inserted disk number eleven and the lessons on how to speak dino continued. The format remained the same, with 'Mr. Rogers' pointing to an object and then telling his viewers what it was. 'This is my arm, this is my head. This is her arm, this is her head.' By the tenth disk three hours later, John had a splitting headache. "If it's all the same to you, I gotta stop now. We can take this back up after lunch." Absorbed in their work, the busy translators barely looked up from their notes. Dan merely said, "Yes," and the four linguists huddled and began comparing their thoughts and notes. John walked out and stretched full length on the sparse grass. When the pounding stopped, he pulled out his cell phone, called Margaret's school number and left her a message. He wanted to see her tonight. The word-smiths remained in the lecture room another hour and a half, leaving only when they were informed that if they didn't come out right now, there wouldn't be any food left.

Margaret was in Sheridan teaching school when the two guardians of the inner chamber were at last removed and began their journey to a New York museum – on loan until a permanent home was built in Sheridan - her father's wish. The heavy hollow cast golden statues looked out of place when they emerged into the sunlight after eons spent in darkness. John, with Mike by his side, felt as though he was saying goodbye to old friends, hoping they would return soon.

"Recovered from last night?" asked John.

"I was right, it is Krell steel. Dick got a report on it. It's some kind of high temp alloy, more like a glass than a solid."

"So what's been going on with you and Karen?"

"Nothing. I tried to talk with her and see about maybe tonight, but she just blew me off. I don't know what her problem is."

"I'm not surprised," said John. "I figured as much. You're gonna have to be satisfied with what you got and forget it. She's just that way. I could tell ya about another gal I knew very much like her, but I gotta go back and start the show."

John started the next showing with two more language lessons. Judging from the assorted odd sounds his viewers were making, the language experts were beginning to pick it up. For an hour after the second lesson they sat writing, comparing notes, and speaking in their new tongue. "How the hell do you guys figure that out," asked an unbelieving John.

"It just comes," replied Dan without an emotion.

John shook his head. "Just how jaded am I to be getting bored with this?" he asked himself. "You up for something different? I'd like to see what's on some of the other disks – if it's OK with you."

"No more than two," said Sarah.

John went to the back wall and pulled out the last disk. It was not a language lesson. For the next fifteen minutes twelve Sapienasaurs manipulated various strange devices from which came even stranger inhuman sounds, almost painful to the ear. "Music to strangle cats by." He said loudly.

When it was over, Sarah added, "Well, it certainly wasn't Mozart. I'd rather listen to Gregorian chants."

"One more?" John asked as he returned to the back wall and pulled a disk from the middle. "Wait a minute, I'm gonna get the others."

In front of the team was a creature that looked like a *Triceratops*, but with only one horn. An unseen Sapienasaur provided a voice-over and his words must have been echoed by the crawler above. Then there was a whole herd of the rhino sized beasts moving slowly, making a low honking sound and grazing on brightly colored flowers.

Einstein's Bones

"It's a *Monoclonius*," announced an awed Karen. "Late Cretaceous."

"I'll be dipped," said Dick slowly. "About two tons worth of the real thing."

They watched as the gray giants with black spots and bumpy hides continued to graze and then fade away.

"Did you get all that," Dick asked the videographer from the Geographic. "Damn. Jesus. We could sit and watch this all day and up to the time we have to leave. My God. I know we all want to, but we do have work to do and so do they," he said as he looked at the team from Princeton. Reluctantly he rose and began to leave. "We'll have to wait and see these others later."

"Oh, John," said Sarah Cooper in her raspy voice, "did you get those copies made that I asked you for, the ones of that book that was on the pedestal? We'd like to start on it after we watch two more disks."

"Just one copy so far. You said you wanted four, correct? Tell you what. You guys know how to work this thing. I'll do the rest while you watch, OK?" He handed the projection duties over to Dan and left in search of Dick.

"I've got Dan running the show in there. Hope you don't mind. And I'd like to go back to town and see Margaret when I'm done making up some copies."

"No," replied Dick. "Not a problem."

Margaret had barely started John's favorite - spaghetti – when he walked into her kitchen. "You're here earlier than I expected," she said. "So how was your day at the office?" she asked with a forced smile.

"You know that's not why I came here. Tell me about last night. Are you OK?"

291

For the second time he saw Margaret cry. She slowly wiped her cheek. "Just what is going on out there? Was it supposed to be you with that woman? I was so humiliated." She stopped and faced John squarely. "Have you been sleeping with her all this time? Tell me. I've seen the way she looks at you."

"Absolutely not."

"Then tell me why I had to see that."

John hesitated. "I guess I should have told you before, but I didn't because there was nothing to it anyway and I didn't want to cause any more problems. She's come on to me a couple of time, but nothing happened. Nothing."

"Has she kissed you?"

"She's tried. She's tried a lot more than that. Took off most of her clothes."

"And you let her? So why didn't you make love to her. It's not like you two have never done it before. She still is beautiful as you've noticed."

John moved close to Margaret and put his arms around her. "Because I love you, that's why." He kissed her. "There's no woman in the world who could make me forget that."

"Well, let's take care right now she doesn't try anything more," said Margaret as she moved towards the phone. She picked up the phone book, found the number she wanted and then said, "room 227 please." There was a short pause. "Is this Karen, Karen Peterson?" After Margaret waited for Karen's reply, she continued. "Well, this is Margaret, you know, Margaret Newcomb. Everybody tells me you're a valuable member of the team and that Dick thinks a lot of you – God knows why. You want to stay on the team, right?" Margaret waited for an affirmative. "Well if you do, if you really want to stay, I'm telling you right now that if I ever hear that you've come anywhere near my man again I'm going to get your slutty little butt kicked out of here and maybe more than that. Do you understand me? I hope so."

She put the phone down and looked at John. "I think that takes care of that, but I'm puzzled," she said as she put her arms around John. "So why was Mike there?"

John forced a short laugh. "You can blame that all on me. Colin told me that Karen would be up there waiting for me, so I figured she just wanted to prove something. So I sent Mikie to prove something else. But that you showed up says she must have been pissed I put her off and wanted to break us up. But I can't figure out the deal with Colin."

"Colin, you said? Maybe I know. I suppose I should have said something about it before all this happened. I didn't talk to him, but Carol told me that Dale said something about Colin doing something with Shunk. Do you figure?"

"What else could it be. Would you have kicked our cute little butts out if it would have been me there?

"In a New York minute. But I sure wouldn't have invited that jerk Shunk back in. How stupid do they think I am?"

He kissed her again. "Feel better. Oh yeah, your gargoyles are on their way. And this. He held up a DVD. "You're gonna flip when you see this."

"It's not the two of them, is it? I saw enough of that last night. And how is your little buddy Mike doing today?"

"He was high as a kite this morning, but he's back to earth now once it dawned on him that last night was last night and there ain't nothing more. I am so sorry you had to go through that. I wish I had a known about that call."

"I'm sorry I doubted you at all. Now go open that bottle of wine and let's watch the movie – if it isn't too long."

"Only about half an hour."

"Do you have Dick's cell phone number?" asked Margaret.
"Sure, why?"
"Might as well take care of Colin, too."
John went into the living room while Margaret made her call.
"So?" he asked when she returned.
"Colin will be gone in the morning."
"What did you say to Dick?"
"I lied. I told him that Colin has been trying to hit on me, that it made me very uncomfortable, and that I would like it if Dick got rid of him."
"I guess Dick knows who the boss is."

Margaret's reaction to the dino music was the same as John's. "That's pretty hard on the ears. Is all the music like that?"
"That's the only one we saw. The next one should be coming up pretty quick. You'll like it."
She watched the animal video in rapt silence. "What were those things?"
"I forgot. I'm not good at names, you know."
"Is that the only copy? If it isn't, I like to show it to the school tomorrow."
"That's why I brought it. We made a lot. Keep it."
"Are you upset about what I asked you the other night about us? Maybe I shouldn't have."
"No, you should have. Been thinking about it – about us. Ya know, hunting season's comin' up and I'm sick and tired of buying an out-of-state license. I figure next year I'll save myself some money and get me a resident one."
She smiled. "That's good enough for me."

Einstein's Bones

Chapter 28

"Jesus Christ, Charlie, don't you think it's about time you got your ass out of the sack? Can't you hear the birdies singing their praises to God – damn it will you ever get up?"

Charlie opened his eyes, saw John standing at the foot of his bed and looked around the room. "So what's the rush?" asked Charlie. "The season doesn't start till tomorrow." He sat up and looked again at his surroundings. "Got to say Margaret has good taste – in home decorating, anyway."

"You did say you wanted an early start for your tour. Besides, I've got breakfast started," said John

"You? Isn't Margaret up yet?"

"After last night she's sleepin' in and it's not a school day, so keep it quiet."

Charlie followed John to the kitchen where John poured him a cup of coffee. "Thanks," said Charlie. "I didn't get a chance to ask you last night, so how are things with you and Margaret? Looks like you two get along pretty good."

"I think so. Next year when we go back hunting in Minnesota I'm gonna have to get an out-of-state license – dang. Make yourself useful and cut that onion for the hash browns, will ya?"

Breakfast was just greasy enough for Charlie. Finished, John was putting the plates in the sink when Margaret entered. "Did we wake you?" asked John.

"Good morning boys. No, I got up just after you did. What are you two up to today?" She looked at Charlie. "Is he taking you on the tour? Any idea when you might be back?"

"Not too late, dear. We're goin' to the lab first then out to the ranch so Charlie can get the crap scared out of him when one of those critters tries to jump in his lap. I think I'll stop by the drugstore first and get him some Depends."

Charlie rolled his eyes. "I have seen them on TV you know."

"You better listen to John," said Margaret. "It's not the same thing. Some pretty tough looking cowboys have left a wet spot on their seats. Dear, you better see if they have the heavy duty ones."

"Time to go," said John. "You want me to bring back anything for you?"

"No."

"Come on over sweet pea and give me a kiss, but not too big a one. We don't want to embarrass Charlie."

"You can do better than that," she insisted after the kiss.

After he complied, he told her how much he loved her and then checked to see if his cell phone was in his pocket. "I'll call you and let you know how we're doing. Love you so much." As he walked out the door, he told her again and blew her a kiss.

"Is that the John I know?" asked Charlie as they started for the lab. "I never saw you like that with Phyllis. Just fight, fight, fight."

"I think I've learned a thing or two and Margaret ain't Phyllis."

"That's for sure."

Sarah and Ming Jen were at the lab when John and Charlie walked in. "How's it going, guys?" said John as he introduced his friend.

Sarah and Ming Jen looked unusually pleased. "We are making some very remarkable progress," replied Ming Jen. "Many gaps, but definite progress. There is still a lot more that we have not deciphered than we have deciphered, but we have enough to have a good idea what it is all about."

Einstein's Bones

John showed Charlie copies of what they were working on – book number one, the book from the pedestal.

"You're really reading this," asked Charlie. "How does it read? Left to right? Top to bottom?"

"Boustrophedonic – that's left to right then right to left – every other line," replied Sarah as she moved her finger over the copy she was working with, and then pointed to her translations.

"And all of this just by the two of you?" asked Charlie.

"Oh my heavens no," replied Sarah. "My husband and his assistant are working on it, too – and there's another hundred with copies all over the world. Without them it wouldn't be possible."

"Can I read some of it?" asked Charlie.

Sarah looked questioningly at John. "How soon do you think?" he asked

"I think we'll have a prelim next week. Until then, you know."

"Sorry Charlie, you're just gonna have to wait. They won't even let me take a peek." John turned back to Sarah and Ming Jen. "Thanks, we'll try not to make too much noise while I show him around."

"They really won't let you?" Charlie asked as he began his tour.

"Nope. They're kinda fussy that way."

"Do they let Margaret? It's all hers, isn't it?"

"I suppose they would if she insisted – either that or walk out. But she knows better than to ask."

There was nothing in the lab that Charlie had not seen, either on TV or in print or attached to e-mails from John. But it does not matter how many photographs you see of King Tut's golden mask, it does not matter how many TV specials you see about the eruption of Mt. Kilauea, it does not matter how many books you have read about Custer's last battle. Stepping on to the actual battlefield for the first time, seeing the red hot lava flow with your own eyes, staring at Tut's mask right in front of you while it stares hauntingly back – that's all different, nothing like what your imagination or mere pictures can prepare you for. Now, for the first time, Charlie Madson looked upon the wonders of the distant past with wide eyes and an open mouth. He reached out to touch a small jewel incrusted statue just inches from him, but pulled back, knowing he was not supposed to put his hand on it. He just looked in silent wonder.

At the end of the tour they came to a long table and on it the complete skeletal remains of an adult Sapienasaur. Charlie looked at it closely and asked, "Are those Einstein's bones?"

"No," replied John. "I think he's in the Field Museum. And anyway this one's a female. But they look about the same."

"You remember how pissed I got last year?"

"How could I forget? I'll try to make it up to you," John said with a laugh.

"You already have."

They left the lab, stopped for lunch, and headed for the ranch.

"It looks pretty deserted now," said John as he parked his truck. "But you should have seen it this summer, especially when we had open house. Everybody and his brother was here."

They walked the short distance to the big gray box. "Wait here a minute," said John. "If they're watching something, I don't want to spoil the surprise."

John entered the lecture room where Dan and Rose along with two nerdy looking assistants were going over their notes. "You got it all figured out yet?" asked John.

Dan was mildly annoyed by the intrusion. "We're working on it, thank you," he replied as he barely looked up.

"Are you done watching for a while? I've got a friend here from Minneapolis and want to show him a couple, if that's OK with you."

"Oh, I guess our work will just have to wait. It's all yours." He got up, and the rest followed, without acknowledging Charlie who was waiting silently by the outer door.

"Right friendly sorts, aren't they," said Charlie once they were out of ear-shot. "Like they never saw me at all."

"Yeah, they are a little hard to take at times."

They entered a lecture room festooned with scattered stacks of papers, three video cameras, four computers, and a collection of used Chinese take-out boxes that hadn't quite made it to one of the trash bins. "And pigs, too. Not what you'd think. John looked down at the floor where a smoke had been crushed out and shook his head. "Jesus."

"Make yourself comfortable, "said John as he handed Charlie a pillow and pointed to the front row center seat. He pulled a sheet of note paper from his pocket, looked it up and down, and asked, "So what's your pleasure? Language lessons? Math? Music? No, I think not. Cooking? How about cartoons? Maybe I'll just surprise ya." He looked down at the paper again and walked to the back wall. "Even I haven't seen this one yet, but they tell me it's pretty good. Don't think it's been aired yet, either. Number six hundred and forty two. Ready. Don't wet your pants."

The instant that 'Mr. Rogers' made his appearance, Charlie jumped back in his seat and blurted, "Oh shit," as the Sapienasaur stood only two feet away and looked him squarely in the eye.

"Warned ya," gloated John.

The Sapienasaur made a few remarks which sounded familiar to John but which he still had no understanding of. The

Einstein's Bones

creature stepped out of the hologram uncovering the image of a blue, brown, and white sphere.

"The earth?" Charlie managed to ask.

"Yup. Sixty five million years ago so I was told."

It looked very much like the earth of today, but not quite. There were the same white clouds and deep blue oceans and small ice caps at the poles. North America was there, but it was joined to Greenland and just touching northern Europe. South America was off floating by itself hundreds of miles from the most southerly point of its northern neighbor, separated from an easily recognized Africa by a very narrow Atlantic ocean. A massive island was suspended off the east coast of Africa – India – hundreds of miles and millions of years from Asia.

The image pulled back to show what looked like satellites transmitting solar energy to the Earth. The image pulled back further to include the moon. "Holy shit, they saw the other side?" said Charlie.

"Keep watching. They told me it gets better."

The camera zoomed out to include the entire solar system and then back in at the individual planets. The rings of Saturn were there but smaller and Jupiter looked just as massive, but without the giant red spot. Mars brought "Holy shits" from both of them. Its clouds were thicker; Olympus Mons sported an ice cap, and narrow bands of green fringed small areas of blue. "Fucking water?" asked Charlie incredulously.

"They didn't tell me about that," said John. "Wow. I always heard that the water on Mars would have disappeared long before that. Guess the experts were wrong."

And the image faded away.

"Well, did ya?" asked John.

"What, piss my pants? Damn close."

Einstein's Bones

"Up for one more? How about a travelogue?"

"They won't mind waiting, will they?"

"They will, but the hell with em, and besides, they know who my main squeeze is." John went to the back wall and pulled out #468. "I've seen it, but I'm pretty sure it hasn't been on the tube yet. He popped it in and once again 'Mr. Rogers' began his presentation. The Sapienasaur's camera panned a landscape dotted with pine trees until it stopped at the half ruined remains of a small group of abandoned buildings made of stone. The style of architecture was simple, reminiscent of second dynasty Egypt. Columns and lintels, no arches, massive. What their tour guide was telling them, John and Charlie could only guess at. Was this the birthplace of their civilization or some sacred site? Some day they might find out. The camera moved on to a stone wall covered with carvings of even stranger symbols, symbols not demonstrated during the language lessons. In the middle of the monument stood a naked Sapienasaur, a shield in his right hand, a sword in his left. In front of him was a smaller version of T-Rex.

"I wonder who won," said Charlie.

"It gets better."

The camera dollied back and panned left. "My God," said Charlie. "A fucking pyramid. Jesus, makes you think maybe Eric Von Daniken might have been at least half right." Charlie compared its size to a nearby pine tree. "Ya got to wonder if there's anything left of it. Any idea where it might be?"

"The disk before this one indicated maybe some place in south east Europe," replied John as the disk faded.

"Can we sneak another?"

"Best not push it with these guys. We can see more later. Ready for a beer?"

Einstein's Bones

Charlie nodded; they got up and walked out past the anxious linguists.

"All yours," said John in passing. "And could you at least try to keep it clean in there?"

The first day of the hunt was nothing unusual – cool and clear blue skies. They drove past the site of the dig over miles of narrow twisting ranch roads until they were at the other side of the ranch, to an area they had never been to before but where the hunting was every bit as good. They took it easy – no rush. By the fourth day they still had not filled out.

At dusk they returned to John's new home. First things first, he greeted Margaret with a kiss. "Missed you out there. You ought to come along tomorrow, it's Saturday."

"And spoil your guy time? No, you two have your fun." She lifted a manila envelope from the kitchen counter. "Got something for you."

"What is it?"

"The preliminary report on the book. You going to read it now?"

"Shower first. You don't have dinner waiting do you?"

"Just pizza tonight."

Out of the shower and in clean clothes, John opened the envelope and pointed Charlie to a stack of hunting magazines. "I'd read this aloud to you, but I'd feel kinda silly." He thumbed through the thirty plus single spaced pages then looked at Margaret. "This is it, huh?" With a Manhattan within easy reach John began to read.

"Margaret,
Enclosed you will find a preliminary translation of book number one, which we have

named, *The Book of Antitoc*. The translation is by no means complete and may never be. We expect to release a somewhat more complete version to the scientific community in several months and to the general public at a later date. As you and John expressed an interest in a "sneak peak", we are giving you this very sketchy translation now. However, for you only we have filled in a lot of gaps with speculations that we probably should not have.

    I suppose that by now you are aware of several problems. The first is that as the spoken language of the Sapienasaurs sounds very foreign to our ears, certain names given are only closest approximation to English that we can give at this time. Also, in the interest of easier reading, we have given modern names to certain more or less universal objects. Thus units of time are stated in minutes and hours. Units of measure are expressed in the metric system. Also, as John may have told you, they used a base eight numbering system, requiring that judgment had to be used when numbers were rounded. Objects as well known to us as they were to them are given by their modern common names. We have taken the liberty of calling their home planet the Earth, their central star, the Sun, their natural satellite, the Moon.

    Animals which were common to them and are known to us are once again given by their modern name. In the cases where animals or other objects were known to them but have, as yet, to be discovered, we have attempted to produce the closest phonetic spelling that we could. In such cases, those spellings will be enclosed by brackets as in the name [Antitoc]. Some notes to ourselves might be in brackets, too. Also, as we will be building a further report from this preliminary translation, some foot notes are included.

At this time, we can not give a definitive answer as to what caused their demise and the demise of the other dinosaurs. Several factors seems to have played a part. Massive volcanic activity in an area of India called the Deccan Traps, the comet or meteor of modern theory, disease and hunger, and possibly war – all these appear to have played a part. All that we can say for certain is that there was a time lag of about five to six years from a meteor impact to the end of their kind.

On a hopeful note, according to *The Book of Antitoc*, the books in the library are a repository of what the Sapienasaurs considered to be the most important of their millennia of learning to be passed on.

Thank you for all of your help and support – from all of the translation team. Dan Kochanowski"

John paused for a refill, then began *The Book of Antitoc*.

"These are the writing of [Antitoc][1] of [Halacartoc] in the hope that the words and deeds of our noble race will not be lost to time. To have lived

---

[1] The correct pronunciation of the name includes a whistling sound

Einstein's Bones

and to have failed is a tragedy; to have lived and to be forgotten is to have never lived at all.

It is the year 36,785 of [Tarwic][2]. Little time now remains before our fate will be decided. It is the desperate hope that some of our race will survive here or on another world. Those among us with faith in our gods cling to the hope that we will be allowed to carry on our existence and continue with the advancements which have been our gift to this earth. I pray that this is so. Others fear that we shall be utterly destroyed, and with us all life on our planet. Will the earth itself be destroyed, leaving only fragments of our world orbiting about the sun? If such be our final destiny, there is yet some small hope that at some time some other form of life might find but a small fragmented remnant of our existence forever floating in the endless reaches of space and time.

I, [Antitoc] am the keeper of records in the library of [Halacartoc], the greatest of our cities. I write this in the belief that our race will end its reign on the earth which has been our home for more than 500,000[3] years. I also write with the hope and faith that the gods will not see fit to destroy all life on our planet. They have created us and surely they can not totally destroy all that they have so created. As they caused us to evolve from lower creatures, so again

---

[2] At the time of publication, no reference to the meaning of "Tarwic" has been found

[3] Expressed as 524,288 in base 8

Einstein's Bones

must they create new races to rise from the ashes of destruction that are now sure to come.

What shall survive, I know not. Of all …. [4]

Perhaps only the very smallest creatures among us will continue to inhabit this planet in the difficult times to come, those creatures which the eye can not see, and yet are the building stones of all life.[5]

How long must these words wait until they are read? It has taken the gods more than a thousand million years to create our race from the simplest forms of life. Might they bestow upon the lowly insects the gift of culture and civilization. Time is my enemy. Time is the destroyer. The earth, with its many motions, will do its best to hide all evidence of our existence. After the destruction which seems certain to come, wind and water and ice will wear away at that which remains. And if those powerful forces have not removed from the surface of the earth all that remains, surely the ground itself will move and in time all that we have built, all that we have accomplished, along with all of our thoughts and beliefs will be buried, out of sight and out of the minds of what may come to follow us.

What follows is a brief account of the events of the last years from the beginnings of our doom until the present. [several untranslated words] There are books to be collected, artifacts to be stored

---

[4] Not translated at this time
[5] Three following sentences untranslated

and the learning room to be completed and filled with the recordings of our sights and sounds."

John read another twenty pages then paused for a second refill. Fifteen minutes later he reached the conclusion.

"In closing, I can only wonder if you will find our history and our civilization in any way similar to your own. Will you be able to learn from both our successes and our failures? If you have not yet faced the crisis of your own destruction, I pray that you will use our knowledge to avoid it yourselves. And finally, if you have not as yet considered the possibility of destruction from the heavens and yourselves, let these words and our meager remains serve as a warning and spur you to prepare.

I thank you, the reader for bringing us back from oblivion and ask that you offer to your gods a prayer for our long forgotten souls [?]. I wish for you the enjoyment of all of the bounties of this planet and that you enjoy, at least, every bit of the success that we once had. May you avoid our mistakes and our ultimate end."

When he finished, he took a slow sip of his drink, and rested his head on the couch.
"Done?" asked Charlie. "So, what's it say?"
"It's not a full translation if that's what you're looking for. Lots of guess work they say. Seems like it'll be a long time before

Einstein's Bones

they can decipher all of it – if they ever can. But they're pretty sure they can have something close in a few months. The last ten pages are something to think about though. From what they've so far pieced together – little bits here and there - what we found is a repository of all the knowledge and some of their most important artifacts they had time to gather up before some big disasters struck. They, the translators, have found references to a long period of massive volcanic activity centered around what's now India – the Deccan Traps possibly and then what they think was a comet or meteor, which I guess comes as no surprise, and then disease, hunger, and probably a war. From the time the comet hit until the old boys turned into toast - their best guess is about five or six years. And there seems to be something about a key to the dino's DNA code. And oh yes, they might not be gone after all, as according to the book, the old boys might just have colonized some planets out there. Here, read it yourself."

"Disease and war," mused Charlie. "Them too? I guess the four horsemen have been around for a long time."

It was the final day of their hunt. John fixed his cross hairs on an antelope, squeezed the trigger, and felt the recoil from his rifle as the animal jumped, took three steps and dropped, joining all the creatures that had shared that spot on the planet since the beginning of life on earth but were now gone. John walked to where the antelope took its last breath and looked down. Two feet from his prize was a skull. Would time forget this skull? Would it forget the antelope's? Would it forget his own? Would some being walk this hill sixty million years from now, look down, and ask himself what it was he saw? And John wished that somehow he could tell whoever that might be that the skull belonged to one of God's great creations, though to anyone living in the present it was nothing more

Einstein's Bones

than the skull of an ordinary cow. John then raised his eyes and looked into a clear blue sky. "Are they still up there someplace? Will they come home some day?"

THE END

Einstein's Bones

About the author

Charles Rice lives in Osceola, WI
He may be contacted at:
charlesrice909@msn.com

Made in the USA
Columbia, SC
04 October 2020